Mr. Reed:
New York City Billionaires Book 3

by Mary Jennings

GET *"The Billionaire's Secret Wife"* FOR FREE

Sign up to my author newsletter to receive exclusive content, sneak peaks and a **free copy of my novella *The Billionaire's Secret Wife*!**

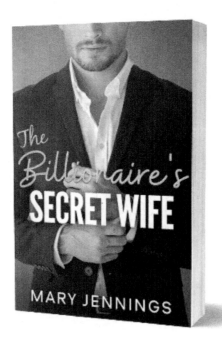

Click maryjenningsauthor.com/secrets to download my free novella!

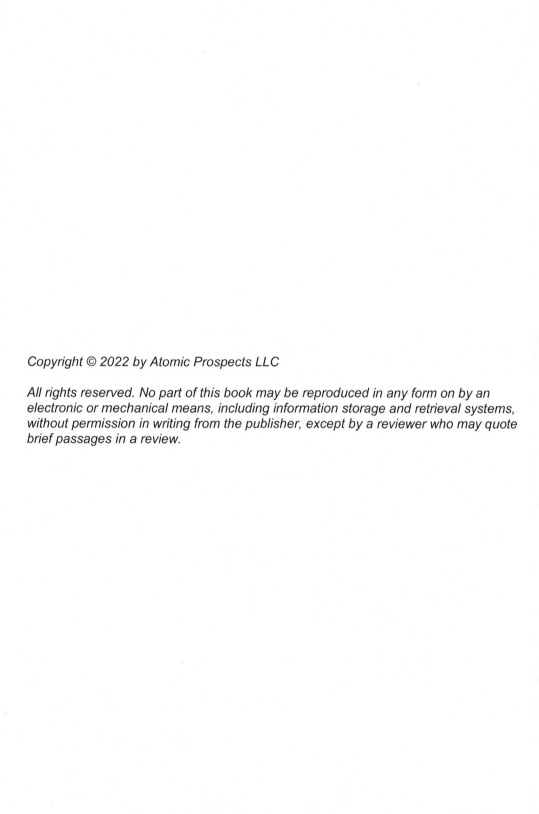

Table of Contents

Chapter One: *Campbell*

"Morning, Daisy! I *love* the outfit. You're always so stylish," chattered Jennie, hopping up from her seat behind the front desk the moment I walked through the pristine glass doors of the executive floor of Reed Capital's main building. "I picked up Mr. Reed's black coffee and your iced Americano."

"Thanks, Jennie. You're an angel," I told her, resting against the glossy marble counter between us. Letting out a slow exhale, I took a moment to catch my breath. It was barely seven-thirty in the morning, but I'd already dealt with a public transportation nightmare thanks to construction taking place on the Q Train tracks that had forced me to transfer twice during my otherwise blessedly convenient and efficient morning commute.

That was New York City for you. Even the locals who were born and raised here never failed to be surprised by the magnificent urban jungle every once in a while.

Normally, I didn't mind a little bit of adventure, but Manhattan's unpredictability had almost made me late to work that morning. Of course, my definition of *late* was what most people considered being perfectly on time, but I liked to get a head start on my days. Early birds and worms, and all that.

"No problem," Jennie answered. "I'm pretty sure we're the first two here."

"As usual," I chuckled. "By the way, your hair is looking particularly shiny this morning. Are you using a new product?"

"Thank you! Yes! You know Vivi down in marketing? She recommended a serum to me," she prattled. "I'll email you the link."

"You're the best," I giggled, then peered down at the organized chaos on top of her desk. "Is that Mr. Holt's coffee order, too? Did he fire another assistant?"

Jennie sighed and slumped down in her chair, which I knew was a sign that she was about to deliver a load of gossip. Early in the morning was pretty much the only time we had to chat like this, since both of our roles at the company were so hectic and we rarely saw a moment of peace once the executives started to arrive. Jennie was the secretary for the entire C-Suite, meaning she managed the bulk of the basic administrative tasks for the highest ranking employees at Reed Capital. Although it sounded like a dull job, it was highly coveted in the world of private equity, where a singular toe in the door could bring you otherwise inaccessible future career opportunities.

Although, my position as an executive assistant to one of the leaders of the firm—the CEO himself, Mr. Mason Reed—meant that I was ranked higher than Jennie, we were thick as thieves. We'd been hired around the same time about two years ago, and since then, had formed an informal girl-power alliance to help each other trudge through our difficult, entry-level roles. We had each other's backs.

That was why Jennie took it upon herself to pick up Mr. Reed's *and* my coffee order on her way into the office, which usually would have been my responsibility. However, the aforementioned Mr. Holt was the CHO, meaning he was basically the king of human resources, though you wouldn't know it from his utter lack of personality and basic human decency. Luckily, I didn't have to deal with him all that often, and he wasn't supposed to be Jennie's problem, either.

"I just felt bad for Michael," Jennie mumbled.

"Michael? Why would you feel bad for *him*?" I snorted.

Michael Hamwell was Mr. Holt's executive assistant. He was a recent graduate of the London School of Economics, not to mention scrawny, snobby, and snide. Michael had only been at Reed Capital for about three months, but that was longer than most of Mr. Holt's assistants had lasted.

Jennie leaned in conspiratorially and lowered her voice. "Don't tell anyone this, but I caught him crying in the stairwell Monday."

"Crying? Why? Did he get a scuff on his Tods?"

Jennie bit her lip to fight back a smirk and tutted her tongue at me.

"Hush, Daisy! He's kind of nice … sometimes. Anyway, I think he's homesick for England. When he noticed I was there, he got really embarrassed and explained that he's 'a little stressed out'. Knowing how awful it must be to deal with Mr. Holt on a daily basis, I couldn't help myself. I offered to take a few things off his plate."

"Jennie!" I protested in a whisper, glancing over my shoulder to confirm that we were actually alone on the top floor. "You have plenty of things on your own plate. If Michael can't handle the role, he should let somebody else have the opportunity."

"You only say that because you're basically superhuman," she joked.

"Not true. I'm just highly—"

"Highly organized, I know. Blah, blah. Anyway, don't worry about it. I really don't mind. Starbucks is right around the corner. It's just one extra coffee to carry in the elevator."

I had a feeling there was more to it, but I kept my mouth shut. Jennie had been particularly sweet to Michael ever since he started, so I had the feeling she was attracted to him, and therefore, offering to shoulder *his* work responsibilities was her way of flirting in this high-stress environment. That was her choice. I didn't know how to politely say to my friend that she deserved much better than a guy who couldn't keep his emotions in check in the workplace, so I decided not to say anything at all.

It wasn't that I hated my fellow EA—that was the business lingo for Executive Assistant—because the truth was I didn't hate anyone. I didn't have time for hatred. Rather, whilst doing some light research on Michael when he was first hired, I discovered that his uncle was the CEO of a hedge fund in London that often partnered with Reed Capital to punt clientele to one another across the pond. In short, Michael was a beneficiary of nepotism. That wasn't to say he wasn't smart enough to deserve the job on his own, but I didn't have much tolerance for people who used advantages that had nothing to do with merit and everything to do with birth.

After all, I was from the middle of nowhere in Vermont and related to absolutely no one of importance, and yet I had managed to work my way into a prestigious role at one of the most successful firms in the city.

What? Like it was hard?

(It was very hard, actually, but that wasn't the point.)

"Well, if you say so," I sighed. "Mr. Holt can't be the easiest person to work for, so I suppose we all deserve a little support once in a while."

"That's funny coming from Mr. Reed's assistant," Jennie dared to joke in a hushed tone.

I snorted. She didn't have to explain what she meant by her remark. Mason Reed, the CEO of Reed Capital, was the grandson of the company's founder, Abraham—also known as 'Abe'—Reed. I had entered the company after the older Mr. Reed's retirement, so I had never gotten to know him personally, but had heard from countless senior employees that he was one of the most pleasant executives in the industry. Abe Reed was patient, energetic, and sociable.

In contrast, his grandson was impatient, moody, and reclusive. Mason Reed wasn't the kind of man who hung around to chat with his coworkers, nor did he participate in office happy hours. He made obligatory appearances at company events and parties, then disappeared like Dracula back into his cave. I'd overheard the more gutsy Reed Capital staff on the lower floors, where Mr. Reed would never dwell, remark on how there always seemed to be a dark cloud hanging over the CEO.

Despite his gruff, antisocial demeanor, Mr. Reed was an ingenious businessman. The charm and confidence he oozed when conducting meetings with clients and partners was unparalleled. It was no wonder why, since he'd taken over the reins at Reed Capital, the company's margins had soared to phenomenal heights.

For all of my critiques about Mr. Holt's behavior, the truth was that *my* job was known to be the most difficult position in the C-Suite. Not only was Mr. Reed the busiest of the executives, he was also the meanest. Legend has it that he went through four different assistants in the span of six months before I was hired. In one of the five rounds of interviews I endured to get the offer, I was told that the role of Mr. Reed's executive assistant required a *very specific type of person*, though no one seemed willing to go into detail about that statement.

Given that I would be celebrating my second anniversary at Reed Capital next month, I suppose I was the right type of person to deal with Mason Reed on a daily basis.

"Daisy. My office," commanded a deep, velvet-smooth voice behind me. I jumped and whirled around at the same time Jennie choked back a gasp of surprise.

Speak of the devil.

Mr. Reed had peered around the corner briefly to confirm that I'd arrived at work, but once his demand was delivered, he didn't wait around for me to follow him. I caught only the barest glimpse of his dark hair and bespoke suit before he disappeared into his office.

"Best not to keep him waiting," I murmured, shooting Jennie a wink.

"You don't think he overheard us talking about Mr. Holt, do you?"

"I doubt it," I replied, shouldering my bag and stepping away from Jennie's desk. "He's not one for gossiping or eavesdropping."

"Alright. Godspeed, sailor," she said, offering me a playful salute.

"Godspeed," I told her, mirroring the gesture and scurrying off to the furthest reaches of the top floor where Mr. Reed's highly coveted private office was located.

It was just as well that Jennie's and my chatter was cut short by my boss. Soon enough, more early birds would start trickling into the office, and the regular on-time staff would arrive shortly after. Both Jennie and I had a daily list of things to get done before actual business hours started, so it was better that we didn't waste too much time enjoying the quiet solitude.

I walked briskly to catch up with Mr. Reed, though he had such long legs that it wouldn't surprise me if he was already back at his desk by the time I made it to him. It was definitely out of the ordinary for him to be at the office this early, but not completely unheard-of. He must have come in at sunrise to beat Jennie.

While most people, including my favorite coworker, were intimidated or downright afraid of Mr. Reed, I'd always steadfastly refused to fall victim to the same frame of mind. Respecting one's employer was good, but fearing him would only make you nervous and clumsy. Nobody wanted an assistant like that.

In truth, I admired Mr. Reed. He was only thirty-four years old, just six years older than me, and was already one of the richest and most successful men in Manhattan. His family came from old money, but most of it was tied up in non-liquid assets, and one quick internet search told you that the vast majority of his net worth came from the hard work he'd poured into this firm.

He was also extremely intelligent. Where most people saw a cold, harsh, analytic man, I saw a person who could look past extraneous details and determine the best course of action in a matter of seconds. In turn, Mr. Reed appreciated people who didn't get hung up on bells and whistles.

I prided myself on being a people person and a fast learner, so it only took me a few days to understand exactly how to earn Mr. Reed's favor and a long-term position at Reed Capital. Once I figured that out, it was smooth sailing. Sure, I had a few bad days here and there, but didn't we all?

In short, Mr. Reed liked people who were organized, efficient, and clever. He didn't like nonsense. He hated wasting time. People who asked too many questions or needed things explained to them a second time annoyed him. Maybe that translated to *cranky and miserable* in some people's books, but after two years of working with the man, I had learned that Mr. Reed's difficult personality wasn't malicious in the slightest. Rather, he had a low tolerance for incompetence.

We had that in common.

The door to his office had been left open, and I knew from experience that meant I was welcome to come in without knocking. Just as I suspected, I found him sitting behind his large, custom-made desk that curved around the back corner of the room. Two walls were made entirely of semi-transparent glass, showcasing downtown New York City's brilliant skyline from the inside, while maintaining his professional privacy from the outside.

"Good morning," I hummed as I entered the office, my heels clicking on the polished mahogany hardwood. "Here's your coffee, sir."

I placed the paper cup on a coaster on his desk. As usual, he grunted in thanks and left it untouched for the moment. Slipping my iPad out of my bag, I grabbed the stylus and opened up the software that the company used for calendaring and event-planning. It took me less than three seconds to be poised and ready to go for whatever series of demands Mr. Reed was going to deliver first thing in the morning. It was something I'd had to do multiple times a day over the past couple of years, so it was basically second nature at that point.

Mr. Reed was a man of few words, so it didn't unsettle me that he was gazing off at a distant point, ignoring me in favor of his thought-filled mind. He had one ankle crossed over his opposite knee and his fingers were folded in his lap. His suit—a Burberry ensemble I had ordered for him last month, since executive assistants were often also personal shoppers—was black, as was his shirt and tie. I remembered the sweltering evening I had gone to pick it up from the tailor after providing them Mr. Reed's measurements (which I had memorized, of course). The monochrome look was chic, especially on a man as handsome as he, but it was also undeniably out of character.

Although I had only noticed a few oddities so far that morning, I knew with absolute certainty that something wasn't right.

Finally, Mr. Reed flicked his blue-eyed gaze to me.

"I need you to come to Connecticut with me this morning," he stated.

I frowned and glanced down at his schedule open on the iPad's screen.

"But, sir, you don't have any meetings in Connecticut scheduled for today," I replied. He did, however, have four back-to-back meetings with very important people on the books that morning.

"Well, it's not a meeting," Mr. Reed muttered. "It's a wake."

"A wake?"

"Is that a problem?"

"No, sir. I'll rearrange your schedule accordingly."

I suppose it was a good thing I'd opted for black trousers and a dark gray silk blouse that morning. I usually liked to wear outfits with a little pop of color, but sheer luck had me dressing in neutral tones that were acceptable for a wake. Maybe Jennie was right; I really was a superhero.

Or, perhaps the universe was on my side.

Either way, I knew better than to hang around and chat with Mr. Reed, so I bustled off to my much smaller office down the hall. Once I was finally able to set my bag down and take a sip of coffee, I started re-coordinating his schedule. It involved a lot of emails with other assistants, who also understood how finicky and last-minute their bosses could be about their daily calendar, so it wasn't a Herculean task.

I'd never been to a wake before. I wanted to ask for more information—mainly, *who died?*—but that was too personal and unnecessary for me to know in order to complete the task. I didn't know anyone who lived in Connecticut, but Greenwich was only a forty-five minute drive away from Reed Capital headquarters if traffic wasn't too bad. It was known to be one of the wealthiest New York City suburbs, but that didn't offer me much in terms of hints.

With his schedule squared away, I smoothed the front of my clothing, grabbed my bag once more, and met Mr. Reed on the way to the elevator. It was a silent journey down, but that was normal. We moved concurrently to the flow of staff, heading out of the building while everyone else was flooding inside. Still, Mr. Reed's presence parted the crowds like the Red Sea, offering us a clear and easy route onto the street where his town car was waiting on the curb.

Mr. Reed's chauffeur, a paunchy old man named Maurice, opened the door to the backseat. Mr. Reed slid in first and I ducked my head to squirm inside with him. I hadn't been on many car rides with him before; none that lasted almost an hour. I assumed my boss wouldn't want to spend the time chatting, so when Maurice pulled out into the Manhattan morning traffic heading north, I reached for my iPad and prepared to get some work done on the road.

However, I couldn't quite curb my curiosity. Something about being in such close proximity with Mr. Reed, in an intimate space where an opaque divider could be pulled up between us and the chauffeur, made me feel on edge. Not in a bad way. Mr. Reed wasn't a creep. I wasn't worried about anything like *that*—and, if I was being completely honest, he was so handsome that I would probably find any flirtation from him to be flattering.

"Sir," I spoke, drawing his attention away from the city dragging by outside the car windows. "May I ask who passed away?"

"My grandmother," he answered simply. "Ruth Baldwin."

"I'm sorry for your loss, Mr. Reed," I answered automatically.

"Don't be," he quipped, pursing his lips in distaste as if he didn't have time for grief or condolences. "She was a heartless woman."

"Oh," I whispered, unsure how to respond to that.

"Regardless, given that I am her eldest grandchild, I need you to attend the reading of the will with me to take notes," Mr. Reed continued. "The Baldwin Estate is substantial, you see."

"I understand. Happy to do it."

I did some quick logistics in my head. Abe Reed was Mr. Reed's paternal grandfather, so that meant Ruth Baldwin was his mother's mother. It was known that Mr. Reed's parents had passed away a long time ago, as had Mr. Reed's uncle, so Ruth had actually outlived both of her children. If my boss really was her eldest heir, he was presumably set to inherit quite a lot today.

Everyone knew that Mr. Reed's family wealth came primarily from his mother's side, but few had borne witness to the physical manifestations of the old money legacy.

I suppose I was about to become one of those few.

Chapter Two: *Reed*

Daisy Campbell was the best assistant anyone could possibly hire. Not only was she Ivy League educated, well-dressed, and impeccably polite, she was also fiercely ambitious and unshakably obedient. On top of that, she was so gorgeous that, when she first entered the room for her interview two years ago, I thought I was being pranked by one of the other executives. I had thought there was no way that the woman in front of me had attended Yale, my alma mater, and interned at Goldman Sachs. She belonged on a runway.

I didn't want to hire her at first. Like most people, I fell victim to the stereotype that because Daisy was attractive and nice, she was also dumb.

She proved me wrong.

I dreaded the day when she inevitably moved on to a more prestigious role and I had to search for a new assistant. Until then, I was determined to take advantage of having her by my side while I still could.

How many assistants would agree to attend a stranger's wake at the drop of a hat with virtually no questions asked? I could tell she was surprised to learn that it was my grandmother who had died, but she brushed it off immediately. Ever the professional.

Daisy spent the drive to Greenwich tapping away on her tablet, arranging nearly every aspect of my life for me so that I could focus on supporting and growing Reed Capital. That was the most important thing. I nurtured my grandfather's company out of respect for him, but also because my career was everything to me. After all, every king needed a kingdom.

Not that I imagined myself a young monarch, but still.

Truthfully, part of me felt like an idiot for bringing Daisy along that morning. A wake was something you attended with loved ones, not your executive assistant.

Of course, the Baldwin clan was not the typical family. I trusted Daisy more than anyone who would be in attendance at the wake and I was going to need some loyal support when old Ruthie's will was read. With her two children previously deceased, the remains of her estate would be up for grabs by numerous greedy cousins. The entire affair would be more a lion's den than a sorrowful memorial service.

I figured Daisy was aware of the basic trivia concerning my family, but I doubted she knew that Ruth Baldwin was one of the richest women on the East Coast. In a matter of minutes, however, she was about to find out.

The iron gates to Baldwin Manor were open when Maurice approached the end of the narrow lane leading to my grandmother's house. If a nine-bedroom, twelve-bathroom home with ten sprawling acres of forest and gardens, not to mention a guest cottage, tennis courts, and an indoor swimming pool, could be referred to merely as a *house.*

I said nothing as Daisy gazed out of the window in silent awe as we pulled around to the grand, double-door entrance. Gravel crunched under the tires to announce our arrival. We were late, but I had done that on purpose. I had no intention of sticking around to gossip with these people. I was here to receive my rightful inheritance and that was it. The sooner I got back to Manhattan, the better.

Several heads turned in my direction as I climbed out of the car, Daisy hurrying after me. As usual, she remained at my elbow, just a step behind me; close enough to be of immediate assistance but not so close it felt as if she was hovering. It wasn't anything I'd trained her to do, but rather a natural habit of hers.

"Don't speak to anyone," I instructed as we climbed the wide front steps.

"Yes, Mr. Reed."

Despite her obedience, there was confusion in her tone. I liked that about her. She did as she was told, but she wasn't always happy about it. That was a good thing. It meant that, although she spent her days following my orders, she had a brain of her own.

I made it less than two steps into the foyer before I was attacked.

"Well, if it isn't the prodigal grandson, the beloved eldest!" boomed a voice from midway up the marble staircase. "Mason Reed, my dear cousin."

I didn't bother keeping the distaste off my face as I shifted to find my cousin making his way down to greet me. He must have claimed the spot on the stairs to have a high vantage point so he could see me the second I walked in.

"Bradley," I said to him, offering nothing more than the barest of nods in welcome.

Bradley Baldwin, whose father had been our grandmother's second child, was a walking train wreck. He was wearing a flashy, borderline theatrical black suit that proved just how desperate for attention he was. More shameful than that was the fact that he sported a deep tan, as if he'd been partying in Ibiza and had taken the private jet to pay his obligatory respects. Knowing Bradley, that was likely the true story.

"Always so serious," chuckled Bradley, clapping a hand on my shoulder roughly. He lacked about two or three inches on me, but he always tried to make up for it with brute force. "Why don't you loosen up once in a while, cousin?"

"Pardon me if I find it difficult to 'loosen up' while attending our grandmother's wake," I remarked coldly.

Bradley pursed his lips. We both knew he didn't give a damn about her, but he didn't want anyone else in attendance to suspect as much. Ruth Baldwin had never been particularly pleasant, opting to express her love for her family by controlling and manipulating them into being exactly who she wanted them to be. That being said, I didn't hate her. When you're orphaned as a child, you learn to be grateful for the semi-tolerable relatives you have left.

"Oi! Marina! Look who it is!" Bradley called out loudly, waving to someone at the end of the arched hallway. At least a half dozen people cringed at his shouting, disturbed that he dared raise his voice in the presence of the deceased.

I fought the urge to outwardly groan as Bradley's twin, my cousin Marina, sauntered over. She was eight minutes older than Bradley, and seemed to have arrived at our grandmother's wake in a much more appropriate outfit than her brother. On the surface, Marina appeared to be the twin with tact. In contrast to her brother, she was polite, witty, and graceful.

However, the truth was Marina was none of those things. She was just a very talented actress. At her core, she was just as rotten and spoiled and shallow as Bradley. I couldn't stand either one of them.

"Mason!" sang Marina with a bright smile, performing brilliantly for the nosy crowd of mourners who filled the manor. "How lovely to see you! Our darling workaholic!"

Before I could stop her, she reached up on the tips of her toes and offered me a casual kiss on either cheek, greeting me the French way. It would have looked ridiculous coming from anyone else considering that our ancestors had no claim to France, but Marina managed to pull it off.

"Hello, Marina," I muttered through gritted teeth.

"Sorry about that," she giggled. "I've been in Paris. Great Uncle Albert recommended me for a summer program at the Sorbonne."

That was a lie. Our great uncle, Ruth's older brother, was too busy drooling over himself in one of the most expensive nursing homes wealth could buy to give a damn about Marina's education. Still, I had to hand it to her. Given that poor Albert was no longer capable of forming complete sentences, no one could question her story. I imagined what Marina was *actually* doing in Paris was more along the lines of what Bradley was doing in Ibiza—the three Cs: clubbing, calculating, and cocaine. If the Baldwin twins loved anything, it was parties, drugs, and scheming.

"How nice of him," I responded to Marina while Bradley stood by with a stupid grin on his face. I didn't bother challenging Marina's lie, and the disappointment she felt about that was apparent in her gaze. My awful cousins were always trying to bait me, but I never fell for their tricks.

"I didn't even know you spoke French, sis," remarked Bradley. Marina rolled her eyes at his comment, but kept her gaze fixated on me.

Yet, the moment I noticed her attention slipping to the leggy blonde behind me, I jumped in before a target could be drawn on Daisy's forehead.

"If you'll excuse me, I'd like to pay my respects now," I said to the twins. I didn't wait for them to say another word before I departed, heading deeper into the house.

The crowd parted for me. I recognized many of the faces, but none of them were as bold as Bradley and Marina to approach me as I made my way through the endless maze of rooms. They all knew who I was, and they also knew I stood to inherit this entire estate and several million dollars' worth of holdings from Ruth Baldwin. Although Bradley and Marina were also eligible heirs, neither of them had a respectable career to boost their credibility.

When my parents had died, rather than being punted out West to my father's sister and her suburban family, I was taken in by his parents. My paternal grandparents were far more affectionate than Ruth had ever been, and although they became my legal guardians, she exercised her control where she could. Her tactics were obvious—promises of a hefty trust fund, priceless professional connections, and a loft apartment in Soho gifted all to coerce me into attending Yale and majoring in finance. The path Ruth wanted me to follow didn't require that much convincing, though my true guardians were always concerned that I wasn't, as they claimed, *following my heart.*

Disgusting. I'd rather follow my head than my heart.

"Those are my cousins," I murmured to Daisy once Bradley and Marina were out of earshot. "Bradley and Marina Baldwin. Twin disasters in designer clothes."

"I see," was all Daisy said in response. I could tell she felt awkward surrounded by strangers in the home of a woman she'd never known, but she dutifully kept pace with me as I located the elaborate display where my grandmother's urn rested in the corner parlor.

Beside her ashes was a black-and-white photograph of her when she was in her twenties, posing like a Hollywood starlet with a demure smile. The room was fairly crowded, but no one uttered a word as I bowed my head at the altar. I wasn't praying—I didn't have time for belief in omniscient beings—but I wasn't a robot. It was certainly unfortunate that she had died, especially since she hadn't reached her eighties yet.

Simply put, I was no stranger to grief. Therefore, I didn't like to dwell on it.

"She was very beautiful," Daisy said quietly. I glanced over to find her admiring my grandmother's photograph with a tender expression. For some reason, the sight of her expressing grief for someone she had never met before caused me to soften slightly.

"Yes, I suppose," I replied.

"Excuse me, Mason?"

Finally. I turned to find the Baldwin family attorney hovering a few feet away.

"Hello, Mr. Henderson," I greeted him. "How are you?"

"I'm well, given the circumstances. I'm very sorry for your loss," he responded politely. He was an honest, dependable man, but he wasn't the most welcome of sights. The last time I had dealt with him, he was helping in divvying my parents' estate, securing my inheritance, and arranging the transfer of guardianship over me.

"Thank you."

"I'm gathering the relevant individuals into the library so I can read Mrs. Baldwin's will," Mr. Henderson explained. He glanced at Daisy, but didn't question her presence.

"I'll head that way now," I told him. "Thank you."

He nodded in thanks and rushed off to locate more of Ruth's immediate relatives. I led Daisy toward the library, which was located on the opposite end of the manor.

"Attorney Henderson, correct?" Daisy whispered. "I believe he's already in your contact list."

"Yes."

"Your cousins are not. Shall I add them?"

"No."

"Got it."

In the library, the so-called VIPs were gathering. Bradley and Marina claimed a spot front and center on the chaise longue before the antique writing desk at the head of the room. I ignored them and opted to stand off to the side by one of the windows. I didn't need to be the center of attention to secure the fortune I had always known would one day be mine.

There were a few others in the room—second cousins and relatives by marriage—but the twins and I were the undeniable main characters.

I looked over at Daisy as Mr. Henderson entered the library and closed the doors behind him, effectively shutting us off from the rest of the house. "Are you going to take notes?"

"I thought it would be tactless to whip out an iPad in the middle of this, so I have my phone in my pocket converting the speech to text," she explained.

Damn, she was *good.*

"Right," I muttered.

"Alright, everyone," Mr. Henderson sighed as he stood behind the desk to address everyone as if it was a podium. He placed a leather portfolio on the surface and opened it to reveal a surprisingly thin document. "First of all, I'd like to express my deepest condolences for each of you. I have been working for the Baldwin family for several decades and have had nothing but profound respect for Ruth. Secondly, it seems she respected me in turn, for I have been formally appointed as the executor of her estate. Thus, without further ado, let's get on with the reading of Ruth Jane Baldwin's last will and testament."

I tensed in anticipation. Though I had no reason to suspect my grandmother had changed her mind in her final days, it was crucial that neither Bradley nor Marina was granted the bulk of her estate. They were fools and plunderers. They would spend the lot of it on Chanel and champagne, and trash Baldwin Manor throwing parties for all of their rich, careless friends.

Their parents had died in the same plane crash that had claimed mine, but instead of being handed off to doting grandparents, they were shipped off to boarding school by their mother's wretched sister, Katrina. Auntie Kat was lurking in the rear of the library probably wondering if, all these years later, she would receive some kind of reward for parenting the brats. I doubted it.

That side of the family couldn't get their hands on Ruth's assets. They didn't deserve it. *I* did. I needed it for Reed Capital.

Or rather, I didn't necessarily *need* it. I could acquire more capital to expand the company from a variety of sources, but believe it or not, a large inheritance was much easier to acquire than a bank loan. It was also preferable to accepting cash from investors in exchange for company stock.

"Let's begin with item number one," Mr. Henderson continued. " 'I, Ruth Jane Baldwin, bequeath two percent of my stock holdings to my granddaughter, Marina Anne Baldwin.' "

Two percent might not have sounded like much, but Ruth had been a savvy investor with a lot of cash to throw around her entire life. In short, my cousin just inherited about a million dollars.

Except, she'd never looked more upset. It was obvious why, especially once another two percent of our grandmother's holdings were bequeathed to Bradley.

They were named early in the will because they would not be receiving anything else. Their visible disappointment was laughable. Did they really think they would be trusted with anything more than that? Our grandmother was no fool. She knew what they did in their leisure time.

I tried not to look impatient as Mr. Henderson continued reading. Tiny bits of my grandmother's estate were chipped off little by little, but each posthumous gift barely made a dent in her fortune.

At last, we reached the end.

" '—hereby bequeath the property at 514 Baldwin Lane, Greenwich, Connecticut and all its contents, the property at 106 Sunflower Drive, Montauk, New York and all its contents, the property at 612 Lee Court in London, United Kingdom and all its contents, the remaining eighty-five percent of my stock holdings, and the entire balance of the Baldwin Trust—currently valued at approximately $42,700,031—to my grandson, Mason Calder Reed—' "

I let out a quiet, subtle exhale. There it was, the moment I'd been anticipating ever since I learned of my grandmother's death. I didn't greet the inheritance with greed, but with respectful eagerness. I hadn't expected her to pass away so soon, but I knew she wouldn't be offended if I considered the inheritance an opportunity.

In my peripheral vision, I could see Bradley and Marina glaring daggers at me, but I ignored them as I nodded in thanks to Mr. Henderson and waited for him to conclude the formalities.

Only … he wasn't finished.

" '—presented to him under the sole condition that he is married—' "

I froze. No. *No.*

That witch.

I should have seen this coming. I should have expected Ruth Baldwin to exercise one final act of control over me in death. She claimed she always wanted the best for me, and I believed she truly thought she was pushing me in the right direction. More often than not, I was more than happy to oblige.

Unfortunately, Ruth and I disagreed on a couple of things. First, she hated that I had taken over the role of CEO for Reed Capital when my grandfather retired. She had wanted him, then also me, to merge the company with an international conglomerate and carry on as the Chairman of the Baldwin Foundation. Basically, my grandmother wanted me to spend the rest of my life being a philanthropist who signed checks and golfed away his days.

Ruth was a traditional woman. She had thought such a path would allow me to settle down and raise a family. That was what she wanted from me more than anything. The Baldwin family bloodline was important to her. Given that neither Bradley nor Marina were procreating any time soon—and thank God for it—she believed it was my responsibility to create a bunch of well-behaved little Baldwins.

Stop fussing around with that silly little firm, Mason, she had once begged me. *You'll stress yourself into an early death with all of that work. There's no need for it. You should find a good wife and take over the foundation instead.*

I knew that was what she wanted for me and I also knew that she was used to getting her way, but I never thought she would go to such lengths as to include a stipulation in her will that would create a barrier to my inheritance.

Unfortunately, it appeared Mr. Henderson wasn't finished reading.

" '—should my eldest nephew be unmarried at the time of my death, the aforementioned inheritance will be available for claim by the first grandchild of mine to be joined in holy matrimony with their partner.' "

I was speechless. So was everyone else in the room.

Well, everyone except Bradley.

"Wait, what?" he barked out like an idiot.

Mr. Henderson sighed. It looked as if he had been mentally preparing himself for this moment, fully aware of the chaos the will's provision was sure to cause.

"The late Mrs. Baldwin has chosen to bequeath the majority of her estate to Mason," Mr. Henderson explained. "However, in order to access the inheritance, Mason must be legally wed. If he is not, he may claim it once he *is* married, but it is also up for claim by either you, Bradley, or your sister, should either of you happen to get married first. I think—well, it is my assumption that Mrs. Baldwin did not intend to pass away this young ... Perhaps she believed Mason would be married by the time she ... Forgive me, Mason, and correct me if I'm wrong, but you are not yet married, are you?"

Screw that nonsense about not speaking ill of the dead. Curse that old woman and her wicked tricks. She knew I would grow nauseated at the thought of my younger cousins getting their hands on her estate if I failed to adhere to her wishes and get married.

One glance at Bradley and Marina revealed they were wearing matching expressions of ravenous glee. They thought they'd lost the treasure they had coveted, but now they had a path to the prize. Neither one of them were married, or even close to becoming engaged, let alone involved in a committed relationship as far as I knew.

But, the same was true for me, as well. We were all in the same boat.

I had only two advantages. The first was that I was quicker and smarter than my cousins.

The second was that I had Daisy.

"No, sir. I am not married yet," I replied to Mr. Henderson, praying that the lie I was about to tell rolled off my tongue smoothly. "However, I am engaged. I apologize that I didn't get the chance earlier to introduce you to my fiancée, Daisy Campbell."

Chapter Three: *Campbell*

"—my fiancée, Daisy Campbell."

Dear Jesus, Mary, and Joseph … *what?*

Despite my best efforts, my cheeks warmed with a blush as every single person in the Baldwin Manor library—which, for the record, looked like something that belonged in a castle on the Scottish moors—turned to stare at me.

My brain worked quickly, doing its duty to solve a puzzle of information as fast as possible.

Bradley and Marina Baldwin were Mr. Reed's cousins, and other than him, the most significant heirs in the room. After just a few minutes in their company, I could tell they were the worst type of people. I couldn't even imagine what kind of horrors would be unleashed if either one of them got their hands on the three houses, significant stock holdings, and forty-two million dollars Mr. Reed's grandmother intended to give to him. So, it was a good thing she chose *him*.

Only, for some reason, he had to be married to claim the inheritance. Since he was single, the inheritance was up for grabs by any one of the three grandchildren if they were married before the others.

It was obvious that Mr. Reed had no idea such a thing would be written into his grandmother's will. He hadn't brought me here with ulterior motives in mind; he simply wasn't the kind of person who would play a trick like that. By declaring me his fiancée, he was thinking on his feet.

And, because I always wanted to be a good assistant, it was up to me to keep pace with him. When I signed the contract two years ago, I had promised loyalty. I really didn't want to let him down.

It took my brain approximately one and a half seconds to process those details before landing on the best possible course of action.

"Your fiancée?" sneered his cousin Marina, a too-skinny brunette with a sharp, steely gaze. "When the hell did you get engaged?"

Play along, Daisy, I told myself.

I stepped closer to Mason and slipped my hand into the crook of his elbow, forcing a soft smile onto my face. To his credit, he didn't flinch when I touched him, though we hadn't shared much more than a handshake since he hired me.

"It's new," I replied to Marina. "He proposed just a couple of weeks ago. We were preparing an announcement, then Mason received the news about his grandmother—"

I didn't need to finish my sentence. Everyone in the room understood that it was uncouth to allow an engagement to overshadow a death. I was shocked by the ease with which the lies tumbled out of me, not to mention how strange it felt to refer to my boss by his first name.

"Weird," muttered Bradley, shifting on the chaise where he sat to get a clearer view of me. I refused to cringe under the force of his creepy, probing gaze. "I didn't know you were even dating anyone, Mason. Where's the ring?"

"It's being sized," I answered smoothly.

"Daisy and I have been together for almost two years, Bradley," Mr. Reed replied with ease. Technically, that wasn't a lie. "However, given that you've spent the majority of that time adventuring to such intellectual locations as Ibiza, Mykonos, and Bali, I'm not surprised you were unaware of my relationship status."

It was a not-so-sly dig at the playboy persona that oozed off Bradley Baldwin in waves. However, before things could get even more tense, I cut in just as Mr. Reed's cousin was formulating a retort.

"We're hoping to set a date for September," I announced. "You'll all be receiving the invitations in your mailboxes as soon as possible."

"Two months from now? That's a rather short engagement, no?" quipped Marina, raising an eyebrow at me.

"Well, she's always wanted an autumn wedding," Mr. Reed explained, placing his hand over mine where it rested on his arm. My breath hitched at the unfamiliar contact, but I had to admit that it wasn't exactly unwelcome. "And, we're too impatient to wait until next September."

"How sweet," the attorney spoke. "Congratulations to both of you. I think we can all be grateful for some happy news during a time of grief. Allow me a couple of days to draw up some paperwork to formalize the engagement. Once that's done, I'll move forward with disbursing the contents of your inheritance, Mason."

"Thank you, Mr. Henderson," he replied. "I appreciate it."

After that, there wasn't much else for anyone to say. Mr. Reed's cousins had lost, almost won, then lost again. He and I had worked together to tell a harmless lie to secure his inheritance, and soon we would be on our way back to Manhattan where everything could go back to normal. Once Mr. Reed received his grandmother's estate, he could claim that things hadn't worked out between us and the wedding was no longer going to happen as planned. Easy-peasy.

As people began trickling out of the library, Mr. Reed started to pull away from me, but I squeezed his arm tightly and leaned in to whisper in his ear, hoping it looked as if I were simply offering him a few tender words.

"Don't let go so abruptly," I whispered to him. "It's not believable."

He cleared his throat loudly as if startled by my proximity, but followed my advice. Instead of yanking his hand away from mine, he slipped it back into his pocket casually. Similarly, I let go of him under the guise of running my fingers through my hair.

"Let's get out of here," he grumbled. "Now."

"Yes, sir."

"Thank you, by the way," Mr. Reed continued under his breath as we maneuvered through the crowded mansion. "I'm sorry for springing that on you. You did well."

It was embarrassing to admit how much I lived for praise, especially when it came from him. Mr. Reed rarely doled out compliments, so when he said something even vaguely kind, it was a big deal.

"It was no problem at all," I assured him. "In fact, it was kind of fun."

"It was the only thing I could think of. Bradley is incapable of monogamy, to say the least, and Marina's longest relationship lasted a grand total of four months, so it was the most effective lie to tell."

"I understand, Mr. Reed—"

"Call me Mason while we're still here," he interrupted. "Just in case."

"Yes, sir—I mean, Mason … but, what about you?"

"What about me?"

"You're actually single, right?" I dared to ask. "I'm not stepping on any toes by being your fake fiancée for the morning, am I?"

For some reason, the corner of his mouth quirked upward ever so slightly into a smirk. He didn't smile often, so I'd learned to pick up on the nearly imperceptible signs of amusement he displayed every once in a while.

"No, Daisy. No toes are being stepped on."

It was the closest I would get to a confirmation that Mr. Reed was single, though I already had my suspicions. How could I not, when I handled his schedule and saw for myself that he worked around the clock. Not to mention the fact that, when I reviewed his monthly expenses, there wasn't a category for personal outings or gifts. For some reason, despite being an incredibly eligible bachelor, Mr. Reed didn't date.

That was strange to a lot of people, including Jennie. She once mentioned that, thanks to the large number of celebrity clients who came to Reed Capital looking for advice on how to invest their wealth, Mr. Reed could easily hook up with a model or an actress. Apparently, he simply chose not to.

It wasn't my place to ask, but I certainly wondered why.

"Let's head out this way," Mr. Reed murmured, nodding his head toward a set of doors leading out onto a sun-soaked patio. "We can cut across the tennis courts and meet my driver at the gates."

"Sounds good."

Unfortunately, before we could make our escape, Marina Baldwin appeared out of nowhere, marching right up to us and blocking our path. A faux smile oozing with spite graced her foxlike face. I'd hoped that the last time I would have to see her was when she ducked out of the library with a dark scowl on her face, her twin brother in tow. At least Bradley was nowhere to be seen at that point.

"Where are you going, Mason?" Marina trilled. "You're not trying to sneak away already, are you? Since I've had the privilege of meeting your stunning fiancée, you have to allow me to introduce you to my boyfriend before you leave."

Mr. Reed snorted humorlessly. "Your boyfriend? What poor victim have you dragged back from France with you?"

Marina forced out a too-loud laugh in response. "You're always so funny! No, no—he's not French. We met in New York a few months ago … hey, Aiden! Babe? Come here for a second!"

Aiden was a decently common name, so when the target of Marina's exclamations rounded the corner, I didn't expect a familiar face. He wasn't just any Aiden from New York.

He was *my* Aiden from New York.

Or rather, Aiden Plourde from Indiana … and he definitely wasn't mine anymore. Once upon a time, though, he was. He wasn't just an ex-boyfriend. A long time ago, I had thought I was going to marry him.

The universe was piling a mountain of unexpected things on my shoulders that day. Unexpected subway maintenance, a road trip to Connecticut, and my first experience with improv. Weren't things like that only supposed to come in threes? How many more heart-stopping moments did fate have in store for me? I wasn't sure I could handle much more.

Once again, my mind processed the situation as quickly as possible so that my problem-solving skills could seek out a solution.

Aiden Plourde and I had met in college. We'd both studied finance, so we swam in the same social circles from the beginning, but we didn't start dating until the summer before our junior year. I loved him. I really did.

When we graduated, we discussed the possibility of marriage like the highly analytical adults we were. I was ready to agree and see Aiden get down on one knee, then realized that our ideas of what marriage entails were completely different. If we got married, Aiden wanted to settle down as soon as possible and start building a family. Naturally, since I would be the one incubating and giving birth to said family, it would require me to give up a lot of my career goals.

Then, when Aiden received a job offer to work for one of the biggest banks in the city, he suggested I might be better off becoming a full-time housewife and stay-at-home mother so that he could focus all his attention on earning money to support the family.

Becoming a wife and a mother were always things I wanted in my future, but not like that. I didn't want to give up my dreams or make any huge tradeoffs. When I told Aiden that I would rather work on establishing my career for a few years before starting a family, he took marriage off the table.

Apparently, he only wanted me as his wife if I was going to make *his* dreams come true, not mine. At that point, there was really no way for the relationship to recover. We just didn't see eye to eye, so we parted ways.

He wasn't a bad person, though. When we broke up, it was difficult, but it was also fairly amicable. The fact of the matter was, sometimes you can find the right person at the wrong time. Maybe if I had met and fell in love with Aiden when I was older and had a successful career of my own, we would have worked out.

Either way, I hadn't seen him in over four years. At first glance, he hadn't changed much, except now he clearly had a lot more money because he dressed a lot better. Plus, there was a Rolex glinting on his wrist like a beacon.

The second Aiden noticed me, he halted briefly in surprise before finishing his journey to Marina's side.

"Daisy?" he gasped. "Daisy Campbell? Is that you?"

"Hi, Aiden," I replied with a nod, having decided that the best response was to act casual and calm. "It's good to see you."

"You two know each other?" asked Marina in a harsh tone.

"Yeah, we used to—" Aiden trailed off, seeming to catch himself at the last minute. For some reason, he didn't want his current girlfriend to know that I was his ex-girlfriend, but that was fine with me. On top of everything else, I didn't need to introduce my boss to my ex-boyfriend.

"We were in the same year at Yale," I answered.

"You're a bulldog, too?" cut in Mr. Reed.

"Yes, sir," Aiden replied with a polite nod, correctly sensing that the man in front of him was older, richer, and more successful than him.

"*Babe*," Marina practically hissed at Aiden, gritting her teeth so tightly, it turned her smile into a snarl. "This is my cousin, Mason Reed and—"

"Reed as in Reed Capital? No way, man! What an honor," Aiden interrupted, reaching out to shake hands with my boss as if he were meeting the president. "What you've done with that firm is really amazing."

"—*and*," Marina continued, desperately trying to maintain control of the conversation. "This is his fiancée, who you apparently already know."

"Wait … fiancée?" Aiden almost choked. "Daisy?"

I couldn't imagine what was going through his head. We had broken up because I hadn't wanted to settle down too young. Now, here I was, still fairly young and allegedly engaged to Mason Reed, a handsome billionaire. Was he regretful? Was he impressed?

I suppose it didn't matter. It was all a lie.

"Yes, it's true," I told him, plastering a smile onto my face. "Mason and I are getting married."

"So soon, too!" chirped Marina, her voice dripping with judgment. "We'll have to remember to leave space in our September calendar for a wedding, babe."

"September? Wow, that is soon," Aiden said, eyes widening in surprise. Then, almost as if it was an afterthought, he added, "Congratulations."

"Thank you," I squeaked out.

Lying to strangers was one thing, but lying to somebody I used to be in love with was a different challenge altogether.

"Well, we should get going," Mr. Reed said. "It was nice to meet you, Aiden."

"You, too," he called out as I was steered away from the happy couple.

It didn't seem right. Aiden was dating Marina Baldwin? Of all people? Sure, he had some borderline misogynist views on gender roles in marriage, but I never thought him to be shallow or cruel. In fact, Aiden was always a very loving and attentive boyfriend to me. He was sweet and romantic and thoughtful. Although I didn't know her that well, I couldn't imagine Aiden would really be into a girl like Marina. So far, I had only seen her act snidely and spiteful, more like a teenager throwing a temper tantrum than a grown woman.

Then again, people could change. Maybe Aiden was into women like that now. Maybe Marina was the ideal candidate for a housewife and had promised him that she wanted nothing more than to dote on him and have his babies for the rest of her life.

I suppose it was none of my business.

We were close to escaping, mere inches away from the side exit Mr. Reed had pointed out before Marina pounced. I could taste freedom and normalcy on my tongue.

Then, a demure, feminine voice stopped both of us in our tracks.

"Mason, dear! You're not going to leave without introducing Auntie Kat to that gorgeous girl of yours, are you?"

At this point, it occurred to me that slipping away from a crowd of Mr. Reed's family members wasn't going to be as easy as either of us had hoped. We should have known better. The notorious bachelor had just announced out of the blue that he was tying the knot with a woman no one had ever met before.

Maybe this wasn't such a good idea after all.

Chapter Four: *Reed*

"Daisy, this is Katrina Greenwood, my—"

As always, Auntie Kat wouldn't allow anyone other than herself to control the conversation. She interrupted me before I could get halfway through a proper introduction.

"Technically, I'm his first cousin once removed," she chattered to Daisy. "I'm his Great Uncle Albert's daughter, but they always called me Auntie Kat."

"It's very nice to meet you, ma'am," replied Daisy politely, shaking Kat's hand.

Every single second she was forced to endure my stupid lie made me feel more ashamed. What was I thinking? This was inappropriate beyond belief. The second we got back to the company, I was willing to bet Daisy would be heading straight to human resources to file a complaint.

She didn't seem disturbed, though—just overwhelmed. I could only tell because she'd been working for me for so long. Auntie Kat was eating her right up without any reservations.

"Mason, darling, why didn't you tell anyone about this lovely angel of yours?" she cooed. "By the way, Daisy, is that your natural hair color?"

"Yes, ma'am."

"I knew it was too gorgeous to be bottle blonde. Anyway, Mason, how can you date a treasure like this for two entire years and not introduce her to the family? Do Abe and Annabelle know? Of course, those grandparents of yours didn't bother to come to Ruthie's wake."

I wasn't a patient man. On a normal day, Auntie Kat drove me insane. Today, while dealing with death and law and a lie that grew more complex by the minute, I could barely keep it together.

"My grandparents are in St. Lucia," I explained. "They couldn't find a flight that would get them here in time, but glancing around the house, it looks like they've sent about ten bouquets of flowers to make up for their absence."

"St. Lucia? How quaint," giggled Auntie Kat. "Anyway, what's with the mysteriousness? You're always so difficult to get ahold of, Mason."

"Ma'am, I think that might be my fault," Daisy chimed in unexpectedly. "You see, most of our relationship has been long-distance."

"Goodness, I understand," she sighed. "Plus, Mason's so busy all the time with that company of his, it's no wonder he didn't get the chance to mention you. I'm delighted to finally make your acquaintance. I look forward to the wedding."

"Thank you, ma'am."

Then, still in character, Daisy reached into her pocket and pulled out her phone. The screen was dark, but she angled it away from Auntie Kat so that she couldn't view it before faking an apologetic smile.

"I'm so sorry. This is so rude of me, but I really have to take this call. It's my doctor," she said to Kat.

"Of course, darling. I won't blame you for it."

Auntie Kat shooed Daisy away playfully. I went along with it, jolting as Daisy grabbed my hand and pulled me along behind her as she ducked out the door at last. She pressed her phone to her ear as I took the lead and guided her around the back corner of the manor until we were out of sight from my nosy relatives. Only then did Daisy slide her phone back into her pocket, drop my hand, and let out a soft sigh.

"That was slick," I told her. "I didn't know you were such a skilled actress."

"Neither did I," she joked.

There was something I wanted to say, but so many lines had already been crossed that I didn't want to push too far into personal territory. Then again, at this point, there was no going back.

"My cousin's boyfriend ... the guy you went to Yale with—"

"Aiden? What about him?"

Marina might have fallen for their not-so-subtle avoidance of the truth, but I knew a thinly-veiled lie when I saw one. Arguably, it was what made me such a good businessman.

"How long did you two date?" I asked.

Daisy blinked in surprise. For the first time, I swear she was speechless. So, I was right. He wasn't just somebody she knew from Yale. She'd had meaningful history with him ... and now he was dating my cousin ... who was related to me ... Daisy's boss ...

Small world.

We stood in the shade of a lush oak tree, one of many on my grandmother's property. There was no one else around, but the echoes of conversation on the main balcony around the corner could be heard between the singing birds and summer breeze wafting through the leaves. As a kid, long before I understood that my grandmother would attempt to reign such rigid control over my life choices, I loved coming to Baldwin Manor. It was peaceful here, the grounds so expansive that I could get lost in them for hours. At least, until the nanny hunted me down.

Daisy groaned quietly.

"I dated Aiden Plourde for three years," she admitted.

She would lie to my family because I needed her to, but she wouldn't lie to me. That was interesting.

"That's a long time."

"We were almost engaged, but—"

"But?"

She shrugged. "Our goals for the future didn't align."

I didn't know that about her, obviously. She was my executive assistant. It wasn't as if we gabbed about our lives over coffee or gossiped while braiding each other's hair.

"It's strange that he would be interested in my cousin," I commented. "Given that he was once in love with you."

"How so?"

"Marina is a miserable wench. You are not."

"I see. Honestly, I don't really know why he's into her either."

"Money?" I suggested.

"He makes seven figures a year."

"Prestige?"

"If that was the case, he could do better than her, couldn't he?" Daisy retorted. The second she realized what she'd said, she gasped and placed her fingertips over her mouth. "I'm sorry. That was rude."

I snorted. I had no idea that the ray of sunshine in front of me was capable of talking smack about other people.

"It was an honest assessment. No need to apologize," I told her.

"I'm wondering … never mind." Daisy bit her lip. She fidgeted slightly as if she didn't know what to do with her hands when she wasn't carrying around her iPad.

"Go on," I urged her, crossing my arms impatiently.

"I'm wondering if it's possible Marina knew about the marriage caveat ahead of time? Perhaps, she's been preparing to secure an engagement for months now," Daisy suggested. "Aiden is traditional. At least, he was when we were together. He'd be happy to get married, especially if forty-two million dollars was involved."

"I considered that briefly, but—" This time, it was my turn to fail to finish my sentence.

The moment Mr. Henderson read that cursed section of my grandmother's will, I had considered all the possibilities. There was no way Bradley was going to get married anytime soon—or at all, even if he went to Las Vegas and convinced a random girl to elope with him. I doubted Mr. Henderson would allow him to cut corners like that.

On the other hand, Marina was not known for maintaining long, committed relationships, but she was also conniving and two-faced. It would be downright foolish if I didn't consider the possibility of her stealing Ruth Baldwin's estate out from under my nose. The good news, I assumed, was that she was currently single.

Marina knew exactly what was going on in my mind, too, otherwise she wouldn't have bothered introducing her *boyfriend* to me. It was her subtle way of letting me know that she wasn't completely out of the game.

Maybe I would have been worried if I hadn't noticed the way Aiden looked at Daisy. At first, I thought it merely that he found her appealing. Daisy tagged along beside me nearly everywhere I went during business hours, so I was used to jaws dropping at the sight of her. But, Aiden's expression wasn't full of surprise as if admiring her for the first time.

To put it bluntly, he looked like a man who was seeing the sun for the first time in years.

Perhaps he once had genuine feelings for Marina, but they paled in comparison to what he obviously still felt for Daisy years later. That's why I had pressed her to explain why their engagement never worked out. *Their future goals didn't align.* That could mean a thousand different things, but whatever had happened between them, he clearly regretted it.

In conclusion, there was no way Marina was going to beat me to the inheritance with a guy like Aiden at her side, who was still in love with his ex-girlfriend years after they'd broken up. Even though that was good news for me, it caused me to feel annoyed. I had no reason to feel possessive over Daisy outside of professional boundaries. Oh, well.

Unlike me, Daisy didn't force me to finish my sentence. Even in our current context, she knew her place.

She wasn't just good. She was perfect.

While I was lost in thought, she'd pulled out her phone again and was frowning at it.

"Sir, I rescheduled your nine o'clock meeting with Mr. Ross to one o'clock, so we should get back on the road soon if we don't want to get caught in the midday rush."

"Agreed. That old man hates tardiness more than I do—"

"Hey, lovebirds! Sneaking around in the bushes at Grandma's funeral? Naughty!" cackled Bradley, stumbling upon us with a lopsided grin. Clearly, he'd been dipping into the liquor supply since learning his fate was sealed in the library. Either that, or he'd been drinking all morning and had finally reached the point where he couldn't help making a fool of himself.

Knowing Bradley, the latter scenario was more likely.

"Mind your business, Bradley," I told him. I placed a hand on Daisy's back to guide her around to the front of the house and as far away from Bradley as possible.

"Where're you going? Are you too cool to be seen around me now that Grandma's money made you a billionaire?" Bradley slurred, toddling after us like a child.

"I was a billionaire at the age of thirty thanks to my own efforts," I corrected him lightly over my shoulder. "How about you head inside and get yourself a glass of water before you embarrass yourself in front of someone less forgiving than me?"

"Screw you!"

I ignored his pathetic rebuttal, pressing more firmly into Daisy's back as I picked up the pace. Seconds later, we rounded the western edge of the mansion near the front lawns. Thankfully, Bradley didn't follow us any further.

"There's Maurice," Daisy murmured, pointing out my town car idling and ready, right in front of the entrance to the house. I swore my driver could read my mind and I was glad for it.

Maurice stepped out of the car as soon as he saw us approaching, opening the door for both of us to get into the back.

Much to my frustration, it appeared we weren't finished with the interruptions yet.

"Mr. Reed! Mason! Wait just a minute!"

The only reason I paused and turned around was because it was Mr. Henderson calling out for me. He was jogging down the front steps, waving to get my attention. I hovered by the open door of the car with Daisy hesitating at my side and Maurice standing nearby.

"Please excuse us," I dismissed my driver, not wanting to risk him overhearing the ridiculous web I'd gotten my assistant and myself tied up in. Obedient as ever, Maurice inclined his head and tucked himself into the driver's seat just as Mr. Henderson came to halt.

It took him a moment to catch his breath. I did my best to exercise patience, keeping an eye on the open doors to ensure no one else was going to stand in the way of our exit. If so, I had half a mind to give Maurice permission to start running people over.

"Mason, I'm so sorry to bother you when you're on your way out, but I thought it would be best for me to tell you this now instead of having to do it over a phone call later," Mr. Henderson ranted, glancing nervously between Daisy and me.

"What is it?" I asked.

"Well, I should apologize for this, but I'm afraid my initial assessment of your grandmother's will was slightly inaccurate," he replied. "A formal confirmation of your engagement to Miss—"

"—Campbell," Daisy offered.

"Thank you. Yes, in regard to your engagement to Miss Campbell, making a formal announcement will not suffice to release the inheritance. It seems Mrs. Baldwin was adamant that the marriage itself be made final before any property can be transferred. I am sorry for not understanding well enough to clarify that earlier, Mr. Reed."

"I see," I sighed.

Mr. Henderson, having no knowledge of the fraud being committed right under his nose, shrugged and offered me a helpless smile.

"It's much ado about nothing, I'm afraid," he said. "But, come September, when you two say 'I do', I can certainly get the ball rolling."

"Right. Thank you for clarifying," I replied. I wished I was as good at faking smiles as Daisy was, but I rarely smiled even when I was truly amused. "I appreciate your diligence, Mr. Henderson. Now, you'll have to excuse us. We really should be getting back to the city."

"Of course, Mason. No problem. I'll have my paralegal send over a copy of the will this week for your records. And, goodbye to you, Miss Campbell—soon to be Mrs. Reed!"

"Goodbye," Daisy breathed.

Then, miraculously, we were able to escape into the confines of my town car. I slammed the door behind me, effectively shutting out the attendees of the wake.

"Step on it, Maurice," I demanded.

"Yes, sir."

As he sped smoothly out of the gravel driveway, I pressed the button on the center console to close the divider between the back and front seats. Moments later, it was just Daisy and me.

I let out a string of expletives, dropping my head into my hands.

Daisy was more eloquent.

"An engagement won't suffice," she said softly. Thoughtfully. Like a scientist observing a perplexing phenomenon. "You actually have to get married to receive the inheritance or one of your cousins will be able to take it from you."

"It seems so," I growled, cursing again. When Daisy glanced nervously at the divider, I shook my head. "It's soundproof."

She exhaled in relief. "Oh, okay. Sir, may I ask why your grandmother would force something like this onto you? It seems cruel."

I rolled my eyes. "Ruth Baldwin is—*was*—a control freak and I was practically her muse. She wanted me to be like every other old-money gentleman."

"What do you mean?"

"You know, marry a perfect wife, have perfect kids, make a few perfect donations here and there, and then die of boredom at a perfectly acceptable age."

"Right."

"This is her way of controlling me from the grave," I grumbled, clenching my hands into fists. Meanwhile, the serene views of New England's wealthiest neighborhood passed by outside the tinted windows. "She knows I can't stand the idea of letting one of my idiot cousins inherit her estate. She probably thought adding that condition to her will would force me to hand over the reins to Reed Capital to someone else and settle down into the life she wanted for me."

"That's insane."

"That's the Baldwin family."

"Mr. Reed, I'm not sure what to say other than that I think, if you put yourself out there, you will find a woman who can make you really happy. There's no reason why you can't fulfill your grandmother's dying wishes and remain CEO of Reed Capital at the same time."

"I don't have time to date!" I protested, hating to hear my voice raise an octave. "It could take years to cultivate a relationship like that."

"I could help—"

"Please, Daisy," I interrupted, grabbing her hand and squeezing it with desperation. I probably looked like a mad man to her, but she didn't cringe or smack me away. "Please help me."

"Of course," she answered, her blue eyes wide with eagerness to please. "What do you need me to do?"

"Daisy—"

"Yes, sir?"

"I need you to play along."

"I'm sorry?"

"They already believe you're my fiancée. They think we're getting married in September. It's just a few more lies. If we follow through—"

"Mr. Reed, I can't—"

"I'll do whatever you want, Miss Campbell," I cut her off sternly. "Consider this a negotiation. If you marry me and help me secure my grandmother's fortune, your wish will be my command. I'll even give you a portion of the inheritance. How much do you want? One million? Two million? Five? Ten?"

"Sir—"

"And, I know you're not going to be my assistant forever, so I'll assist you in getting a job working for the president of the country, if that's what you want. I have connections," I continued. One of the best ways to convince someone of something was to give them no opportunity to argue. Coupled with offers Daisy couldn't reasonably refuse, I thought I had a good shot at this. "Hell, I'll even make *you* president. Please agree to this."

From the outside, I was almost positive I looked utterly pathetic. Here I was, begging a twenty-something-year-old to pretend to love me and fake a marriage with me so I could gain access to a dead relative's property, which I had been promised to be the recipient of in the first place. Was this what my grandmother wanted? She wanted me reduced to a fool, begging on my knees in front of my subordinate?

"I—" Daisy was speechless. I was screwed. The second Maurice brought this car to a halt, I was certain she was going to throw herself out of it, run away, and never show her face at Reed Capital again.

It was time to tap into my last-resort options. Daisy Campbell, like most bright ingenues who had been on the gifted and talented track since kindergarten, lived for approval. People like her thrived on positive feedback from their superiors. They *needed* it.

Daisy was a sucker for praise.

"You're an incredible assistant," I said, ignoring the nausea I felt delivering the corny flattery as I continued to squeeze her hand. "I consider myself very lucky to have hired you. Honestly, I don't know what I'd do without you. You do more for me than most executive assistants. I know this is a lot to ask, but just consider it another contract the company is trying to win. We just have to play our cards right, which you always do so well, and we'll reap the rewards of our hard work at the end of the day. Name your conditions and I'll do my best to fulfill them."

"Jesus Christ," she whispered, wriggling her hand in my grasp.

"Sorry," I said, quickly letting go of her.

"No, it's just … I don't think you've ever said that many sentences in a row to me. Your communications are usually monosyllabic."

Was that why she looked so freaked out? Because I was saying more than one sentence at a time?

Two years of knowing her, and her mind continued to baffle me.

Chapter Five: *Campbell*

I was absolutely floored. I didn't think the day could get any more insane, but I was wrong. Not only had I been asked to attend a wake with my boss for one of his family members, but I had played along to ensure that he would secure the inheritance promised in his grandmother's will. Which meant pretending to be part of a romantically involved couple with Mr. Reed, the CEO of the company where I worked and the hottest billionaire in New York, in front of his entire family.

Not to mention … my ex-boyfriend.

I still couldn't believe Aiden was dating Marina Baldwin, Mr. Reed's shallow, spoiled cousin. Who had he become in the years since our breakup? I didn't have the energy to fret about it.

I didn't have the capacity to think of much else besides the handsome man sitting beside me in the car, who also happened to be my boss, practically begging me to keep up the charade even now that we were past the boundaries of the exquisite Baldwin Estate and pretend to marry him.

Except, pretending wasn't enough.

According to what Attorney Henderson had said, formal proof of an engagement wasn't enough to entitle Mr. Reed his money. We actually had to get married. There had to be legal documentation of our marriage.

The highly logical and emotionless part of my brain was screaming at me from the dusty shadows where it usually lived. It was trying to tell me that this wasn't my problem. Just because I was Mr. Reed's executive assistant, didn't mean I was obliged to assist him in every single aspect of his life. In fact, I was only contractually obligated to help him with professional issues related to his position at Reed Capital.

But, there was a reason that little voice was often cast aside. I didn't believe in only looking at the world with pure logic and no emotion.

The truth was, I wanted to help Mr. Reed with his dilemma. Despite his difficult personality, I deeply respected him. I admired him. On top of that, I was loyal to him and didn't want to let him down. Even if it wasn't my concern whether or not he would inherit millions of dollars from his deceased relative, I felt invested in the situation. After all, I'd just met his awful cousins. Bradley was a train wreck with a fake tan and a playboy persona that I was certain couldn't be cured and Marina was a snide, disingenuous princess. Maybe they had good sides, but I considered myself an expert in reading people. If Bradley and Marina had redeemable qualities, they were buried deep.

Mr. Reed, on the other hand, was an honest, hardworking man. He didn't act like an old money brat. He cared about the work he did, the company he was growing, and the people he employed. In the two years I'd been by his side, I'd witnessed a lot of surly attitude and snippy impatience, but I had also caught glimpses of the pure, genuine heart he kept hidden deep inside himself. The last thing I wanted was for him to be forced to forfeit the majority of his grandmother's estate just because he wasn't married. What a ridiculous condition!

"Please say something," Mr. Reed murmured.

I hadn't noticed how long I'd been silent. Usually, my thought spirals were quick and efficient.

"Mr. Reed, are you seriously asking me to marry you? Legally?"

I had to make sure I wasn't utterly delirious.

"Yes," he answered. "I just need the documentation. I know it's probably not the way you were picturing your future wedding, but we don't have to think about it like that. It's just a … mutually beneficial contractual arrangement."

Wow. Romantic.

"Right," I sighed.

"It can be annulled right after the deposit is made into my account," he insisted. "Neither of us will have to become an official divorcee."

"It will have to be believable," I told him. "If it was as easy as simply getting documentation, we could go to the courthouse and elope right now. So could Marina and Aiden."

Mr. Reed nodded. "Mr. Henderson wouldn't allow an elopement. The will clearly stated a traditional marriage ceremony was necessary."

"There will need to be a wedding," I whispered. My stomach flipped, but I couldn't figure out the dizzying swirl of emotions that had caused it to happen.

"It can be small. Intimate, as they say," Mr. Reed suggested.

"I'll have to tell my parents. I can't get married—no matter the reason—and hide it from them."

He frowned for a moment, deep in thought.

"We can tell them that we met at work," he replied. "And, when we get the annulment, you can tell them I was the bad guy in the breakup."

He took my hand again. Part of me wished he would stop doing that, but then, a more significant part of me couldn't hide that I wanted more. All the soft, subtle touches we'd shared inside the mansion—his hand at the base of my spine, my hand tucked into the crook of his elbow—made my skin tingle. I wasn't supposed to feel that way about him. He was my *boss*. It was inappropriate.

Of course, I'd always found Mr. Reed attractive. It was impossible not to. He could have been an actor or a model if he wanted to, with his strong jaw, piercing eyes, and thick hair. In the early days of being his executive assistant, I had to remind myself daily that developing a crush on him would only spell disaster for me. Eventually, I shook it off.

Unfortunately, those old, dormant feelings were starting to bubble up again now that topics such as dating and marriage and love were being thrown around.

"Mr. Reed—" I sighed, letting my voice trail off. I wanted to say yes. I wanted to help him. Not because of my stupid little crush, but because I truly believed in him. I wanted to see him continue to be successful, not only because it would benefit me, but also because he deserved it.

"How about you call me Mason?" he suggested, his tone oddly timid. "I think that, given what I just put you through, it's only fair that we're on a mutual, first-name basis, Daisy."

I rarely used his first name. If I did, it was only in the context of referring to him as Mr. Mason Reed. He was never just *Mason.*

But, I didn't hate the idea of being more casual with him.

Mr. Reed—or rather, Mason—shifted in the seat to face me more directly. I wondered if he was about to give me one final business pitch before demanding I draw a conclusion, but then, my brain fizzled as his knee gently nudged my thigh. It was an accidental touch, one that I expected him to immediately pull away from.

He didn't. He kept his leg resting there, pressing ever so slightly against mine. Was he doing it on purpose? Was he, the least flirtatious person I'd ever met, encouraging me with physical connection? Or, was he so consumed in the desperate moment that he didn't even notice the touch at all?

I closed my eyes and pinched the bridge of my nose. I already knew what my answer was going to be. If I was being completely honest with myself, I never considered the opposite path. The ability to say no to people in need wasn't written in my DNA.

Taking a deep breath, I opened my eyes and stared at Mason as if he were a business partner, not my superior, and we were brokering a particularly hard bargain.

"Okay," I said. "I will do this."

"You—"

"—but I have one major condition," I carried on, daring to speak over him for the first time ever.

Mason visibly deflated with relief, his greenish-blue eyes lighting up in a way I'd never seen before. He was happy. I was making him happy.

That was all I ever wanted to do.

"Name it," he replied.

"Nobody at Reed Capital can know about this," I softly demanded. "My reputation is very important to me, as is my future career path. If anyone finds out that I'm *involved* with the company's CEO, regardless of the fact that it's not true, people will think that I'm the type of person who sleeps my way to the top."

Mason furrowed his brow with concern, as if it hadn't occurred to him that was a possibility. I wasn't surprised. He was a man. They usually didn't have to worry about stuff like that.

"I understand. Of course. I agree to your condition. Anything else?"

"I would like you to pay off my student loans."

At that, Mason let out a small breath of laughter. "Fine. I'll pay off your future children's student loans, too. Is that all?"

"I'd also like you to give Jennie a promotion and a raise," I added.

"Jennie? Who?"

"Jennifer James, the C-suite secretary."

"Right. Miss James. She is a valuable employee … sure. I'll arrange it."

"Good."

The barest ghost of a smirk danced across his features. "Would you like to add anything else to the list? I think it's clear that you have all the power in this negotiation."

There were plenty of things I could ask for. I could ask him to give me a promotion and a raise just like Jennie, but I wanted to earn those things the old-fashioned way. The only reason I vouched for my friend was because I feared her hard work went unrecognized. Anyone who paid attention to Jennie knew that she deserved to be much more than an overworked and underpaid secretary.

I could have asked for money. With my help, Mr. Reed—*Mason*—stood to inherit forty-two million dollars in cash, and the majority of Ruth Baldwin's stock holdings and a significant amount of real estate. If I wanted a piece of that pie, it would be easy to ask for it.

The thing was, I didn't really care about money or net worth or glamorous properties. They were nice to have, but that wasn't why I worked hard. Rather, I wanted to make a name for myself in this world, and for everyone to know that I wholeheartedly earned it all by myself. I wanted people to know that a skinny little girl from a small town in Vermont could become successful without all the privileges that many others were born into.

Mason couldn't give that to me. That was the whole point. Nobody could give it to me. I had to obtain it for myself.

I shrugged. "That's it."

"Seriously? Don't you want some of the money?"

"No, that's okay."

He raised his eyebrows at me, lips parted slightly in surprise. Maybe he'd never witnessed anyone turning down the offer of money in his life.

"Okay, then. We have a deal?"

Mason stuck out his hand to shake mine. I didn't hesitate.

"Deal," I answered, slipping my hand into his and shaking firmly.

At that exact moment, the chauffeur merged onto the highway, and at the last second, stomped on the brakes to avoid careening into a traffic jam that hadn't been visible until the last minute. I jolted forward, but Mason instinctively threw out an arm across my stomach to soften the impact.

There was a tap on the barrier between the front seat and us, a wordless apology from the driver. Mason reached out to tap back, indicating that it was all right, but the barrier remained in place. When he turned back to me, I was a bit breathless.

"Thanks," I whispered. "But, I'm wearing a seatbelt."

"It was impulse," he admitted. "My apologies."

"It's okay."

A beat of silence flooded between us. My stomach was fluttering from the ghost of his hand pressing against it protectively. Outside, it looked like traffic heading back into Manhattan was dragging particularly slow. We wouldn't be back at the office for at least half an hour. The urge struck me to whip out my iPad, check my email, and confirm his schedule was still on track, but I temporarily ignored it. It didn't seem like the right time.

Mason cleared his throat. "So, I guess we're engaged."

"I guess so," I laughed.

"Thank you, Daisy. I mean it. I don't know how to explain how grateful I am, but I think it's safe to say that not everyone's assistant would go to such lengths for them."

I shrugged. "I trust you."

It was a simple explanation, but I hoped it got my point across. It was the most succinct way I could summarize why I decided to agree to something as insane as a fake marriage with my boss.

He smiled. A real smile. They were so rare and fleeting that I almost thought it was a trick of the light. It faded within seconds.

"Thank you," he said gruffly.

Then, with a quiet exhale, he rested his head back against the seat. He made a grunting noise in the back of his throat, a familiar sound that I had learned to recognize as an indication of his being extremely stressed out, but trying not to show it. I didn't blame him. He was in a position just as precarious as mine, if not more so.

If anyone found out that the CEO of Reed Capital had coerced his assistant into legally marrying him so that he could secure a fortune, he'd be seen as the sleaziest guy on the East Coast. Never mind that there was no coercion involved and I had totally consented to the situation. He was my superior, he was older than me, and he basically held my professional fate in his hands.

On top of that, his grandmother had died. No matter how complicated their relationship had been, I was sure that was also taking a toll on him.

I suppose that was why I reached out and placed my hand on top of his knee. It was the first gesture of comfort I could think of.

Mason tensed and lifted his head to meet my gaze.

"Sir—" I mumbled.

"Yes?"

"I—please don't let this stress you out more than necessary. It's my job to make your life easier so, as usual, you can count on me."

The corner of his lips twitched upward. "As usual. Thank you, Daisy."

"Also—"

"Yes?"

"Your tie is a bit crooked."

"Oh." With a slight frown, he grabbed the knot of his tie and tugged it toward the middle of his collar, only making it crooked in the other direction. "Better?"

"Not really. Let me help."

Mason held still as I scooted closer and carefully took hold of the knot in his tie. It was made of mulberry silk, one of the most expensive types of silk in the world, which I knew because I was the one who had ordered it for him. It felt like cool water beneath my fingertips, yet my skin was on fire as I carefully readjusted the loop around his neck. His throat bobbed as he swallowed, light stubble dusting his jaw. My eyes traveled upward until they met his, one hand still loosely gripping onto his tie.

It was only then that I realized just how close we were. Our faces were mere inches away. I couldn't help pausing to admire his thick eyelashes. It was funny to think that someone as dominant and masculine as him could have such a pretty feature as dense, fluttery eyelashes.

"What's so funny?" he asked me, his voice low.

There was a note in his voice that I didn't recognize. Over the past two years, I'd gotten to know the intricate nuances of Mason's tones. I knew when he was annoyed, tired, satisfied, or whatever else.

But, this was new.

"Nothing," I answered. There was no way I was about to tell my boss how much I liked his pretty eyelashes. I'd rather roll myself into oncoming traffic.

I loosened my grip on his tie and was about to back away, but he reached up and closed his hand over mine on top of his chest to stop me. I froze.

"You're a beautiful woman," he said. "I hope you know that. Whichever man you *actually* marry in the future will be very lucky."

He thought I was beautiful? For some reason, it had never occurred to me that I could be physically appealing to Mason beyond being dressed appropriately for work. Sometimes, it was hard to remember that he was a human male like all the others.

"That's very nice of you to say, Mr. Reed."

"Mason. Call me Mason, Daisy."

"Sorry ... Mason."

The second I said his name, it was as if something snapped. What had once been mere tension was now electric, unbearable suspense.

It was the stress of the day, I told myself. We were both a little panicky and desperate. We were deeply connected in so many ways, but the novelty of this proximity, of these timid touches, was enough to trigger something primal within both of us.

Before I knew it, we were kissing. His lips were softer than I expected, but his kiss was anything but. Mason didn't waste time with polite buildup, instead kissing me fiercely as if he were ravenous for my lips. I lost myself in the reckless heat of the moment, wrapping my arms around his shoulders and slipping my tongue past his lips.

He groaned, low and guttural. Not for the first time, I was glad that the barrier between the chauffeur and us was apparently soundproof. As he maneuvered the car slowly but surely closer to midtown Manhattan, Mason and I were consumed in our own world.

Grabbing my waist tightly, he tugged me closer. My body instinctively knew what he wanted, so I flung off my seat belt and lifted myself up, hooking my leg over his hips so that I was straddling his lap. I gasped for air between kisses, our ragged breathing hitting a staccato rhythm. Mason trailed his large hands down my hips. He grabbed my ass firmly through my trousers, squeezing tightly.

An inferno of heat raged through me, causing me to roll my hips against him. As I did so, I could feel his hardening length through the fabric of his pants pressing against my inner thigh. Goosebumps erupted on my skin.

He was … *big.*

I felt like a madwoman, as if something wild and uncontrollable had been unleashed. Where was my composure? My professionalism?

Either way, I didn't care. I just knew I wanted him. I wanted this.

I rolled my hips again, dropping my forehead onto his shoulder. Mason cursed, moving his hands only briefly enough to push my blazer off my shoulders and onto the floor of the car, then returned them to my butt.

"Again," he crooned, guiding my desperate motions against his body into a continuous pulse of my heat against his. The friction was torturous.

I let out a whimper, clinging onto him for dear life. There were layers of clothing between us, but that didn't stop the tingle of desire between my thighs growing stronger each time I thrusted against him. But, I didn't want to be the only one getting something out of this ridiculous, ill-advised tryst.

"Can I touch you?" I whispered.

"Please," he growled.

I wasn't one to ignore polite orders, so I slid my hands down his front. A metallic *clink* followed seconds later as I undid his belt, then quickly unbuttoned and unzipped his pants. He shifted beneath me as I dipped my hand under the waistband of his briefs and coaxed his erection out.

I'd already felt how large it was, but seeing it with my own eyes made my heart skip a beat.

"Jesus Christ," I cursed out loud before I could stop myself.

"Let's leave God out of this," Mason suggested gruffly before capturing my lips in another kiss.

I stroked him as I started up my own movements again, building my climax with just the help of his thigh and the seam of my trousers. I knew that if I paused for even a second to think about what I was doing in the back of that car with Mason Reed of all people, I would start freaking out.

And, it felt too good to stop.

I rubbed him in tandem with stuttering hips, but as I got closer and closer to the edge, I lost the tempo. Collapsing against him, Mason let out a long, low moan as I picked up the pace for both of us.

I wished I was naked. *No, I didn't.* Yes, I did.

I wished I could feel his skin against mine. *Stop that.* I didn't want to.

I wished he was inside me. *Shut up.* I couldn't.

My mind was at war with itself, that highly logical party pooper inside my brain trying to beat down the part of me that just wanted to feel good. It had been so long since I'd been intimate with someone, so long since I'd even kissed a man. I hadn't realized how much I missed it.

When my climax struck, I inhaled sharply and pressed my face into the crook of his neck to stifle the shout I wanted to let out. It didn't seem right that I was able to unravel like that while still fully clothed, but I suppose not being touched in ages could do that to a woman. Either that, or Mason just had that effect on me.

Either way, when I caught my breath, I realized that I was still pumping his length in my hand. The dark-eyed, furiously needy look on his face told me that he was dangerously close.

Without hesitating, I wriggled off his lap and sat back down in my seat. A flicker of disappointment in his gaze told me that he was convinced for half a second that I wasn't going to help him finish, but that immediately faded when I ducked my head and took him in my mouth.

Chapter Six: *Reed*

Damn it. Shit.

My cock was in her mouth.

My … her … Daisy …

The trip to Connecticut wasn't supposed to end like this. When I woke up this morning, I had thought I would be millions of dollars richer and my assistant would still be simply that—my assistant. Now, we were in the back of my town car, her lips wrapped around my erection, and she was bobbing her head eagerly in my lap.

Not to mention the fact that we were literally engaged to be married.

This isn't right, I thought to myself even as I gripped a fistful of her hair and closed my eyes in ecstasy. *There were at least seven HR violations happening at this very moment.*

Stuff like this didn't happen in real life. This was a fantasy, a movie plot. I'd always been able to acknowledge that Daisy was unfairly sexy and demure, but that was only because I wasn't blind or stupid. Never in a million years did I plan to act on it. That was sick and twisted.

"Daisy," I panted, using her hair to tug her head off me as I reached my climax. "Daisy, I'm—"

She lifted her head just as I dissolved into a wave of pleasure that struck me dumb for several seconds. I clapped a hand over my mouth to stifle my groan as I came onto her hand.

And then, she smiled at me. It was a timid grin. Nervous. She was afraid she'd done something wrong, that returning my kisses and not stopping things before they went too far was the wrong decision. It was as if she believed she'd just failed a test.

"I … I … oh, my God," she breathed, glancing down at my lap as I tucked myself back into my trousers. "I'm so sorry."

I chuckled. "What are you sorry about? I'm the one who just—"

When I trailed off, Daisy looked at her hand as if she couldn't believe her eyes. "It's okay. I have tissues."

As she fumbled in her purse for a packet of tissues to clean up the mess, I tucked in my shirt. Comically, I realized I'd been locked safely in my seat belt the whole time.

I looked out the window for the first time since we'd left my grandmother's estate. With a jolt, I noticed that we were only a few blocks away from the office. Despite getting caught in traffic, time had sped up in the heat of the moment.

"That was good timing," I muttered under my breath.

Daisy quickly fixed her hair, running her fingers through her long, blonde waves and smoothing down the front of her shirt. She collected her blazer from where it lay in a heap at her feet. As she pulled it on over her blouse, I caught sight of an embarrassed blush on her cheeks.

"I'm sorry," she said again, avoiding my gaze as she gathered her things.

"Why are you apologizing?" I asked, genuinely curious. Normally, she wasn't like this. "What do you have to be sorry for?"

She bit her lip. "I got … carried away."

I snorted. "There was more than one person involved in that scenario, Daisy. If I didn't want it to happen, I would've stopped it. I mean that."

"But, just because you kissed me, didn't mean that I needed to—"

"I'm serious," I interrupted sternly. "You're making me feel like I let you take advantage of me or something. I was a willing participant in that."

She glanced away as we pulled up to the curb in front of the high-rise that housed Reed Capital headquarters. "It was a mistake. I don't want you to think that I was waiting for the opportunity to—or that I think about you like—"

"Look at me," I commanded, fed up with this blushing, stuttering version of my executive assistant. She obeyed instantly. "There has never been any point in the last two years when I questioned your professionalism, and I hope that you can say the same for me. What just happened was both of us allowing our stress to get the better of us. We can forget about it and pretend it never happened, if you'd like."

Daisy exhaled in relief. "Yes, please."

There was no way I could force myself to lose the memory of her lowering her head between my legs, but I would at least try not to dwell on it. While I was in the workplace, at least.

"Good. It's done."

I waited for her to answer my handshake. After a brief pause, she did.

"Moving on," she sighed, turning away from me to let herself out onto the sidewalk.

"Our agreement is still in place, yes?" I asked before she opened the door. "That little moment didn't endanger anything, did it?"

Daisy chuckled quietly. "No, Mr. Reed. Don't worry. I'm still your secret fiancée. I won't let you down."

"Good to hear."

"Yes, now come on," Daisy replied, her demeanor changing like a flipped switch back into the no-nonsense, efficient assistant I knew well. "You have a meeting in five minutes."

"Shit," I hissed, quickly stumbling out of the town car after her and rushing into the building.

***

The rest of the work day passed normally, except for the fact that I couldn't stop thinking about Daisy. Not in a stupid, daydreamy way. I was just keeping an eye on her.

After we arrived back at work and parted ways, me to my typical endless string of meetings and her to the little office she used to run my life, I decided to leave her alone. Giving her space was the best course of action. It was what I did at the end of most difficult business deals. After someone made a difficult decision, it was natural for them to panic a little bit. An intellectual knew hovering wouldn't help.

It wasn't that I was worried Daisy was going to back out of the marriage. It genuinely seemed as if she wanted to help me with the nasty situation my grandmother had left behind for me to deal with. In fact, Daisy never said no to me. Not once in two years had she complained, even when I was fully aware that my demands were pushing the limit of possibility. She was a people pleaser, a textbook formerly gifted kid who lived for praise.

And, that was why I was worried.

During a brief respite between scheduled obligations, I paced the hardwood back and forth inside my office. I hadn't seen Daisy for hours. Part of me was starting to question if that scene in the car actually happened or if I had fallen asleep on the ride back and dreamed it.

Only, physically speaking, I knew it was real. I hadn't touched a woman—or been touched by a woman—like that in longer than I was willing to admit. My body was relishing the release of tension even if my brain was anguishing over the details.

Was I a monster? Was I taking advantage of her? Knowing that Daisy was unlikely to refuse anything I asked of her, had I subconsciously clung on to that and used it to my benefit? Was this manipulative and cruel of me?

For all I knew, she was downstairs talking to Human Resources, preparing to press charges and claim that I was a predator. She'd have a decent case. I was her superior, the man who metaphorically signed her checks, and I had brought her to a personal family event, placed her in an awkward situation where she basically had no choice but to agree that she was my girlfriend, begged her to marry me so that I could inherit money, and then made the first move in the back of the car.

What the hell was wrong with me?

Nervously, I poked my head out of my office. Down the hall, I heard the distinct sound of Daisy's musical laughter over the normal hustle and bustle of the executive floor.

"Of course, Mrs. Chae!" I heard her chirp. It sounded as if she was on the phone with one of our oldest clients, a rich widow from Seoul who had too much money and no idea what to do with it before she enlisted the help of Reed Capital. Now, thanks to me, she was even richer.

At least Daisy sounded normal. She was always so cheerful, so friendly. It didn't matter who she was talking to. Even when young, misogynistic douchebags showed up for consultations on what to do with all their outrageous trust funds, Daisy took their leers and wandering eyes in stride. I didn't know how she did it.

Right … people pleaser.

I checked my watch. It was four-thirty. The office closed at five. Most of the staff on the lower floors went home the second the clock struck the hour, but the C-suite was usually active for a few more hours.

Trying to calm my frayed nerves, I sat at my desk and opened the email from Mr. Henderson with the details of my grandmother's will and final requests. Except, reading it pissed me off all over again, so instead I busied myself with fulfilling one of Daisy's contractual requests. She wanted the secretary to get a promotion and a raise. That was easy enough. I didn't mind doing it. I just had to make sure there was a proper position available for the girl and make the transition seem natural.

I was able to think for about two minutes before my phone started ringing. It wasn't the office phone on my desk, but my personal cell phone. When I grabbed it and looked at the screen, I cursed out loud.

The name *Bradley Baldwin* was shining brightly up at me.

"What do you want?" I answered. "Some of us have jobs."

"Hello to you, too, cousin," snickered Bradley. "You can't possibly be too busy for family, can you?"

"I'll give you five seconds before I hang up."

Another idiotic cackle met my ears from the other side of the line. I rolled my eyes at the empty room.

"I just wanted to call and properly congratulate you on the engagement. I didn't get a chance to speak with you before you left the wake. You really hurried out of there, didn't you, Mason?"

"Thanks," I grumbled.

"You know, I didn't even know you were dating—"

"Well, I don't post every detail of my personal life on the internet like you. It's called having class."

"Right, right. I'll make note of that. Anyway, you'd think at least *somebody* in the family would've heard about that pretty girl of yours. What's the matter? Does she turn into an ogre when the sun sets?"

Something about hearing Bradley refer to Daisy as a *pretty girl* with that slimy tone of voice made me want to punch my fist through the drywall. I choked back the urge.

"It's hard to get ahold of you when you're gallivanting around the world on the family's dime," I bit back. "My apologies."

"It's strange," Bradley mused. He clearly wasn't listening to a word I was saying, merely taking the opportunity between my responses to taunt me like a moron. "I thought you were, like, a lone wolf or something. Or, asexual. I mean, how many girlfriends have you had in your life? Negative three?"

"Is there a point to this call or can I hang up now?"

"Marina says you've been dating that chick for two years, man—"

"How about you mind your damn business, *man*?" I snapped.

Without waiting for a response, I hung up and slammed my phone down onto my desk. I knew I shouldn't have bothered answering. Bradley lacked the brain cells to hold a productive conversation no matter the context.

In the silence that followed, I heard another echo of Daisy's voice from down the hall. It sounded as if she was talking to one of the other executives, her tone bright and chipper.

I couldn't take it anymore.

With a huff, I punched the button that would connect me to the phone on her desk. The muffled conversation floating through my office door stopped short. She picked up after the first ring. For some reason, the thought of her stopping mid-sentence in order to rush to pick up my call quelled my frustration the slightest bit.

"Yes, Mr. Reed?" she answered.

"Can you come to my office?"

"Yes, sir."

She hung up. It was a normal exchange, one that often happened multiple times a day. Yet, given the morning we'd had, it felt different this time.

It took her less than a minute to bustle her way into my office. She paused in the doorway, iPad in hand, ready to perform her duties as my executive assistant. If not for the briefest flicker of uncertainty in her gaze, it would have appeared as though she and I had never shared that sordid moment in the back seat.

"Come in. Close the door."

She obeyed, stepping inside and quickly shutting us off from the rest of the executive floor.

"What can I do for you?" Daisy asked automatically.

"Sit down," I told her. Once again, she did exactly what she was told without hesitation. "How are you doing?"

She frowned in confusion. "I'm sorry?"

"How are you?" I repeated. "I'm checking in regarding the events of earlier today."

"Well, I received the estate documents from Attorney Henderson's paralegal, Yuna. I'm building a spreadsheet with an itemization of the contents of the estate, and I've reached out to Ruth Baldwin's account manager at JP Morgan to confirm—"

"That's not what I meant," I cut her off.

Daisy bit her lip, lowering her gaze. "Right."

I wasn't sure if I was going to regret what I was about to ask her, but I knew I needed to do something about the awkward tension between us. I needed the inheritance, but I wasn't sure I was willing to sacrifice my assistant for it. Daisy was too perfect. It was rare to find someone like her, professionally speaking.

"I'd like to invite you over to my place for dinner tomorrow night," I said.

"What? Your place?"

"Yes, I'm assuming you have my home address. I'll have my chef prepare something. Do you have any food allergies?"

"But, sir … why?"

At least she wasn't handing in her resignation. That was promising.

"I think it would be a good idea for us to discuss the details of my grandmother's deal and our ensuing arrangement outside the context of the workplace," I explained. "We should talk about it as equals. If it makes you uncomfortable to meet at my home, I can book a private dining room at your restaurant of choice."

Daisy shook her head. "No, it's okay. It doesn't make me uncomfortable. Sure—I mean … yes, sir. I'll put it in my calendar. What time?"

"Does seven work for you?"

"Yes, sir."

"Great."

She shifted in her seat. She wasn't used to being asked to sit down in my office, instead always ready on her feet to receive my demands and flit off to the next place she needed to be.

"Anything else, Mr. Reed?"

There were a dozen different things I wanted to say to her, but I didn't know how to put them into words. I also wasn't convinced that it wouldn't make her visible nervousness a thousand times worse. She was spooked.

And yet, she still wasn't running away.

"No, Daisy. You may go."

She scurried out of my office so fast, it was as if she didn't want to be there in the first place. She'd never been like that before. In fact, Daisy was pretty much the only non-executive in the whole company who didn't tremble with fear at the sound of my voice. If that had changed, I was screwed.

It was all bloody Ruth Baldwin's fault.

Chapter Seven: *Campbell*

Poppy Maxwell, my best friend from college, threw her head back and cackled loudly. "It's always the ones you least expect."

I pouted at her over the salted rim of my margarita. "What's that supposed to mean?"

"You know exactly what I mean," she giggled. "Goody-two-shoes, never breaks the rules, always says 'yes, sir' and 'yes, ma'am'—of course you'd end up in a situation like this!"

"You're one to talk!" I whined. "You're just as much of a goody-two-shoes as I am."

Poppy smirked and put on a fake Southern-belle voice. "That's where you're wrong, Miss Daisy. I'm hardly an angel."

"You're an attorney at one of the most successful law firms in the city," I quipped.

"So? Just because we're both successful doesn't mean I'm as strait-laced as you. I've prioritized my womanly needs so that I can be a millionaire by the age of thirty *and* not become sexually repressed."

"Hey! I am not sexually repressed!" I protested.

We were in a loud, busy bar on the Lower East Side, so my words weren't in danger of being overheard. After the day I'd had, beginning all the way back with my public transportation issues, I desperately needed a drink. Luckily, Poppy wasn't too busy with her hectic career to join me and listen to me rant.

"Oh, please," she teased me. "When's the last time you had sex? Not counting this morning?"

"I didn't—we didn't—technically ... God, I don't even know."

With a groan, I dropped my head into my hands. Poppy tutted her tongue and reached out to pat my arm.

"Honestly, I think it's kind of sexy," she replied. "Like, as your friend, I'm really proud of you right now. You've never done anything scandalous in your life, so it's about time. That being said, as an attorney, I am a little concerned about the legal ramifications of conducting an affair with your boss—"

"It's not an affair!" I protested. "I already told you. He needs help and I just happen to be the most available candidate for the situation."

"Seriously? He doesn't have, like, a girlfriend or two? He's Mason Reed, after all. I bet there are a million women begging for the chance to suck his—"

"Jesus Christ, Poppy!" I hissed.

She snickered. I took a large gulp of my drink, but the burn of the alcohol was slow in calming my frayed nerves.

"I can't believe Aiden was there," Poppy continued chattering. "Although, I'm not all that surprised to hear he's dating someone like that. What's her name again? Marie? Macy?"

"Marina."

"Right. Marina. You know I was never the biggest fan of Aiden Plourde, so the fact that he's cozying up to a bitchy, old-money heiress is basically exactly what I expected."

I pursed my lips, drumming my fingers on the tabletop. Poppy and I had known each other since our freshman year at Yale when we were randomly paired together as roommates. We were thick as thieves, both of us from small towns in the middle of nowhere and fiercely ambitious. The best part was that, because we had never pursued the same career field, we never had to compete with each other. We could cheer one another on from the sidelines.

Since we'd known each other for so long, Poppy was the only other person who knew the dirty details of the demise of mine and Aiden's relationship. It was true, she had never liked him much, but she held her tongue for the most part. When we finally broke up, though, she was free to speak her mind. I didn't mind. Obviously, Aiden and I didn't end things on the best of terms, but I preferred to move on with optimism rather than dwell on the negative things in my past. Despite that, it was validating to know that my best friend agreed I was better off without him.

"Aiden can date whomever he wants," I said to Poppy. "I really don't care. Considering everything that happened today, it's pretty low on the ranking of things that have me freaking out."

"What is there to freak out about?" Poppy asked. "I thought you said you both reached an agreement."

"We did, at least in terms of the marriage. We'll get it annulled as soon as he gets the money. It's just that I can't stop thinking about the fact that I made out with my boss in the back of his town car."

"Didn't you like it?"

"Yes."

"And, didn't he?"

"It seemed so."

"And, you agreed that it was just a one-time, heat-of-the-moment thing?"

"Yeah, but—"

Poppy wiggled her eyebrows at me suggestively. "But, what?"

I ran my fingers through my hair in exasperation. "I can't stop thinking about it."

"Of course you can't. Your boss is sexy as hell. Any normal person would've been begging for the chance to jump his bones from the moment they were hired."

"But, I was never a 'normal person', as you say. Mason isn't just attractive. He's clever and fair-minded. He runs his company incredibly well, and it's obvious that he truly cares about Reed Capital and its employees. I've always admired him in a professional sense and knew that I didn't want to allow any other forms of admiration to ruin the possibility of me working for him for many years to come. But, now—"

"Now—?"

I sighed heavily. "I mean, I tried all day to forget how stupidly good that little hookup was and I thought I was doing a pretty good job of it. Except, just when I thought I was about to make it through the rest of the work day without having to see him again, he asked me to come to his office and shut the door."

"Oh, this is better than a porno," murmured Poppy with a devilish smirk. I flicked her on the arm, but she only laughed and swatted me away.

"It was maddening," I groaned. "He invited me for dinner at his place, but not in the context of romance. It's going to be like a business meeting, which is fine, but the entire time I was shut away in his office with him, I couldn't stop thinking about the possibility of us … of him—"

"Go on," Poppy coaxed me.

I blushed furiously. "Honestly, I had this image in my mind of him throwing me on top of his desk and finishing what we started in the car."

"Whew!" she swooned, fanning herself as if it was getting too hot in the bar. "My innocent, hardworking Daisy was having thoughts like *that*?"

"It's never happened before, I swear! Never. I've always been so good at ignoring how handsome he is and … ugh. I don't know what came over me. I practically ran out of the room once he dismissed me because I was so ashamed of myself."

"You want to know what I think?" Poppy asked.

"I know you're going to tell me either way."

She ignored the playful dig. "I think you have no reason to be ashamed, Daisy. You're human. Don't forget that. We're nothing more than barely-evolved jungle animals with hormones and instinctive urges. It's totally normal to indulge a little fantasy about someone you find attractive. It doesn't make you a bad person or any less good at your job. Plus, it's not as if he stopped you from—*you know*—so it's safe to say he wanted it, too. I'm sure he's had some naughty thoughts about you in the past couple of years. Like, look at you, Daisy. You're gorgeous."

I gulped. I hadn't considered that before. The idea that Mr. Reed—or Mason, or whatever I was supposed to call him inside the privacy of my own mind now—might have experienced fleeting thoughts about me in compromising situations once or twice over the past couple of years startled me. It wasn't that I was upset by the possibility of it, but rather that it simply didn't sound plausible. He was so rigid. So cool and logical.

"I don't think that's helping," I muttered. As Poppy gazed at me with a mixture of concern and amusement, I downed the rest of my margarita and gestured at the waitress for another one.

"I think you need to calm down and loosen up, Daisy," Poppy offered. "The way I see it, this could actually be a blessing in disguise."

"How so?"

"Well, you really do have the upper hand here, so you can negotiate pretty much anything you want out of this marriage agreement. Plus, even though it's fake … who knows? Maybe this is the beginning of a beautiful love story."

"You're joking."

"Think about it! There's all this unresolved sexual tension between the two of you. You already spend every day together, and now you also have to pretend to be engaged. You'll get the chance to see a side of Mason Reed you wouldn't otherwise witness, which is not a bad thing in the slightest. I can see it now; you're going to fall for each other. Just go with the flow, girl. Trust the path that the universe has placed you on. He's basically a prince, Daisy, and you're as pretty as a princess. It's like a fairytale."

The waitress dropped off my drink with a silent nod as Poppy finished her monologue. I gulped down half of it in the span of a few seconds and fixed Poppy with a firm stare.

"That's ridiculous."

"Open your mind, Daisy!"

"It's not that I don't think that sounds lovely, because it does. It's not as if I'm jaded. You know that. It's just … Mason is definitely not Prince Charming. He's allergic to love."

Poppy scoffed. "That's impossible. You can't look as good as he does and not have a few notches in your headboard."

I shrugged. "It's true, though. I've never seen him date anyone. I'm the one who handles his schedule, remember? I'd be the first to know. I actually can't even picture it. He's so focused on the company."

"Career-obsessed birds of a feather," Poppy crooned. "It's a tale as old as time."

"I'm not obsessed with my career," I argued lightly. "It's just my number-one priority. Same for him."

"Sure, sure. Go ahead and defend your sexy boss's honor."

"You're insufferable," I moaned, but I couldn't help cracking a smile.

Poppy had always been like this. Even though she'd always been ferociously ambitious, she was also very good at not taking things too seriously. She believed that going with the flow and listening to her heart was the best way to achieve her goals. I suppose it worked out for her, but I wasn't like that. I couldn't simply believe that there was an ambiguous higher power nudging me in a particular direction. I was the kind of person who wanted complete control of the journey taken in this life.

"Everything's going to be okay, Daisy," Poppy said. "Don't lose sleep over this. In fact, I'm sure once you get a full night of rest, you'll wake up tomorrow morning feeling much calmer about this whole thing. Plus, you have me for support, as always. Also, if there ever comes a point where that delectable CEO of yours starts to make you feel uncomfortable, I can whip out a harassment lawsuit in, like, ten minutes. I've got your back either way."

"Thanks," I chuckled. "I appreciate it. I don't think the lawsuit will be necessary. I can't believe I even agreed to this in the first place. I thought I was just going to help him out with some note-taking at the wake and … I walked out of there as his fake fiancée. I played along with almost no hesitation. What's wrong with me?"

"Nothing's wrong with you," Poppy insisted. "You just have a praise kink."

"Excuse me?"

"Like, duh. Maybe you don't climax every time somebody says *good girl*, but you're definitely a people pleaser. I get it. I'm the same, to an extent. They curse us to be like this when we're young, innocent, so-called gifted kids. We spend our whole childhood and teenage years being praised for how smart and special we are that it becomes our primary source of motivation. Thus, we don't really know how to structure our lives or careers or relationships around anything else."

"That's pretty deep."

"It's true. Trust me. I started going to therapy, so I'm basically the most enlightened person you know."

"Right."

Poppy smiled, her expression devoid of her usual mischief. "Be honest with me, okay? You feel like you're supposed to regret the decision to play along with this inheritance scheme, right?"

"Yes."

"But, you don't, because–"

"Because, I didn't want to let Mr. Reed down. Also, his cousins are walking disasters. It doesn't seem fair that they could get their hands on their grandmother's money just because Mr. Reed has been too focused on building the company to settle down and find a wife."

"But, it's literally not your problem."

"I know that—"

"I'm not judging you," Poppy interrupted gently. "I'm just saying. Anyway, let's say you call the whole thing off. What then?"

I frowned deeply. "Then, Mason would be disappointed and angry. He wouldn't get his inheritance and I would probably be fired for being the reason why."

"Well, I doubt that. You can't fire an assistant for not wanting to marry you," she replied. "Although, New York is an at-will state, so I suppose he wouldn't really need a reason to fire you if he wanted to."

"Thanks, Poppy. This is really helpful."

"My point is—you're not going to back out of this, are you? Even though it all feels crazy and stupid, you're going to forge ahead and see it through, right?"

Pinching the bridge of my nose, I nodded reluctantly. "Yeah, I am. It feels like the only way."

"Exactly. Thus, because you haven't completely given up and fled the country, I feel like there's a part of you who wants to see where this ends up, both professionally and personally. You're curious. I think that's a good thing. Trust me on this one, Daisy. For once in your life, go with the flow."

Go with the flow. She had a point. I couldn't think of a single instance in my life when I'd gone with the flow. I never left anything up to chance, not even when I was a child. If I wanted to do something, I didn't leave it up to the universe to decide if it was the right path for me. I blazed my own trail. That was how I'd gotten accepted with a full scholarship to Yale University, how I beat everyone in the senior class for a coveted internship at a top bank right after graduation, and how I ended up as the assistant to the CEO of Reed Capital. I took aim for what I desired and shot a clear bullseye. I forced the flow to go with *me*.

Still, it was hard to deny that Poppy had a point. After all, I'd never been faced with a circumstance like this before. It wasn't something I could plan for. It was one of those unexpected things that came out of left field, a curveball that I typically had plenty of emergency strategies to adjust for. Not this time, though. This was entirely unique.

So, maybe Poppy was right. Maybe the only way to deal with the pressure of a secret fake marriage with my boss, who I was also now apparently unable to deny my intense attraction to, was by going with the flow. For now, sitting back and letting things fall into place was probably the only way I'd be able to figure out how to navigate the complex nuances.

"Fine," I sighed at last. "You're right. Attorney Maxwell wins the debate. If the flow comes knocking at my door, I'll go with it."

"That's my girl," she said, squeezing my hand encouragingly. "You're a good person, Daisy. You're smart, too. Smarter than most other people in this damn city. I'm confident that, no matter what, you'll come out of this with some kind of happy ending."

"Thanks, Poppy."

"That's what I'm here for. Now, the real question is … what are you going to tell your parents?"

I groaned. "Don't remind me."

She burst out laughing. "Hey, you're lucky. Your parents are nice and chill. Didn't they meet at Woodstock?"

"Yeah—"

"I'm sure they'll be fine about it as long as you convince them you're actually in love. Meanwhile, my mom would have a fit if she found out I was marrying a guy in two months and I'd been keeping the relationship a secret for two years. Unless the guy was, like, a billionaire doctor with seven PhDs or something."

"Yes, your mom is rather strict," I mused.

"That's one way to describe her," Poppy chuckled. Mr. and Mrs. Maxwell were kind people, but while Poppy's father was more a backseat driver in terms of parenting style, her mother was definitely a helicopter parent. It was clear she just wanted the best for her daughter, though. "If you need me to help break the news or back up your story, don't hesitate to ask. I'm a lawyer, after all. I get paid all day to lie."

I rolled my eyes at her joke. "I thought you got paid to oversee corporate mergers and acquisitions."

"That, too."

"Thanks for coming out at the last minute, Poppy. I know you're even busier with work than I am most of the time."

"That's what friends are for," she replied with a shrug. "If our roles were reversed, I know you'd do the same thing for me. Unfortunately, my boss is an ugly old geezer, so I suppose I'll have to keep living vicariously through you."

"I suppose so."

Part of me wished I had a boss like Poppy's—unattractive and on the brink of retirement. It would make this whole thing a lot easier. Poppy's boss was already married and I assumed his grandparents had passed away decades ago, considering that he himself was a grandfather at this point. If Mason was like that, the only thing I would have to worry about was being a good executive assistant, plain and simple.

Life was full of hurdles and challenges, though. One of my obstacles just happened to be the fact that the guy I worked for was hot, rich, single, and evidently attracted to me. At least, attracted enough to initiate a desperate kiss when he was extremely stressed out.

Normally, things weren't this complicated for me. I was so good at organizing my life, so good at keeping things tidy. Usually, Poppy was the one texting *me* with a man-related crisis on her plate.

How did my life turn into such a confusing mess in just one day?

Chapter Eight: *Reed*

Suffice it to say, I didn't have guests over often.

I didn't have time to entertain, nor did I have much interest in it. If I wanted to be around people outside of work hours, I would go to a bar. Given that I considered every hour of the day an opportunity to be productive, I didn't see the point in wasting time indulging in Manhattan's nightlife. That was a scene better suited for my cousins.

Luckily, even though I didn't have many visitors, I also didn't spend much time at home beyond sleeping and eating. I had a cleaner who was hired to tidy up the townhouse I owned in Greenwich Village on a weekly basis, and I occasionally hired a chef for evenings when I wasn't eating dinner with a client or picking up takeout on the way home.

In short, there wasn't much preparation to do for Daisy's arrival. It wasn't as if I had to impress her. She had managed almost every detail of my life for the past two years. If anything, it was strange that she hadn't yet seen the inside of my house.

I started pacing back and forth in the foyer at quarter to seven. I couldn't sit still. I was agitated. Nervous, too. Not because Daisy was coming over, but because I was worried that she *wasn't* going to show. Work that day had been as normal as it usually was, yet I couldn't shake the feeling that our agreement to forget what had happened in the town car was not working out for either one of us.

How could I forget it? It was one of the biggest mistakes of my professional career. Initiating a kiss with my executive assistant could easily be the reason Daisy chose to back out of everything. Then, not only would I lose the most efficient and valuable staff member at Reed Capital, I'd also lose my opportunity to overcome my grandmother's ridiculous demands regarding the inheritance. Thus, my company wouldn't get the forty-two million dollar investment that could broaden its horizons in ways I could only fantasize about.

That's why I needed to be alone with Daisy outside the context of the workplace. We needed to disentangle ourselves from the nuances of our professional roles so that we could discuss the deal we had brokered as equals.

I was dressed more casually than I would be at the office, though my khaki trousers and blue collared shirt were, in my opinion, perfectly appropriate for a dinner meeting on a pleasant summer evening.

At five minutes to seven, the doorbell rang. I halted my pacing and nearly cracked a smile. Daisy was always punctual, which meant that she was always five minutes early. It was something we had in common, one of the many reasons why we worked so well together.

I answered the door. For a minute, my brain fizzled like an egg in a frying pan. Daisy was wearing a white sundress that hugged her perfect curvy-but-slender body. Her blonde hair was pulled back into a classy French twist and she wore a simple gold necklace on her elegant throat. She looked like a literal daisy. I'd never seen her dressed so … daintily? At work, she was usually in structured, tailored attire like everyone else. At first, I almost didn't recognize her.

She looked pretty.

I almost scoffed at myself as soon as my brain formed the thought. Daisy's undeniable beauty was not the point that evening.

Clearing my throat, I stepped aside and gestured for her to come in.

"I didn't wear white on purpose, I promise," she said in lieu of hello, timidly stepping across the threshold.

"What?"

She smoothed down the front of her dress. "White … weddings—"

"Oh, right." Somehow, it didn't occur to me that this would be the first time I would see Daisy dolled up like a queen outside the workplace. She was going to be my fake bride, after all.

Daisy bit her lip, glancing around the first floor of my townhouse.

"It's not what I expected," she mused.

"Really?" I asked.

"Yeah, it's kind of cozy. Comfortable," she explained. "I pictured a place with bare, Scandinavian-style furnishings and maybe some weird art."

"Weird art, huh?" At least she was acting like her usual cheerful, talkative self. I relaxed slightly.

"Don't rich people just hire art buyers to fill their homes with random modern art they can brag about to all of their rich friends?" Daisy replied with a shrug, moving toward one of the paintings hanging on the wall above the fireplace in the formal lounge.

"I'm not sure if I'm the best person to ask about the standard behavior of people within my tax bracket," I remarked.

A breath of laughter escaped past Daisy's lips. "This is a Cézanne, isn't it?"

"Correct," I answered, coming to stand behind her. I wasn't aware she knew anything about art—or at least enough to identify an original piece by a famous French painter—but I shouldn't have been surprised. Daisy was certainly not a one-trick pony.

"Wow. It's lovely."

I could practically hear the gears whirring in her head as she attempted to calculate how much the painting that casually hung in my house was worth. In truth, I had no idea the exact value, but I estimated it would fetch at least a few million at auction.

"It belonged to my mother," I told her in order to clarify that I didn't personally blow that much cash on an old painting. "Follow me."

Daisy wandered along after me as I led the way to the back of the house, where a pair of antique doors opened up to a private backyard. Last summer, in desperate need of fresh air in a private space, I had hired an architect to build a Mediterranean-style patio. A crew of landscapers planted some leafy trees and vines for privacy, and I had my own outdoor haven in the middle of Manhattan.

"This is so peaceful," Daisy said when she stepped outside. "If I don't look up, I don't even feel like I'm in New York."

I nodded, my nerves returning without explanation. Leading her to the table set up under a veranda, I pulled out a chair for her. Chivalry wasn't inherently romantic, after all.

"I'll admit ahead of time that I don't cook much, so I had the chef prepare the spread. Spanish tapas, I think."

"That sounds great."

There was a hotel-style cart laid out next to the table, laden with various dishes and a pitcher of homemade sangria. The chef was already gone for the evening, as per my instructions. Daisy and I were the only two people in the entire house. I didn't want to risk anyone overhearing the smallest snippet of our discussion. I wanted to ensure that, when I presented the marriage certificate to Mr. Henderson, there would be no one who could unravel the truth and ruin everything at the last second.

I sat across from Daisy. She wore a subtle smirk of amusement on her face as she took in the sight of the large and impressive meal.

"What is it?" I asked.

"Nothing."

"It's not nothing."

Daisy shrugged. "I've never eaten a meal cooked by a private, personal chef. We've lived very different lives, you and I."

There was no judgment in her tone, but the barest hint of self-consciousness struck me. Usually, I was an expert at determining the perfect meal and setting for business meetings depending on who the client was. Most people didn't realize how important the small details were. Had I already messed up the evening?

"We can order a pizza instead, if you'd like," I suggested.

At that, Daisy laughed. It was bright and colored with surprise.

"You eat pizza?"

I furrowed my brow. "Of course I eat pizza. I'm a New Yorker, aren't I?"

She smiled and fell silent.

Don't think about the excruciating curve of her collarbone or the gracefulness of her delicate shoulders, I urged myself. *Don't think about her big, blue eyes. Don't remember the way they looked up at you before she closed them and lowered her head into your lap ...*

"Shall we serve ourselves?" I suggested.

Daisy nodded. "Sure."

As we quietly filled our plates with the various dishes on offer, the awkward tension continued. For the first time in my life, I didn't know what to say. I don't know what had gotten into me. This was my ideal stage, the place where I shined. You could put me across a dinner table from anyone in the world, give me an hour, and I'd have a trusted business partner or client figuratively eating from my hand.

Unfortunately, Daisy was apparently an outlier.

I uttered the first thing I could think of in a desperate attempt to dissipate the discomfort that hung heavy in the summer air around us.

"You say we've lived different lives," I began. "Since you attended my grandmother's funeral, I suppose you have a more detailed insight into my life than I have into yours. Tell me about your family. You're from Maine, correct?"

All I knew about Daisy's background prior to her college years was that she was from some random place in New England. In my opinion, it was acceptable to share personal anecdotes during business meetings to break the ice.

Though, the more I tried to convince myself that this was purely business, the more I wondered if that was the most accurate way to view the situation.

"Vermont, actually," Daisy corrected me. "There isn't much to tell. My childhood was pretty normal."

"What does 'normal' mean to you?" I pressed, filling her glass with sangria.

"You know, small town suburbs. My mom Sharon was a schoolteacher, and my dad Jim retired from being a mailman last year. I'm an only child. All in all, we're a fairly ordinary American family."

I understood that what she described was, in fact, the typical situation for most people in this country. Yet, I'd never experienced anything like it. I was fully aware of the fact that I had been fed with a silver spoon all my life, but it's often hard to identify your privileges when you don't know any different.

The downside to asking someone to share personal anecdotes was that the general expectation was for you to share something in turn. Daisy had told me about her parents, so I owed her a little detail about mine. The thing was, it was common knowledge that they were dead. You don't become one of the youngest billionaires in New York without sacrificing a significant amount of privacy in the process. Even if I were a nobody without a penny to my name, everyone would know what had happened to my parents. My mother was a Baldwin, after all, and my father came from a long line of successful men who invested well during the Industrial Revolution. In most cases, being absurdly rich made you a public figure as much as being a politician or musician did.

Therefore, Daisy already knew who my parents were. She knew that Benjamin and Rose Reed had died in a private jet crash over twenty years ago when I was only twelve years old. She was also well aware of the fact that Daniel and Jane Baldwin, my uncle and aunt, were also casualties of the same accident. They were Marina and Bradley's parents, but being orphaned in the same way hadn't helped us form a special bond. If anything, it made me want to be as far away from them as possible.

Even though anyone, including Daisy, could do a quick internet search to discover all those things in a matter of seconds, I felt inclined to offer something to the conversation in turn.

"I'm sure you know that my father was an investment banker and was working with my grandfather to build Reed Capital prior to his death," I began. "But, while everyone thinks that my mother was merely a trophy wife, she was actually an artist. A painter."

"Really?"

It was a well-kept secret, but I figured Daisy deserved to know more about me than the average person given that she'd agreed to become my fake wife.

"It's true," I told her. "She used to sell her paintings under a pseudonym, then donate the money to charity. She admired the impressionists the most."

"Hence the Cézanne," Daisy mused. Her gaze drifted past the patio doors back into the house. I could already guess what she was thinking. She was wondering if any of the pieces on display in my home were painted by my mother, but it appeared that she was too timid to ask.

"I have a few paintings of hers," I answered her unspoken question. "But, they are all in storage."

Daisy took a sip of sangria. "I see."

Another beat of awkward silence. This wasn't like us. Obviously, it wasn't as if we gabbed like schoolgirls together, but I couldn't remember ever feeling an ounce of awkwardness within the natural quiet that settled between us on a daily basis.

"Shall we move on to discuss the details of our arrangement?" I asked.

"Oh, yes," Daisy replied, leaning over to grab the tote bag she carried with her everywhere. "I brought the trusted iPad so I can take notes."

I nodded, feeling more at ease as she pulled out the stylus and set the tablet on the table beside her plate.

"It's imperative that we keep our story straight," I said. "Of course, my family already thinks we've been dating for two years and that, for a portion of our relationship, we were a long-distance couple."

"I think the best plan of attack will be for us to have two separate stories," Daisy suggested. "One that we can use for your family and one for mine. My parents will likely be satisfied with the vague explanation that we met at work. You can tell them that you work in the C-suite with me. Technically, it's not a lie. I'm pretty sure they don't remember the name of the company I work for, so I won't have to explain why it matches your surname."

"Yes, that's fine. I'd rather you not have to explicitly lie to your parents on my behalf," I responded. "However, if anyone in my family discovers that you really do work for me, I think that will be toeing too close to the reality that you attended the wake as my assistant, not my fiancée."

She nibbled bits of food as she scribbled notes on the screen, nodding almost to herself as she did so. In many ways, it felt like we were truly at work.

"Agreed," she replied. "We can tell them that I have some kind of non-corporate job. Something like … a piano tutor?"

She gestured to something inside the house. When I turned to look, I realized she'd spotted the grand piano positioned by the window in the back parlor. It was a family heirloom, but I didn't play.

"Sure," I agreed. "What if they ask you to play something on the off chance we're forced to attend another family event in the next two months?"

Daisy shrugged. "I can play. I took lessons for almost fifteen years."

"I didn't know that."

"Well, it wasn't necessary information to include in my job application."

"Right. Fine. That's suitable."

"By the way, you're going to have to meet my parents," Daisy continued. "We can take a weekend trip to Vermont, but there's no way they're going to wait until the wedding to meet you for the first time."

I cringed internally. The idea of lying to her parents' faces in their own home didn't sit well with me, but it was necessary. Anyway, it was inevitable that Jim and Sharon Campbell were going to despise me eventually. Once Daisy and I annulled the marriage, I'd be nothing more than the flaky man who had toyed with their daughter's heart.

I hated the thought of it. I was neither flaky nor a womanizer, but having two random small-town people hate my guts wasn't the worst fate imaginable. Not when the alternative was forfeiting the inheritance.

"Okay, fine," I said to her. "You handle my schedule anyway, so just book the trip for whichever weekend works best for both of us."

"Got it."

"Then, there's the matter of the wedding planner," I continued. "I have a trusted connection from Yale—a woman named Pat Maybell who has done quite a few private yet high-profile weddings. She can be discreet and I believe she'll mind her business if it occurs to her that there might be a thread of falseness in this arrangement."

"Okay … sure."

Daisy set down the stylus and settled back in her chair, staring off into the distance with a slightly shell-shocked expression.

"Are you alright?"

Her blue eyes flicked over to me. "I can't believe I'm getting married. I mean, I know it's not real, but still."

"I get it," I replied. "I never planned on marriage. At least, not this soon. It's strange. All these things that I never wanted to bother with are suddenly popping up because my grandmother wanted to have the last word. Are you sure you don't want to back out?"

It pained me to ask. The possibility that she might take me up on the offer caused my anxiety to spike.

"I'm sure," Daisy answered, clear and confident. "By the way, I told my best friend about this. She's the only one who knows and I trust her to keep the secret."

I flinched. "Are you certain?"

"She's an attorney at Chen, Wong, and Montgomery. Discretion is in her job description."

I raised my eyebrows in surprise. That was one of the most profitable, exclusive corporate law firms in the nation. Their biggest client was Disney, so that said a lot.

"Okay," I sighed. "That's fine."

"Her name is Poppy. She went to Yale, too. You can meet her if you'd like."

"Sure, sure. All in due time."

"Right."

I cleared my throat and shifted to fish something out of my pocket. It'd been burning a hole in there for hours. "Last but not least, there's the matter of the ring."

Daisy grew still. "I forgot about that."

"No worries. I've taken care of it," I said, holding out the little red box with the classic Cartier branding on it. "Here."

Instead of taking the ring box from me, Daisy pursed her lips at me.

"Seriously?" she asked.

"What?"

"You're just going to toss it to me … a Cartier diamond … across the table like that?"

"I—" What did she expect?

Only, I realized exactly what she expected. Even if this was a contractual deal between colleagues, she expected a proper proposal. I suppose that was fair. If I were a young woman, I would probably balk at my careless delivery as well.

With a quiet sigh, I stood up from the table and approached her chair. She shifted to face me, eyes wide with a whirl of emotions I couldn't quite decode. I flipped open the box, the massive diamond within instantly catching the light of the setting sun.

Then, without further ado, I got down on one knee.

Chapter Nine: *Campbell*

Never in a million years did I ever expect to see the image before me.

Mason Reed, CEO of Reed Capital, also known as my employer, was down on one knee in front of me. In his hands was a tiny red box lined with white satin. Cradled within the soft material was the largest diamond I'd ever seen in my life. It was oval cut, pure as glass, and cushioned on either side by two small emeralds. The band was simple, crafted from white gold by the look of it.

It was beautiful.

Although marriage had always been something I assumed would happen to me one day, I'd never given much thought to the ring. In my head, as long as the man I was getting engaged to was the love of my life, it didn't really matter what I wore on my finger. When I was briefly and unofficially engaged to Aiden all those years ago, he was still in the process of saving up for the ring when we broke up, so this moment was unlike anything I'd experienced before. Now that it was happening, I realized that there was a small part of me that wanted my ring to be pretty. Somehow, miraculously, the one Mason was presenting to me was exactly my taste.

"Jesus Christ," I whispered. "It's huge."

"It was my mother's," Mason explained with a casual shrug. "It was the best I could do on short notice, but I can get something else if you prefer."

"No, it's—" I trailed off. The engagement ring belonged to his deceased mother. It was the ring his father had proposed to her with. The meaning behind that wasn't lost on me, yet Mason appeared unbothered by the gravity of it. "It's gorgeous."

"Good. Great," he muttered. "Anyway—Daisy Campbell, will you do me a huge favor and marry me for the sole purpose of helping me acquire a significant amount of money and assets?"

Something about the tension of the moment had Mr. Reed, the epitome of coldness and crankiness, cracking a joke. I burst out laughing at his sarcastic tone.

"Yes, of course," I answered. "I'll marry you."

Mason smiled. It was small, subtle, existing more in his eyes than his lips.

"Thank you," he replied.

He took the ring out, setting the box aside on the table with our unfinished dinner. Holding out his hand as if waiting for me to hand him his coffee, I realized he was going to put the ring on me himself. With a nervous flip of my stomach, I slipped my left hand into his waiting palm.

The band was cool as he slid the ring onto my finger. It was heavier than I expected, but it fit perfectly.

"What are the chances?" I murmured, holding out my hand to admire the grandiose gem.

"It looks nice," he offered, still down on one knee. "You'll have to take it off at work, obviously, but at least we won't have to bother with having it resized."

"I'll take good care of it," I promised him. "You can trust me."

"I know I can."

I cleared my throat and abruptly turned away, unable to meet his gaze for any longer. It was hardly a romantic moment, but all I could think about was throwing myself into his arms.

Nervously, I started chattering. "So, is that everything? I'm sure we'll have more to add to the notes as things come up here and there, but—"

Though I wasn't looking at him, I was aware of Mason standing up from the ground at last. He cut me off with a soft, simple command.

"That's enough for now, Daisy."

I stared up at him. "Okay."

"Actually, if you'd like to wrap up dinner, I was wondering if you'd play something for me."

"Play?"

"On the piano."

I blinked in surprise. He wanted me to play the piano for him? Over the past two years, he'd asked me to do a lot of things, but never to entertain him. Only, it was clear that this wasn't just a request made out of the desire to be amused. Rather, he seemed purely curious.

If my fake job as his fake fiancée was being a pianist, then I suppose I owed him a little bit of proof that I could tell the lie well enough.

"Yes, sir," I said automatically, standing up. When Mason's mouth curved into a smirk, I bit my lip and fought the urge to blush furiously. "I mean … sure."

Poppy was right. I was such a people pleaser it was embarrassing.

Wordlessly, Mason turned and led the way inside the house. With his back turned, I grabbed my glass and quickly downed a gulp of the sweet, fruity sangria before scurrying after him.

The grand piano, which was obviously vintage and very expensive, rested in the corner of a cozy sitting room decorated with earth tones and soft furnishings. It was painted black, gleaming in the fading daylight filtering through the arched windows. Mason stood aside, gesturing for me to make myself at home on the antique piano bench.

"I don't play, but I have a guy who comes and tunes it once a year," Mason explained as I took a seat. "It belonged to my grandfather—not Abe Reed, but the one on the Baldwin side of the family—and it's the same old man who's been taking care of it for about forty years now. I suppose he wasn't always an old man, but I keep wondering if he's going to retire anytime soon. He's been traveling between the piano's various homes for decades now."

I smiled at the story. My family didn't have heirlooms like this. My mother had a few pieces of jewelry passed down from her grandmother that would eventually get handed down to me, but that was it. The ring on my finger was undoubtedly worth ten times all the Campbell jewels. We certainly didn't have a priceless piano that we passed down from one generation to the next. It probably cost a few thousand dollars just to transport it safely between locations. I couldn't imagine.

I lifted the cover and gently rested my fingertips on the smooth ivory keys, fidgeting nervously. I was rusty, to say the least. I'd been telling the truth when I mentioned that I'd taken piano lessons for a decade and a half, but it had been at least a couple of years since I actually sat down and practiced. Hopefully, my boss was unfamiliar enough with classical music that he wouldn't be too harsh of a judge.

"Any requests?" I asked.

Mason was perched on the windowsill nearby, backlit by the bursts of orange and pink that filled the sky outside.

"Surprise me," he replied.

I decided to go for a classic, a popular melody most students had memorized and even inexperienced listeners could identify. Playing from memory, I gently pressed down on the keys. As promised, it was in tune. The room had great acoustics as well, but the piano itself was constructed with a level of quality that many other instruments didn't have. The sound it produced was clear, true, and flawlessly responsive to the weight of my touch.

When I finished the short tune, I paused and glanced over at Mason. It was difficult to read his expression, but at least he didn't look horrified.

"Debussy," I said.

Mason nodded. "*Clair de Lune*, right?"

"Yes."

"You have it memorized?"

"Yes. It's not a very difficult song."

His lips twitched into a smirk. "I see."

I thought about what Poppy had said the other night over drinks. She insisted that I should go with the flow. Right now, the direction of the flow was hard to determine. The atmosphere switched from professional to personal to downright awkward … to something that felt too strong and nerve-wracking and delicious to name. I wanted a dozen different things in that moment.

Most of all, however, I wanted Mason to know he could trust me. Not just as his assistant, but as his partner in fraud, and—dare I consider it—as his friend. I didn't think Mason Reed had many friends. He had hundreds of friendly business contacts, but I was almost positive he didn't have anyone he would consider his confidante. Whom did he talk to when he needed to rant out his frustrations? Whom did he lean on when he needed a bit of emotional support? Even the strongest and most independent people in the world needed friends. I firmly believed that humans were social creatures.

Maybe, instead of fooling myself into thinking there was anything romantic about this arrangement between him and me, it was best to view it as a blossoming friendship. Even if he would never admit it out loud, I got the feeling that Mason could use a friend. I could be that for him.

"Do you want me to show you?" I asked him.

"Sorry?"

"The song. I can show you how to play it."

"I don't even know how to read music."

"That's okay. Neither does Paul McCartney. There are actually quite a few famous musicians who don't bother with sheet music and all those technicalities," I explained. There was plenty of room on the piano bench, so I scooted over and patted the space next to me. "Come on."

Mason hesitated. "We really don't—"

"Come *on*," I dared to interrupt. I'd never spoken over him before, let alone given him a command. My stomach flipped with a flutter of fear.

Yet, Mason did as I said. With a resigned sigh, he sat beside me. There was barely an inch of space between us. We were closer than we had been in the town car, but at least we weren't in a small enclosed space. Not that the large, airy room did anything to ease the tension.

"My hands are probably too big," he muttered, lifting one hand and resting it on top of the keys.

"Nonsense," I replied. I forced myself to ignore the memory of what those large hands felt like on my body. "Okay, so the song involves playing chords and individual notes at the same time. I'll show you the chords, alright?"

"Sure."

"Put your index finger on this key," I instructed him. "And then, rest your thumb here … your middle finger should go there … you'll hold that for four counts—"

Careful not to make contact, I pointed to the keys. Mason did his best to follow my instructions, nodding quietly.

"Then, you'll add your ring finger to make a different chord," I continued.

This time, Mason fumbled slightly, furrowing his brow in confusion. Automatically, I reached out and moved his hands for him, applying pressure to indicate he should press the keys. He tensed almost imperceptibly when I touched him, but he didn't pull away. Instead, he allowed me to guide his hand in the right position, the large diamond on my finger sparkling brightly the whole time.

"Like this?" he asked, his voice softer than I'd ever heard before.

"Yes, perfect. Now, I'll play the notes with my right hand. Ready?"

"I guess so."

I kept my left hand over his, tapping for him to play the chord as I began with the melody.

"Now switch to the other chord," I murmured. He was a bit clumsy as he did so, and I slowed the tempo to allow for the fumbling.

It wasn't a particularly graceful rendition of "Clair de Lune", but it was at least somewhat recognizable. I grinned when we finished.

"See? Not so hard," I told him.

Mason chuckled, pulling his hands back and resting them on his thighs.

"If anything, that only made me more convinced of its difficulty," he remarked.

"Oh—"

"It's all right," he laughed quietly. "I'm fine with being a one-trick pony. You are a very accomplished young woman, Daisy. You should be proud of yourself."

Once again, I wasn't prepared for the compliment. He rarely offered them. I had gotten used to simply assuming I wasn't doing anything wrong because he wasn't outright criticizing me at any given time.

When my eyes locked onto his, my heart jumped into my throat. There it was again—that magnetic pull that I didn't think was possible to feel from him. The attraction I'd been denying for almost two years. Did he feel it too? Would he walk away before either of us could act on it? What lengths was he willing to go to in order to prevent another heated moment between us?

Apparently, the answers to those questions were *yes, no,* and *none,* because the only thing Mason did was shift ever so slightly closer. My breath caught as he lifted his hand to my face and brushed back from my forehead a strand of blonde hair that had escaped from the twisted updo. He looked as though he was barely holding himself back, lips parted as he hovered mere inches from my face.

"Last time, I made the first move," he whispered. "This time, I'll leave the ball in your court."

What? Had I heard that correctly? Was I merely hallucinating what I wanted to hear? Did I *really* want to hear that?

Of course I did. Who was I kidding?

"Are you sure?" I asked.

"Yes."

Normally, I'd waste a well of mental energy weighing the pros and cons of jumping his bones. I'd analyze the situation from a thousand different angles as fast as I possibly could before landing on the best possible decision. However, when I was with Mason like this, my mind didn't work as efficiently as it usually did. I couldn't get my thoughts to settle down long enough to be logical.

With him, it was primal. Instinctive. Something had unlocked between us a few days ago, something that had been buried deep for ages, and it wasn't easily put back to rest.

Without sparing a single thought, I closed the distance between us and kissed him deeply. That was my answer. The ball was in my court and I chose to play the riskiest game.

But, I couldn't bring myself to care. It felt too good to go back now.

Chapter Ten: *Reed*

I didn't mean for it to happen again. It wasn't part of the plan. In fact, I was almost afraid to touch her just in case it finally scared her off.

And yet, there she was … wearing my mother's engagement ring, glowing golden in the sunset, playing a romantic tune on my grandfather's piano. She was the one who offered me the space beside her, the one who placed her hand over mine. She was the one who smiled at me as if I genuinely brought her joy, as impossible as that seemed.

So I gave her a choice, because I knew I couldn't stand to resist her a minute longer. I'd been holding myself back from the second I opened the door and saw her on my front stoop.

I didn't expect her to give me that wordless *yes*. I was prepared for her to push me away. Surely, a woman as bright and shining as her wouldn't make the same mistake twice with a man as sour and antisocial as me.

I was wrong. Daisy paused for only half a second before she leaned in to kiss me. Just like the first time, my body responded instantaneously. I craved her like a man left to starve in the desert. I wanted her with such force it threatened to drive me mad.

She wrapped her arms around my shoulders, pressing herself as close as she could to me while we were still sitting on the piano bench together. Her body was petite, but not fragile as I gripped her narrow waist tightly. At my touch, she whimpered softly in the back of her throat, but I could tell that it wasn't a protest.

It was better than before. Better because we weren't trapped in a moving vehicle with my chauffeur on the other side of a thin divider. Better because we were alone in this stupidly large house of mine, which made my mind whir with countless possibilities.

Then, at the memory of the last time we kissed like this, I remembered that I still owed her a favor.

Breaking apart from the kiss, I rose from the bench and placed my hands firmly on her knees to spin her away from the piano. I knelt on the smooth floorboards in front of her, this time on both knees instead of just one.

She stared down at me breathlessly. "What are you doing?"

"Paying you back," I answered simply.

Her forehead scrunched up in confusion, but when I gently coaxed her legs apart, I watched her eyes grow wide as she realized what I meant. A soft pink blush rose to her cheeks as we both recalled the way she so eagerly took me into her mouth.

"You don't have to—"

"Quiet," I hushed her.

As usual, she did as she was told.

In the back of my head, I was shouting at myself to stop. This was the exact thing I was trying to avoid happening again. There was a panicked voice in my mind that was insisting I was taking advantage of the situation. That I was manipulating my employee, that I was being a douchebag.

But, she wasn't stopping me. Not just because she was afraid of my reaction if she did, but because she wanted me to do this. I could see it in her eyes.

Daisy bit her lip, bracing herself on the bench as I spread her thighs open. My hands roamed up the velvet-smooth skin of her legs, pushing up the hem of her dress slowly. She was wearing light pink panties, delicate and hemmed with lace. I didn't know how someone as sweet and feminine as her managed to be as sexy as she was, but it made me feel like a brainless caveman.

I pushed the flimsy fabric aside, grabbed her hips, and lowered my head to her center.

The moment I pressed my lips to her inner thigh, a sharp gasp escaped her, followed by a soft moan. I couldn't help the smirk on my face, but I wasn't in the mood to tease. My impatience to taste her urged me onwards.

It was fitting that she was named after a flower because she blossomed the second my tongue touched her. She was like sweet nectar flowing from between perfect petals. I couldn't get enough of her.

At one point, she shifted backward, her hand reaching for something to hold onto but landing on the keys. The harsh, dissonant chord echoed around the room, but neither of us flinched or snapped out of it. She merely readjusted and tangled her fingers in my hair, pressing me closer.

Much to my surprise, it didn't take her long to start completely falling apart. Her heavy breaths turned into desperate panting. I had to tighten my grip on her to stop her from squirming.

"Mason, I'm … I'm—"

The sound of my name on her lips coupled with the fact that she couldn't even get a complete sentence out was enough to confirm that I was definitely not going to be satiated once this so-called repayment was complete.

Daisy inhaled sharply and trembled, the muscles of her slender thighs tensing on either side of my face. I didn't pull away until she was whining under her breath and fidgeting away from the overstimulation. When I finally sat back on my heels, she readjusted herself on the bench and pulled her dress back down over her thighs. The sight of her breathless and blushing reminded me of a very insistent firmness in my trousers.

Only, that was going too far. Foreplay in the heat of the moment with my employee-slash-fake-fiancée was one thing, but going all the way seemed completely reckless. There was no going back from that.

Not that there was any going back from this.

I let out a groan of frustration and stood up, pacing away from Daisy.

"Damn it," I muttered.

"What's wrong?" she asked softly, almost nervously.

I whirled around to find her gazing at me with wide eyes, knees pressed tightly together and hands clutching the edge of the bench tightly as if she was about to be chastised. I'd already figured out that a woman like Daisy couldn't stand the thought that she might have done something wrong. Seeing her looking at me like that—so eager to please—outside the context of the workplace did something to me that I couldn't describe. It was like fire in my veins.

"That wasn't supposed to happen again," I sighed.

"Right."

"I don't want you to get the wrong idea."

Daisy cocked her head to the side at my admittedly vague statement. "What do you mean?"

"I don't want you to think that this is all part of an elaborate, long-term master plan to seduce you," I explained, feeling like an idiot as I said the words aloud. "I'm taking advantage of my assistant in more ways than one and it doesn't feel right, but I hope you know that I didn't hire you because I thought an opportunity like this might come up someday."

Inexplicably, Daisy burst out laughing. I stared at her, unsure if she was laughing at me for being a moron or if she was losing her mind from the pressure of the current circumstances.

Still smiling, she tried to explain her outburst. "If there are two things I've learned about you in the past two years, it's that you hate wasting time and you don't mince words. If you wanted to seduce me, you would've done it on the day I came in for my interview."

I shouldn't have been surprised that she knew me so well. It was her job.

"That's a fair assessment," I remarked.

"Don't worry," she said, standing up and self-consciously smoothing out the wrinkles in her sundress. "I'm not egoistic enough to believe I would ever be the subject of anyone's master plan. Whatever's going on here—whatever this is between us—materialized practically out of nowhere, from my point of view."

I breathed a sigh of relief. "Yes, it seems like that is the case."

"Although, I should admit that I've always thought you were handsome," she continued, bashfully glancing down at her shoes. "Objectively, I mean. Like, in the beginning, I wondered why you weren't dating a gorgeous foreign model or something, but then, I realized it's because you have more passion for your career over anything else ... and I admire that."

"You think I'm handsome?" I wanted to bash my head into the wainscoting the second I uttered it aloud, but I didn't know what else to say.

What kind of alpha-male billionaire questioned a woman when she said something like that to him? Only, it wasn't that I didn't believe what Daisy said was true. I was fully aware that I was decently attractive. Rather, it seemed odd that she, specifically, would be attracted to me. I assumed she would go for someone more gentle and nerdier, like that ex-boyfriend of hers who'd gotten himself tangled in my cousin Marina's web.

"Yeah," she replied with a shrug, as if it were obvious.

"Is that why you wanted the job so badly?" I dared to joke.

Daisy snorted. "Excuse me?"

"Well, if I recall correctly, you were *really* determined in your interview."

She mockingly gasped as if scandalized, reaching out to smack my shoulder lightly. "I was determined because I wanted the job, Casanova. It had nothing to do with you."

"Sure."

Watching her lips curve into a smirk made it even more difficult to stop myself from throwing us both to the floor and spending the rest of the night rolling around naked on the parlor carpet.

"I didn't know you could be like this," she said.

"Like what?"

"Funny."

I barked out a laugh. "Ouch!"

"No, I just mean that I barely see you smile at work, so I figured joking around wasn't your thing."

"So, you think I don't have a sense of humor?"

"No, every intellect has one," she replied. "More like I didn't think your humor would be so flirtatious."

I couldn't help laughing. "You think I'm flirting with you?"

"You just went down—"

"Right, right," I chuckled, cutting her off before she made my hard-on any worse. "Well, anyway, I think we should establish some ground rules regarding this newfound physical intimacy."

"Sure. Like what?"

"Like … Do you want it to keep happening?" I lowered myself onto the nearby chaise longue, hoping that the new position would disguise the insistent bulge in my crotch region.

Daisy blushed. "Do you?"

"I asked you first."

She sighed. "Honestly, I'm worried that this will jeopardize my career."

"I see. You mentioned before that you're hesitant to risk rumors spreading about your work ethic. You don't want people to think you haven't earned your success the right way."

"Exactly," she replied. "But, we're already keeping so many secrets—"

Glancing down at the diamond ring on her finger, she trailed off.

"Would you like to know what I think?" I asked her.

She nodded eagerly. "Please."

What did I think?

Honestly … screw it. I wanted her and she was my fiancée. We were actually going to get married. Even if there was no romance involved and the marriage would be annulled immediately, we were now engaging in a relationship that transcended the realm of workplace appropriateness. She was gorgeous. She had an amazing body. We had undeniable physical chemistry. It wasn't as if I had feelings for her.

"I think that we might as well have fun in the meantime if we have to go through all this nonsense," I said. "Clearly, there's mutual attraction. I think denying it would only add to the stress and jeopardize the stability and secrecy of the arrangement."

Daisy took a step toward me. "That's a fair assessment."

It took me a second to realize that she was mocking me. I'd always known she was incurably cheerful and bubbly, but I didn't think she was this playful.

"You agree, then?"

Another step. As she drew closer, it occurred to me how futile it was to hide how badly my body was hungering for her. All she had to do was look down. At this point, there was no point trying to keep it from her.

"I agree."

"Good."

"Good," she repeated, taking one more step closer.

As she stood before me, slender and graceful between my knees while I sat beneath her, she reached behind her back with both hands. For a moment, I didn't understand what she was doing, but then I heard the unmistakable sound of a zipper being undone. Daisy held my gaze as she undid the back of her dress without a problem, the fabric around her breasts and rib cage loosening. When the zipper was all the way down, she moved her hands to the sleeves, pulling the frilly things down her arms. She did so without a single word or second of hesitation. It was almost casual, the way she undressed for me. In truth, it was probably the sexiest thing I'd ever seen.

At last, she let the flimsy sundress drop to the floor. It pooled at her feet. She kicked off her heels and lost a couple of inches of height while she stood there, dressed in nothing but those pink panties and a matching bra. My mouth went dry.

"Well?" she murmured.

"What?"

"It's your move now. I'm metaphorically tossing the ball back into your court."

"Understood," I muttered.

She was right when she said I didn't like to waste time. If she was leaving it up to me to make the next move, I wasn't going to mess around for a second longer. Overthinking was a waste of time. It was better to act on instinct. Doing so had rarely failed me before.

I stood, causing the distance between us to close instantly. She gasped, but she didn't step back, instead reaching for my shoulders to hold herself steady. Grabbing her hips, I lifted her off the floor and she automatically wrapped her legs around my waist. She was even lighter than I expected; it required no effort at all to carry her into the hall and toward the staircase.

"Where are we going?" she asked, her lips pressed close to my ear.

"My sex dungeon, of course."

"What—oh, another joke?" Daisy laughed loudly, burying her face in my shoulder.

"I'm dead serious," I quipped.

She lifted her head and furrowed her brow at me as I climbed the stairs. When I saw the look of confused uncertainty on her pretty face, I couldn't stop myself from cracking a smile. Realizing that I was being sarcastic, she pouted.

"You need to work on your comedic delivery."

"Yes, ma'am."

"Ooh, I like the sound of that."

I snorted. "Don't get used to it."

"Yes, sir."

I laughed. She was witty. I liked it.

By that point, we'd reached the top of the stairs. Luckily, my bedroom was on the second floor, though it wouldn't have been a problem to continue carrying her all the way up to the roof deck if I wanted to. But, just as she mentioned, I was impatient, so I kicked open the door at the end of the hall and dropped her on top of my bed.

She landed with a quiet gasp, gazing around to take in the surroundings—the king size bed, the balcony overlooking the rear garden—snapping back to attention when I yanked off my shirt and climbed on top of her as she scooted backward toward the pillows at the headboard.

Her body felt so small underneath mine, but not fragile. Despite her name and her sweetness, it was clear that there was nothing fragile about Daisy. She was fierce and determined when she wanted something … including me. She reached for me as if it were something she had been yearning for longer than she realized. I suppose that was true for both of us.

We kissed ferociously, her hands roaming down the bare skin of my chest to my stomach, fumbling with my belt and the zipper of my pants. I moved my mouth down to her jaw, trailing kisses along her throat as she slipped a hand beneath my waistband and palmed my erection through my briefs. Instantly, the memory of the last time she touched me there ignited a wildfire within me.

I grabbed her hands and held them against the pillows above her head. She gazed up at me with wide, blue eyes that should have appeared innocent, yet were anything but when paired with her impatient pout and the way she wriggled her hips beneath me.

"Are you sure?" I asked.

"One hundred percent. Yes. I give my consent. I want this. Blah, blah … can you please just take off your pants?"

"Since when are you the boss of me?" I asked, ducking my head to press my lips to the rise of her breasts over the top of her bra. "Is this the kind of wife you'll be to me? Pushy and demanding?"

"Well, if I can't tell you what to do at work, I thought I'd take the opportunity—"

It was impossible not to grin. "Nope. No matter the context, I don't take orders."

"I was afraid you'd say that," she sighed, though the sound quickly turned into a moan when I moved lower, trailing the tip of my nose down the center of her stomach until my lips reached the waistband of her panties.

I pulled them off without ceremony, tossing them over my shoulder as Daisy went ahead and removed her bra by herself. I crawled backward and stood at the edge of the bed, sliding off the rest of my clothing. I watched Daisy's eyes trail down the length of my body. There were a hundred things wrong with what was happening, but somehow that made it even more intense. It felt dangerous.

I'd never been much of an adrenaline junkie before, but this woman might have the power to convert me.

"Like what you see?" I smirked.

She rolled her eyes. "Obviously."

I crawled back onto the bed, hovering over her as she adjusted herself beneath me. I wanted nothing more than to devour her right away, especially since the foreplay downstairs had created an obvious dampness between her thighs for me. However, some things were more important than desperate passion.

"Are you on birth control?" I asked, trying to focus past the feel of her fingernails grazing gently down my back.

"Yeah, I have an IUD," she replied. "What about you? Are you—?"

"Are you asking if I'm on birth control?"

Daisy giggled. "No, I meant … are you clean? As in—?"

"Oh. Right. Of course. Yes."

"Cool. Me, too."

"Cool," I mocked her gently. Before she could bite out a retort, I kissed her deeply, lowering my weight onto her.

Using a hand to guide myself into her, she made a subtle sound of discomfort in the back of her throat when I started to press against her. I froze instantly, breaking the kiss.

"Sorry," she murmured. "It's been a while, and you're not exactly small. Not even average-sized, actually."

"Do you want me to—?"

"No, no, it's okay. Just go slow."

"No problem."

That was a lie. As I buried myself deep inside her, it was excruciating to go slow, but the last thing I wanted to do was hurt her. She furrowed her brow with pain, biting her lip as she adjusted to my size. After a minute, she closed her eyes and pressed the back of her head into the pillow, her chest curving off the mattress as she let out a soft moan.

"God—" she breathed.

"Should I stop? Are you okay?"

"No, that wasn't—it's not—it's good now. Don't stop. Keep going."

I didn't need to be told twice. Bracing myself on one elbow, I used my other hand to grab the back of Daisy's thigh and create a good angle for both of us as I started thrusting as gently as I could manage. She squirmed, clinging on to me as she whimpered in my ear.

She said it had been a while since she'd slept with someone, but I failed to mention the same was also true for me. I was paying the consequences of that right away, putting all my effort into not climaxing too soon. It was agonizing; Daisy felt so good that I could barely keep myself together. Not to mention the sounds she made, biting my shoulder to muffle the loudest of them.

"You're so sexy," I blurted out between heavy breaths.

"Mm," was all she offered in response.

After that, thinking straight was impossible. I prided myself on being a level-headed man, but this version of Daisy—this woman who was less well-behaved than I thought—did something to my brain. She messed it up in a good way. I enjoyed the mental numbness, indulging the physical ecstasy that I hadn't tasted in so long.

Without hesitating, I lost myself in her.

It was hours later when I was left alone with my thoughts again, but my solitude wasn't absolute. It wasn't even close to midnight yet, but Daisy was fast asleep on the sheets beside me. She slept on her stomach, her golden hair splayed out across the pillow, breathing serenely in the darkness.

I couldn't sleep. Even after hours of rolling around under the covers with her, I was restless. It was enough to make me wish that I could flush away my mind again. We both had to be at the office tomorrow, but I suppose it wasn't a big deal for her to spend the night. It wasn't as if she was going to get in trouble with her boss for running late. I was the only person she had to answer to at Reed Capital.

Unsure how light of a sleeper she was, I carefully climbed out of bed and slipped my trousers back on. I left the belt on the floor, letting my pants sit low on my hips as I made my way downstairs. Needing some way to distract myself from the infuriating tornado of thoughts in my head, I decided to busy myself with cleaning up the mess we'd left behind on the patio. If the pigeons hadn't already claimed the remnants of our dinner, that was.

Except, just as I was about to step out into the humid night air, my phone started vibrating loudly with a call from where I left it behind in the back parlor. I retrieved it quickly, shocked that I had been able to stay away from work-related responsibilities for this long.

The minute I saw who was calling, I scoffed out loud. It wasn't work. It was Bradley, yet again. Considering the late hour, I imagined he was already drunk and on his way to an exclusive club. In fact, no matter what time zone my fool of a cousin was in, it was guaranteed that he was partying his life away.

I ignored the call, but a text came in just a few seconds after the screen went dark again.

What's up, cuz? I'm in Vegas! Thinking about eloping with the first drunk girl who wants me, and getting my hands on a cool forty-two million bucks. Thoughts?

Cursing under my breath, I took a seat on the piano bench and typed out a reply to his ridiculous threat.

Henderson would never fall for it, I responded. *Nice try, though.*

If claiming our grandmother's inheritance was as easy as eloping with a stranger, Daisy and I would have already gone through the legal motions days ago. But my cousins, the family attorney, and I knew that Ruth Baldwin wanted a real marriage, a genuine relationship. It was literally written in the fine print. Bradley could understood that, even with his significant lack of crucial brain cells, so he was just being annoying. I shouldn't have bothered responding.

While Daisy slept soundly upstairs, I fiddled with my phone in the silence of the vast, lonely first floor. This was a big house. Although it usually had a staff member of some type wandering around the place during the day, I was the only person who slept here. It was kind of nice to know there was someone else dreaming within these walls.

Another incoming text jostled me out of my embarrassingly tender thoughts.

I'm surprised Henderson is falling for YOUR charade, Bradley had written back. *You're not fooling me or Marina. This isn't over.*

That definitely wasn't deserving of a response. He was drunk and pathetic, trying to project his own insecurities onto others. Even if neither Bradley nor Marina believed that Daisy was my fiancée, they had no way of proving otherwise.

"Idiot," I muttered under my breath.

Chapter Eleven: *Campbell*

I'd never been happier in my life for the weekend to begin. The past week had easily been one of the most stressful weeks career-wise, and in terms of my personal life. Not only was I secretly engaged to my boss, but I had also slept with him and spent the night at his house after the fact.

When I woke up the morning after that euphoric evening, a delicious ache in my hips, it had taken several minutes to remember where I was. The sight of the engagement ring sparkling on my finger in the morning sunlight was enough to jog my memory, though. That, and the fact that Mason was shirtless and snoring gently beside me.

I ended up wearing the same outfit as the night before to work that day. It was a little more girlish and casual than what I would usually dare to wear at Reed Capital, but once I got to my little office, I located a spare blazer to shrug on over the top of the frilly sundress sleeves.

The entire day, the diamond that once belonged to Mason's mother burned a hole in the bottom of my bag. Coupled with the fact that my boss had quite literally been inside of me the night before, which I'd rather face death than admit to anyone other than Poppy—I was jumpy and anxious all day. We'd ridden into work together, his chauffeur picking both of us up in front of Mason's townhouse with a noticeable question in his gaze. Luckily, it wasn't totally out of the ordinary for us to arrive at the office at the same time.

"Cute dress!" Jennie had chirped at me as Mason carried on without a backward glance toward his office the second the elevator doors slid open.

"Thanks," I had answered, trying to stop my gaze from lingering too long on his retreating back. "I thought I'd give casual Friday a try."

"Oh, please," my coworker laughed. "You look like you belong on a runway. That's hardly casual. You're too humble. By the way, here's Mr. Reed's coffee order."

"Thanks, Jennie," I murmured, accepting the drink along with my usual iced Americano. I didn't stick around to chat, but I took comfort in the fact that Jennie wouldn't take it personally. Sometimes we were just too busy for it. That was life at Reed Capital.

Part of me didn't want to bring Mason his coffee, even if it was something I did almost every single day first thing in the morning. For some reason, switching roles so suddenly and dramatically left me feeling so overwhelmed I could barely think straight. I made my way to his office woodenly, as though I was operating on autopilot.

I knocked on the doorframe. When Mason, dressed in a full suit, glanced up from his desk, my heart squeezed. His wavy hair was still damp from the shower.

The shower that we had shared together, indulging in one another's bodies in the steaming bathroom with little care for the passing minutes. It was a miracle we made it to the office at our typical early time.

But, I couldn't think about those things when I was under the roof of Reed Capital's headquarters. He wasn't Mason here. He was Mr. Reed, the CEO.

"Yes, Daisy?" he inquired, raising an eyebrow at me.

It was only then that I realized I'd been gaping stupidly at him for several long seconds without saying anything. At least the grouchy impatience that was always present in his tone was a bit lighter than usual.

"Your coffee," I blurted. "I have your coffee."

"Thank you."

Trying not to stumble over my own feet, I scurried into the room and placed his coffee on the same coaster as I always did. Clearing my throat, I begged myself to get a grip. I had promised him I would help with his grandmother's inheritance, but I wasn't going to be able to keep that promise if I was incapable of compartmentalizing my thoughts appropriately.

I straightened my spine. "You have a meeting with Mr. and Mrs. Reese at nine, followed by a meeting with the representative from Santander who called last week, then a luncheon with the Maywell Foundation at one. Maurice will pick you up at half-past noon and I've already sent the donation check to them ahead of time."

"Thank you, Daisy."

"Your travel arrangements for the Forty Under Forty Conference in Chicago next week have also been confirmed and forwarded to your email," I continued, reciting from memory as I fumbled for my iPad inside my tote bag. "Then, you have that meeting with Singapore this afternoon. I blocked out two hours because Mr. Wang is known to be particularly chatty. Also, Ms. Laurent is waiting for a call back regarding her late father's corporate holdings. She won't accept any other consultant."

"Thank you. I'll call her."

"Also—"

"Daisy, breathe," he interrupted. His voice was so gentle, it barely sounded like him. "I can take care of myself for the next ten minutes, I think. At least go put your bag down in your office before doting on me."

"Yes, sir."

I practically ran away. The second I reached the sanctuary of my office, I closed the door and sank into my chair to do some deep breathing exercises.

Going with the flow was a lot more complicated than I'd thought it would be. It wasn't as if I regretted the night I spent with Mason. In fact, it had easily been one of the best nights of my life. The best sex I'd ever had, too. There was no denying that.

Now that the sun was up, reality felt like a slap in the face. I was living a double life. In one version, I was Mason's fiancée. I was a piano teacher, a devoted partner, and the woman who wore his mother's old wedding ring on my finger. In the other version of my reality, I was still Mr. Reed's executive assistant. I had to take care of him in more detail than a wife would ever be expected to, which was part of the reason why I was such a good fit for the role of fake wife in the first place.

At least I wasn't alone in this. Mason was also stuck in the middle, pretending to be my future husband to his family while simultaneously maintaining his authority as my employer to all others. At the same time, we were venturing into a world of physical passion that neither one of us expected to have to navigate. It was the world's most delicate balancing act.

But, I could handle it. I could handle anything.

You've made it this far in life, I reminded myself. *The only way is up.*

That little voice had a point. Life wasn't going to get any easier than this. No matter the source of my stress, I was an ambitious woman who had chosen a challenging path. If I couldn't handle it, I was weaker than I thought.

All I needed was to make it through one more work day, then I could take the weekend to center myself. When Monday came around again, I was confident I would have absolutely everything under control.

Much to my relief, Mr. Reed—or Mason—or Mr. Reed … or whomever he was supposed to be inside my head—had such a busy day that I didn't have to risk making a fool of myself in front of him again. Once he finished his conference call with some business partners in Asia, he would head out to meet an old Yale classmate, who was now a very influential politician, at the Metropolitan Club. It was one of the most exclusive private clubs in the city and also where Mr. Reed was known to secure his most lucrative deals and wealthiest clients.

I knew he wouldn't be back in the office, enjoying the rest of his afternoon with overpriced cigars and whiskey.

See you Monday, he wrote to me in the subject line of an email as a simple goodbye. It was the same thing he sent most Fridays when he left the office before me, but it was hard to deny that even the small details felt different now.

After that brief note from my boss, the rest of the day passed blissfully fast. I declined the usual invitation to get drinks with the rest of the C-Suite administrative staff and headed straight home. Nobody blamed me for claiming that I was too exhausted to socialize, even if it was out of character for me. Being Mr. Reed's executive assistant allowed me the privilege of making such excuses for myself without scrutiny. Nobody questioned how tiring working for Mason could be.

On Saturday morning, I woke early. I'd planned to forgive myself if I happened to sleep in until late morning, thinking that I deserved a rest after the hectic week I'd had, but my conscious mind had other ideas.

I awoke in the quiet solitude of my one-bedroom apartment on the Lower East Side. Most people didn't know that being an executive assistant was a difficult or lucrative career, but my six-figure salary was earned with blood, sweat, and tears. It afforded me a decent apartment in a stylish, youthful, and safe neighborhood with enough disposable income left over to treat myself often.

Once I paid my dues at Reed Capital and was offered the next rung up on the career ladder, I might even be able to afford a two-bedroom. Living comfortably in Manhattan came with a steep price tag, but I was an adamant believer that it was wholly worth it.

I loved New York. I loved that when I climbed out of bed and flung open the curtains, there were pigeons cooing on the fire escape outside my window. I loved the constant hum of activity even in the middle of the night, the unexpected bursts of racket punctuated by bursts of pedestrian laughter and chatter. I loved the little bodega on my street corner that sold niche foreign snacks right next to Lays potato chips. I loved the fancy art galleries and grimy dive bars sitting next to each other on the narrow streets.

I loved it so much that even when I was wiped out from a stressful week at work, I couldn't stand to stay indoors.

Despite my mild mental breakdown at the office yesterday, I was in a good mood that morning. I told myself it had something to do with the sunshine, but I was fully aware that it was also because I'd gotten laid for the first time in over a year. The last guy I'd slept with was a random blind date that Poppy had set up for me with a new attorney at the firm. We dated for a couple of months, but it never amounted to anything.

Before that, I'd had another dry spell following my big breakup with Aiden. We had dated for so long, yet it had been ages since I'd thought about those old days. In spite of the fact that it hadn't ended well between us, the relationship itself had generally been good. I did love him. That was real. Back then, I was convinced that sex with Aiden was as good as it could get. We had great chemistry in the bedroom, so intimacy with him was hardly disappointing.

However, now that I had something else to compare it to other than a random, short-lived, pseudo-relationship …

To put it bluntly, I had no idea what I was missing.

For a man who didn't date, Mason was an unfairly skilled lover. The way we collided together in his sheets felt cosmic. It felt like something that couldn't be contained by this planet, by this solar system.

It was that good.

Then again, I didn't want to get carried away. I was a practical woman, so I didn't often let myself be consumed by daydreaming. I preferred to live in the moment.

Humming under my breath, I practically danced my way into the shower, then got dressed in a coordinating cotton shorts-and-blouse ensemble. Leaving my iPad behind, I left the apartment with a tote bag that weighed as light as a feather. It was oppressively hot outside, but that was Manhattan in July. I didn't mind it. A little bit of heat and sweat never hurt anyone.

I spent the majority of the morning wandering around the local farmer's market and perusing my favorite independent bookstore. I never minded spending time by myself. If I wanted to hang out with Poppy, I could have called her and coaxed her out of the hangover haze I was sure she was suffering under, but I was enjoying my own company that morning.

And anyway, in New York City, you're never really alone.

At one point, I passed by an upscale boutique that specialized in lingerie. I'd wandered all the way up into Nolita, accidentally toeing the borders of the West Village where Mason lived. I couldn't stop myself from wondering if he was home. Despite it being a Saturday, I knew he had a conference call scheduled for this afternoon with a potential investor, but that didn't mean he wasn't spending the morning out and about. Was there a chance I might run into him? I doubted it.

I felt silly for hoping it would happen, too. If we unexpectedly crossed paths on the busy streets, who would I be to him? What version of me did he see first? His assistant? His fake fiancée? The woman he'd slept with a couple of nights ago? Which one of those people did I want to be most of all?

As I stepped into the lingerie store with the intent to merely browse, my automatic thought was that I wanted Mason to still see me as his employee, first and foremost. My career was the most important thing to me. That was why I'd gotten myself tangled up in this situation in the first place. I didn't want to let Mason down because my future depended on his opinion of me and my work ethic.

Still, there was a tiny part of me that hoped he was also incurably occupied by his desire for me, just as I was for him. I hoped we were walking a two-way street.

The shopkeeper was busy assisting a trio of women by the front of the shop, so I perused the stock on my own. They were high quality pieces, ranging in style from pretty and delicate to sexy and provocative. I tended to lean more toward the former, but I suddenly found myself wondering what kind of lingerie Mason preferred. From the way we spoke at his house, it was clear that we'd given up on trying to avoid the attraction between us, which meant that we were probably going to sleep together again.

Would it be inappropriate if I asked my boss what panties he wanted to see me in? Yes, definitely. But if my boss was also my fiancé … where did that leave us?

Puzzled, I frowned at a matching set made of soft mesh and cleverly placed embroidery, leaving very little to the imagination while still somehow coming across as inarguably classy.

Just as I was about to check the price tag, my phone rang.

I yanked it out of my pocket, thinking it was Mason needing help with something work-related since I'd spent many weekends over the past two years being on-call. However, when I saw the number on the screen, I realized I didn't recognize it. Spam calls were supposed to be filtered directly to my voicemail, so there was a chance it was a client or colleague who hadn't been saved to my contacts list.

"Hello? This is Daisy Campbell," I answered quietly, moving to the corner of the shop.

"Daisy! Hey, how's it going?" asked an oddly familiar male voice on the other end of the line. "It's Aiden."

"What?"

"Aiden Plourde. I figured you'd still have the same number," he chuckled.

My ex-boyfriend was calling me? More importantly than that, my ex-boyfriend still remembered my phone number? Just because we ran into each other at Ruth Baldwin's funeral didn't mean I ever expected to speak to him again. Sure, he was dating Mason's cousin, but from what he'd said about her romantic habits, that wouldn't last long.

"Hi, Aiden," I replied, unable to keep the confusion out of my tone. "Is everything okay?"

"Of course! I just wanted to call and properly congratulate you on your engagement," Aiden chattered cheerfully. "I would've done so earlier this week, but I've been so swamped at work ... anyway, congratulations, Daisy."

"Thank you," I responded automatically.

"It's crazy to think you're getting married, and to Mason Reed, of all guys! I mean, he runs in really exclusive circles. Even some of us fellow financial guys can't get ahold of him! It's funny, you know? I always thought you were a career woman."

Instantly, my mood soured. I never expected Aiden to become the type of ex who delivered snide, backhanded remarks as if they were nothing more than casual remarks. Clearly, he'd changed a lot in the past few years. Was he jealous? Did he see me on the arm of New York's most eligible billionaire bachelor and instantly think I had gone back on my claims that I wanted to work on my career before settling down? That was why we had broken up, after all.

And, now what? He was mocking me?

"I suppose you didn't know me as well as you thought you did," I quipped. "I don't have time to talk right now, though, so—"

"No, wait!" he protested.

I froze, raising my eyebrows at a display of neatly folded satin panties in every color of the rainbow. "Yes?"

"Sorry. I didn't mean for that to sound like I was a jealous ex or whatever. It's just that I was so surprised to see you, Daisy. You know, I've thought about you a lot over the past few years. I'm really happy to see that you're doing well."

He thought about me often, yet this was the first time he was calling in all that time? I wasn't buying it.

"Aren't you dating Marina Baldwin?" I asked coldly.

"Well, yes, but—"

"Perhaps you should be spending more time thinking about her, not me."

I didn't wait for a response, hanging up without hesitation. If Aiden was going to launch into a speech about how he'd made the biggest mistake of his life and desperately wanted me back, he'd obviously forgotten that I wasn't a gullible fool. Aiden only wanted me because he couldn't have me. It was a tale as old as time.

Slipping my phone back into my pocket, I grabbed the embroidered mesh outfit I'd been admiring earlier and marched right to the register without glancing at the price tag.

Aiden Plourde was greedy. He craved status above all else. It wasn't honest success or pure fulfillment he was after. He just wanted everyone to think he was the top dog, and he happily let me walk away because I wasn't willing to devote my life to boosting his image. However, now that someone like Mason had me as his trophy, Aiden saw value in me again.

But, I was more than just a trophy to Mason. I knew at least that much was true. He was cranky and difficult more often than not, but he didn't lie. Mason meant it when he admitted to admiring my intelligence and ambition. He valued me as more than a pretty trinket. I wasn't sure I could say the same for Aiden. It was wildly transparent of him to be dating one of the richest old-money heiresses in the country. Furthermore, if he was bold enough to call me and claim that I was consistently on his mind, he clearly didn't care that much about Marina. I suspected she was just a status symbol to him.

I almost felt bad for her.

Exiting the shop with the most risqué lingerie I'd ever owned, packaged neatly in a pretty red bag, I headed home with my head held high.

The romance between Mason and me might be fake, but the mutual respect was incontestable. Apparently, that was something Aiden and I had never had.

Chapter Twelve: *Reed*

"—considering that almost four trillion dollars in assets are currently being held in private equity by high-net-worth individuals, the benefits of investment in private companies are undeniable—"

"—which is exactly why we want to avoid discussions of the company going public! In this day and age, venture capitalists are far more dependable than the stock market—"

"—and that means nothing when we look at the astronomical cash flow the company could experience if it went public—"

"—*potential* cash flow, you mean. Have you considered the absolute nightmare you'll be trapping your shareholders in if the company's financial reports are public? The standards are strict. You'll need to shell out hundreds of thousands just to amass a legal team skilled enough to combat the shareholder lawsuits alone!"

"Gentlemen, gentlemen," I sighed, placing my hands firmly on the table. "Please, let's circle back to the original goal of today's meeting. Mediation."

Normally, I didn't mind watching lesser businessmen fight like schoolchildren. It was a subtle boost to my own ego to know I'd never make a fool of myself like that in front of others. Today, however, I was in a particularly impatient mood and the issue on my plate was downright annoying.

Not to mention, it technically wasn't my problem.

Reed Capital was a consulting firm at the heart of it. We represented private equity firms that represented investors who wanted to dump their millions into private companies and reap the rewards of almost tyrannical control over them. More often than not, we never dealt with the companies themselves, but sometimes we were dragged into chaos merely because we were a part of the puzzle.

Today, there was an anxious investor, a frustrated private equity firm representative, and an uncertain company executive sitting at the conference table before me. Unable to solve their dispute amongst themselves, they'd turned to the consultant who brokered the partnership in the first place for guidance.

Lucky me.

While Daisy sat patiently in the corner of the room, tapping quietly on her iPad as she dutifully took notes, I turned to the company executive sitting on my left.

"Mr. Burns, I understand that you're interested in taking your company public," I began, using my diplomatic voice in hopes that we could wrap up this blasted meeting before I gave in to the urge to bang my head against the wall. "While there are undeniable benefits to doing so, your investor's concerns are justified. May I speak from personal experience?"

"Of course," Mr. Burns replied, clearly relieved that my taking the floor meant that he was no longer being cursed out by his investor.

"Reed Capital is a private company," I continued. "We have private investments that we handle in-house. I have found that remaining private has allowed this company of mine to grow much faster and more freely than if I had taken it public the moment I inherited it from my grandfather. In fact, I'd be bold enough to claim that, if I allowed myself to become distracted by the time-consuming IPO process, I wouldn't be a billionaire at the age of thirty-four."

Mr. Burns inclined his head respectfully. It was as much of an agreement as I was going to get out of him, but I could see from the look in his eyes that I'd convinced him.

I turned to his primary investor next.

"Mr. Shang, I think your argument would be best paired with a cost-benefit analysis with ten-year projections on Mr. Burns' company if he chooses to stay private versus going public," I remarked lightly, a subtle criticism of his stubbornness laced in my words. "I'll have my finance team prepare it for you at no cost."

"Thank you, Mr. Reed."

Lastly, I nodded at Jackson Gallagher on the other end of the table, who was a longtime colleague of mine. He owned the private equity firm that funneled Mr. Shang's money into companies like the one Mr. Burns owned. Yet another Yale graduate, he'd been taking a seat in my conference room for years now.

"Mr. Gallagher, I think you'd agree with me on this. No matter the industry, commerce is ever-changing. Although, it's my personal opinion that Mr. Burns' company should remain private for now, there is no guarantee that going public won't benefit him in the near or distant future."

"I absolutely agree," Jackson replied with a grin. "That's why it's so important that we keep these lines of communication between the investor and the recipient, as well as our minds, wide open."

"Couldn't have said it better myself," I said, clapping my hands together. "Now, are we all finished here? I don't know about you boys, but I've got a case of the Mondays and could really use a walk in the park. How about you three head down to the lobby together and I'll meet you there?"

Jackson snorted quietly, but neither Mr. Burns nor Mr. Shang caught it. Instead, they let out twin sighs and nodded in unison, standing up and filing out of the room.

On his way out, Jackson paused to clap me on the shoulder.

"Classic," he murmured.

I rolled my eyes. "Good to see you, man."

"You, too, Mason. Until next time."

"Take care."

Because Jackson had been working with me for a while, he knew that my walk-in-the-park suggestion was a go-to, harmless hustle of mine. Whenever Reed Capital had a difficult partnership on our hands, I liked to send the involved parties a few blocks north to Central Park. Fresh air did wonders for the spirit. Although I promised I would catch up with them, I never did. Instead, I would always make an excuse and send our best marketing representative in my stead. Usually, he would come back with a new retainer, a handful of business contacts, and increased earning potential for the company. He was that good.

With the irate men gone, Daisy stood and meandered over to me. She was wearing a skirt that hugged her figure tightly, and now that I was actually allowing myself to acknowledge how sexy she was, I had to admit that her outfit choices were driving me crazy. Nobody should be allowed to look that good in professional business attire.

"Shall I send Bill down?" she asked. Of course, she knew all about the walk-in-the-park hustle.

"Yes, but—"

"But give them time to soak in the awkward tension before we send Bill in for the rescue, yeah?"

"Exactly."

"I'll tell him to give it exactly six minutes."

"Make it seven."

"Yes, sir."

I left the conference room with Daisy following obediently behind me. After the weekend, I was a bit anxious about how things would stand between us when we came back to the office. Last Friday, despite starting out with a mutual exchange of mind-blowing oral sex in the shower before we rode into work together, the vibe was tenuous. Daisy was stuttering and stumbling over her words, and even I was struggling to readjust my perspective from the bedroom to the workplace.

Yet, this morning, Daisy had arrived bright and early ... and as normal as ever. She was chipper and charming, graceful and efficient. There was no blush on her cheeks when she addressed me as 'Mr. Reed', nor did she zone out when doing something as simple as bringing me my coffee.

It was as if she reset her brain over the weekend and was back to her original factory settings.

I secretly hoped that didn't mean she no longer wanted to sleep with me. I wasn't ready to let go of that part of our arrangement yet. She was far too exquisite to forget that easily.

Back in my office, I settled down at my desk while Daisy battled with the copy machine in the corner. I had no idea what she was doing, but I'd learned to trust the process when it came to her muttering under her breath and banging her fist on top of the machine.

"Can you write a new scanner into the next quarterly budget?" Daisy grumbled.

"What's wrong with it?"

"It hates me."

"It's not sentient. It's incapable of hatred, Daisy."

"Personally, I don't know why you bothered humoring that Kodak rep," she complained, ignoring my commentary. Her back was turned to me as she crouched in front of the large machine. It took every ounce of determination within me not to look directly at her ass. "This thing is all bells and whistles—no reliability. There's nothing wrong with the classics, Mr. Reed. A Xerox would be just fine."

"That Kodak rep's uncle happened to be on the board of one of the biggest private equity firms in New England. I had to offer him something in exchange for the contact," I explained.

"Well, your transactional networking habits are making my job more difficult than it needs to be," she scoffed. Her complaint was followed by a dull *thunk* as she yanked out the toner cartridge roughly. "Do you want color-coded personal expense reports or not?"

When I started laughing, she threw a mocking glare over her shoulder. Daisy knew as well as I did that I didn't give a damn if my personal expenses were color-coded. It was she who insisted on the organizational flair.

This was different. Traditionally, I was the one barking and growling at something while Daisy lightheartedly untangled the metaphorical knot with a smile. The shift definitely had to do with the nuance of our new relationship, but I didn't dislike it.

She was lovely to look at even when she was annoyed at me.

"Daisy, just let the IT guy deal with it," I sighed. "There's no need to get toner all over your suit for the sake of my expense re—"

Suddenly, the voice of one of my least favorite people cut me off.

"Hey, hey! Surprise! What's up, cuz?"

I tensed as Bradley, wearing a ridiculous designer tracksuit, sauntered into my office with a wide smile on his face. Daisy was on her feet fast as lightning, thinking quickly enough to clasp her hands behind her back to hide the fact that she wasn't wearing the engagement ring. I didn't know where she kept it when she was at work, but I trusted her to keep it safe.

"Who the hell let you in here?" I grumbled, not even bothering to stand up to welcome my cousin properly.

"The pretty chick at the front desk, man. All I had to do was say I'm family and she let me pass," Bradley chuckled. "Nice place you've got here, by the way. Shame I've never been invited to see it myself."

"Why are you here?" I snapped. "You can't just waltz into my company in the middle of the day, especially not dressed like that. I know this is an unfamiliar concept to you, but Reed Capital has a reputable image to uphold."

My insult fell on deaf ears. Bradley's gaze was roaming around the space a little too curiously, as if deciding what he wanted to grab and run out the door with.

When his eyes landed on Daisy, his jaw dropped.

"Well, hey! I didn't see you at first!" he exclaimed, waving at her like an idiot. "Daisy, right? What are you doing here? Fixing your man's printer?"

Daisy hesitated for only half a second. It would have been impossible to catch if I didn't know her as well as I did.

She let out a bubble of girlish laughter. "Huh? Oh, no. I was just in the area and was thinking about him, so I thought I'd stop by and say hello."

The door was wide open, but my office was positioned in such a way that foot traffic didn't ever pass by on accident. As long as no one was bold enough to pop their head in without warning, they wouldn't catch Daisy sauntering over to me and placing a possessive hand on my shoulder. It was the girlfriend type of touch, not the assistant kind, but it was necessary.

"How romantic," Bradley cooed. "Anyway, I was also just in the area—"

"I thought you were in Vegas," I interrupted.

"That was days ago," he guffawed as if I'd told the funniest joke in the world. "Bradley Baldwin moves fast around this big, beautiful world."

I cringed at the way he referred to himself in the third person. "I'm about three seconds away from calling security, Bradley."

"Chill out, Mason. God, Daisy, how can you have the hots for this guy? Dude's got a stick shoved all the way up his—"

Daisy cleared her throat loudly to muffle the crude word. "I happen to like mature, focused men with polite social skills."

"I'm sure," Bradley chuckled. He came forward, digging around in his pocket for a minute before dropping a small rectangle of thick stationery on top of my desk.

"What's this?" I muttered, grabbing the paper.

"Marina and I thought it would be nice to host a memorial gala in Grandmother's honor. It's sponsoring some kind of charity. I don't know. Marina's being a control freak and barely giving me the details, but you're obviously invited," Bradley babbled. "Both of you."

"If we agree to attend, can you remove yourself from my office and agree not to say a single word to anyone on your way out, including the poor girl at the front desk?" I sneered.

"Sure, cuz. No problem," he smirked, already backing toward the door. "See you this weekend."

When he was gone, I dialed the head of security. While I asked him to confirm Bradley's exit and to ensure he was never permitted to enter again, Daisy removed her hand from my shoulder and took a look at the gala invitation.

"That was close," she mused quietly once I was off the phone.

I let out a long exhale and sat back in my chair. "I should've told you this before, but he and Marina have been on my case about this wedding. It's childish crap. They don't believe it's real, and it sounds like they're hell-bent on exposing us."

"Exposing us?" Daisy repeated, keeping her voice low. "Can Bradley even say his ABCs?"

I smirked. This new sassy side of her was amusing. "I'm assuming Marina is the brains behind the operation. He's just the messenger boy. Either way, this gala is fair play. As the intended primary inheritor of my grandmother's estate, I can't exactly refuse to attend an event being held in her honor. Neither can my fiancée."

"So, Marina and Bradley get to make themselves look like the more devoted grandchildren for throwing an elaborate soiree, but you're still the only one who is actually getting married," she replied. "What do they actually get out of this?"

I shrugged. "They probably think they can catch us slipping up. They'll be trying to convince everyone that our relationship is on the rocks, that the wedding isn't going to happen, that we're not a real couple. Just nonsense and gossip, but all eyes will inevitably be on us. I know how Marina works. She goes for the psyche."

"Interesting."

Daisy was biting her lip, but her expression was hard to read.

"I hope you didn't have any important plans this weekend," I said to her. "I know it's a lot to ask, but we can consider it practice for the big day."

"It's no problem," Daisy insisted, handing the invitation back to me. "I don't have any plans. It's just that I've never been to a charity gala before."

"It's just a bunch of rich people bragging about how rich they are."

"I figured. I guess what I mean is … it's black-tie. I don't have anything to wear."

"Right," I responded, shifting to retrieve my wallet from my back pocket. I pulled out my personal platinum card and handed it to her. "There's no limit on the card, so buy whatever you need. Just add it to your beloved color-coded expense report."

Daisy cracked a smile. "No limit? Seriously? I'm not buying a gown. I'm buying Google."

"Good luck. I already own significant stock in Google."

"Of course you do."

Chapter Thirteen: *Campbell*

"You charged *how much* to his credit card?" Poppy gasped, staring at the garment bag lying on the end of her bed as if it were a stolen priceless artifact.

I shrugged. "Thirty-four thousand dollars."

"Daisy—"

"What?"

"*Daisy—*"

With a sigh, I flopped onto the mattress beside the bag and grinned up at my best friend. When I'd told her about the memorial gala, which was a not-so-subtle trap set by Mason's spiteful cousins, Poppy insisted on my coming over so that she could help me get ready.

"Okay, but listen, I have a very good explanation."

She crossed her arms. "I'd love to hear it."

"So, when Mason whipped out his card and told me to go wild, I knew I couldn't just buy any dress, you know? Like, the Baldwins are old, *old* money. The kind of people with untraceable foreign assets and bespoke everything."

"True."

"Even if I bought something fresh off the runway worth eight semesters at an Ivy League institution, it wouldn't be good enough," I continued. "If I want to show those people that I'm the real deal—which I'm not, but whatever—then I have to wear something meaningful."

"The suspense is killing me, Daisy."

"So, I did some research—"

"Naturally."

"As it turns out, Ruth Baldwin wasn't just any old rich lady. She loved her luxury designers, but favored one in particular more than any other."

"I'm intrigued," Poppy hummed. "Which one?"

"Dior."

"No shit."

Poppy's wide-eyed stare grew wider still as she cast another look at the garment bag between us. I grinned proudly.

"It's true. She loved Dior. Can you blame her? The important detail here is that Ruth was a longtime friend of John Galliano despite being about fifteen years older than him."

"Who?"

"The creative director of the House of Dior until about a decade ago."

"Can you please just reach the punchline, Daisy? You're killing me," she whined.

I tutted my tongue at her impatience. "In 1997, Galliano's first year at Dior, he designed a couture gown that he named the Ruthie Dress."

Poppy's jaw dropped. "We're talking about *vintage* Dior?"

"We sure are."

With a flourish, I lowered the zipper of the long bag and revealed the contents within. Poppy gasped dramatically, clutching her hands over her heart. The Ruthie Dress was difficult to track down, but not impossible. I had managed to find one in good condition online. One trip to the tailor, who jumped into action the second I flashed Mason's credit card, and the dress fit me like a glove.

It was made of pure satin dyed a deep turquoise. The natural sheen of the fabric revealed glimmers of blue and green depending on the angle of the light, which meant that it would complement both my blue eyes and the emeralds on my engagement ring. Despite being made in 1997, it wasn't outdated. The dress was simple and chic with a pleated bodice, delicate sleeves that fell just off the shoulders, and a long skirt that spilled down to the floor like a waterfall. It was the kind of gown that would have looked good a hundred years ago and would undoubtedly still look good a century from now.

Plus, anyone who knew Ruth Baldwin well enough would know exactly what I was wearing right away. When I asked Mason for final approval on the purchase, he recognized the gown immediately and applauded my diligence. He hadn't been expecting me to treat the search for a gala dress like a work assignment, but I was delighted to have impressed him.

Poppy whistled low, lightly running her fingers over the fabric.

"Daisy Campbell, you are an evil mastermind."

"Thank you."

"Alright, let me pick my jaw up off the floor so I can start working my magic on your hair and makeup."

***

When Mason's town car rolled up to the sidewalk outside Poppy's building, my hair was pulled back into an elegant crown of curls fixed into place with tiny pearl pins. We decided not to have my makeup be dramatic and to let the dress do most of the talking. I was wearing a pair of silver heels—also Dior, of course—and carrying a matching clutch.

The true star of the show was inevitably the ring. It was huge without being gaudy, noticeable without being distracting. Chances were high that many people would recognize it as the ring that once belonged to Mason's mother, which would help to solidify the charade that our relationship was real.

If Marina and Bradley were going to learn anything about me that evening, it was that I didn't do anything halfway.

"Jesus Christ," Poppy whispered from where she was perched in the windowsill, staring down at Mason as he climbed out of the car. "That is seriously the hottest man I've ever seen in real life. Can I take him for a spin after you guys get a divorce?"

"Be my guest," I joked. Watching over Poppy's shoulder, I had to admit she was right. Mason looked incredible in his tuxedo, which was also Dior, but a more recent design. His hair was combed back from his face with the perfect amount of gel. Even from the window, he looked incredibly dapper.

He disappeared from view as he approached the stoop. The sound of the doorbell rang throughout the apartment and Poppy dashed away to let Mason into the building using the intercom system. I waited nervously by the door. When I looked in the mirror, I felt like a princess, but what if it wasn't good enough for him? What if the whole ensemble wasn't as perfect as I hoped it would be?

I wanted him to be satisfied with the effort I'd put into this last-minute gala. Deep down, I also wanted him to think that I was beautiful.

A soft knock on the door made me jump. Poppy was hiding around the corner, having agreed to save the introductions for another time.

When I opened the door, I felt a flutter in my stomach at the sight of Mason in a tuxedo. He looked incredible, jaw freshly shaven and eyes glistening with brightness. The scent of his aftershave floated off him tastefully without overpowering bystanders.

He grew still when he saw me, lips parted slightly as his eyes roamed up and down my body. The gown showed off my figure while still leaving quite a lot to the imagination.

"You look beautiful," Mason said in lieu of hello. His tone was comically matter-of-fact, as if he were commenting on the weather. "Perfect, actually. You look perfect."

I was relieved he didn't use words like *suitable* or *adequate*.

"Thank you," I replied. "You look very handsome."

He didn't acknowledge the compliment, instead simply holding out his arm for me to take. "Shall we go?"

"Yes," I answered, slipping my hand into the crook of his elbow just as I had the first time at his grandmother's funeral. Goodness, things had moved quickly since then.

"I thought you lived on the Lower East Side," he commented as we stepped into the elevator.

"I do. This is my friend's place. Poppy—the one I told you about. She helped me get ready."

"And, you didn't introduce us?"

"She's ... shy."

"Well, it's probably best to leave the introduction for another time anyway."

Once we piled into the infamous car and set off for the ballroom where the gala was being held, things took on an oddly businesslike tone. Mason spent the short drive telling me what to expect ahead of time.

"We'll make our appearance. I'll sign a donation check. Then, we can get out of there. We won't have to stay long, though the sight of you in that dress deserves to be appreciated the entirety of the evening."

Once again, his compliment was delivered so factually that I almost didn't realize he was expressing admiration. I took it in stride. Mason didn't date, so he was therefore unaccustomed to telling women they looked nice.

As it turned out, a charity gala was exactly what Mason described: rich people bragging about how rich they were. The venue itself was a marvel, housed in a massive building with Greek columns and a dramatically large entrance. There was quite a large crowd milling around by the doors waiting to get in, but when Mason and I emerged from the backseat of the car, they parted like the Red Sea.

I'd never had so many pairs of eyes on me before. Instinctively searching for support as we made our way up the grand steps, I reached for Mason's hand. He entwined our fingers today. Even though he likely saw the gesture as nothing more than show, I was grateful for his firm, steady grasp on my shaking hand.

Once inside the first set of doors, a woman I recognized as Mason's Aunt Katrina—or Auntie Kat, as she had introduced herself at the wake—approached us with a teary-eyed smile.

"Oh, Daisy," she cooed, holding out her arms for a hug as if we were close friends, rather than two strangers who'd briefly met only once before. "That dress is perfect. Where did you find it?"

"Thank you. Online, if you'd believe it. I thought it was fitting."

The older woman blinked her watery eyes and held my shoulders as she stepped back. I still hadn't let go of Mason's hand, though his aunt had yet to acknowledge him.

"It's a very thoughtful gesture," replied Auntie Kat. "And here I am, looking like a fool in off-the-rack Marchesa."

"But, you look absolutely stunning," I insisted.

"You're too kind, sweetheart," she sniffed. Finally, she turned to Mason. "My dear boy, you better be treating this angel of yours well."

"Yes, ma'am."

"I don't doubt it. Abe and Annabelle raised you well."

She reached up to gently pat Mason's cheek before quietly excusing herself.

"She seems different than last time," I commented once she was out of earshot.

"She gets sentimental when she drinks," Mason explained as he guided me toward the entrance to the ballroom.

"I see."

"Hey, Mason! It's the king and queen of the ball!" shouted Bradley from across the vast, high-ceilinged room.

"Speaking of drunkards," Mason grumbled.

Bradley lumbered toward us, dressed in a tuxedo that would have otherwise looked decent on him if not for the garish, bright purple bowtie, which was crooked. Behind him, a familiar dark-haired girl with sharp eyes and pursed lips followed closely. Marina looked lovely, especially in comparison to her brother, but the fact that I knew how poisonous her heart was ruined the effect. Still, I couldn't even imagine how much the velvet petal pink dress she wore cost her. It was an oddly cheerful choice for a memorial gala, but I suppose she had a good reason for it. I had a feeling that a woman like Marina never did anything by accident.

I plastered a polite smile on my face and held on tighter to Mason as his spiteful cousins pushed their way through the busy ballroom. A string quartet positioned on a small stage in the corner played a melancholy tune, but it was too early in the evening for people to give up on mingling to dance just yet.

"Hello, Mason," sneered Marina before turning her gaze upon me. "And, it's Daisy … right?"

I fought the urge to roll my eyes. She knew what my name was.

"Yes," I answered. "And, you're Marie, right?"

"Marina," she sniffed.

"My apologies," I replied bashfully as Mason cleared his throat to stifle a chuckle at my purposeful mistake. "Marina. It's so nice to see you again. That dress is beautiful."

"Thank you. Grandmother's favorite flower was peonies, so I thought the color was perfect. I'd love to know how you managed to get your hands on a Ruthie Dress, though. It's vintage, no?"

"It is, yes," I told her. I didn't offer the same tidbit of information that I had to Auntie Kat, which was that I miraculously located it online. From the way Marina was observing me as if she were a predator and I was her prey, I wanted her to squirm internally about how I was able to find such a perfect gown for the occasion.

"I see a big diamond on that finger! Finally!" chortled Bradley, his eyes zeroing in on the engagement ring that glittered at my side.

"Let me see!" gasped Marina.

I lifted my left hand to allow her a better look, hyper aware of several bystanders craning their necks to catch a glimpse of the massive stone as they pretended to casually pass by.

"I wanted something simple," I chattered, forcing out a playful giggle. "But Mason insisted on spoiling me."

"That's my Aunt Rose's ring," Marina whispered, staring wide-eyed at Mason. Bradley was already losing focus, wandering off toward the nearest waiter with a tray full of champagne flutes.

Rose Reed. That was Mason's mother's name. However, before she married his father Benjamin Reed, she was Rose Baldwin—Ruth's daughter. I assumed Marina would have known her very well.

"Yes, of course," Mason replied. "What else would I have used to propose to the love of my life?"

I hated the way my stomach flipped at his statement. I knew he didn't actually see me as the love of his life, but he was so convincing. Who could have guessed that Mason Reed was such a talented actor?

It was hard to tell what Marina was thinking from the look on her face, especially since this was only the second time I'd met her. It seemed as though, at the sight of the ring on my finger, all the snark and spite had melted out of her. The smirk on her lips formed into a thin line.

She was convinced. If she'd had doubts that Mason was serious about getting married, seeing Rose Reed's diamond on my hand had proven something to her. She'd fallen for it … but she wasn't happy about it.

"Of course," Marina said to Mason before clearing her throat. "Excuse me."

Without another word, Marina stalked away. Bradley was nowhere to be seen at that point, leaving Mason and me alone on the fringes of the curious crowd.

"Let's dance," Mason suggested, pulling me toward the center of the ballroom as the string quartet began playing a new song. "Before somebody else pounces on us."

"You dance?" I replied automatically.

He grinned devilishly. "Of course I do. I'm a heathen, Daisy."

"Good to know."

When his hand rested on my waist, I felt a delicious chill go up my spine. Placing my hand on his shoulder, we joined the dozen or so couples swaying to the soothing, somewhat mournful melody. He held me close—not so close that there wasn't an inch of space between us, but close enough that we resembled any other couple who was madly in love.

"We can dance for a little while, get some drinks, say hello to a couple of my family members, and then get out of here," Mason spoke quietly in my ear.

"Sure. I don't mind sticking around if you want to, though."

"I definitely don't want to."

"Right … Can I ask you a question?"

Mason locked eyes with me. "What is it?"

I urged myself not to hesitate. "Do you ever want to get married one day? For real?"

For some reason, he frowned at my question. "Why do you ask?"

I shrugged. "I'm just curious."

"It's not in my plans," he replied. "It never was. Marriage, love, romance … it's a waste of time in my eyes."

"A waste of time?" I gasped. "You can't be serious."

"I've rarely seen marriages that last," Mason explained matter-of-factly. "My paternal grandparents, the ones who raised me, got divorced and I saw how much trouble both of them went through. They're friendly now, but it turned their lives upside down for years. I'd rather sink my company into the hole before putting myself in a situation where that would be a potential risk."

"Just because your grandparents got divorced doesn't mean you will. Love can last."

Mason furrowed his brow at me as if I'd said something foolish. "Love never lasts."

I fell quiet. It was hard to be held by him like this, to feel the chemistry pulsing between us, knowing that he didn't believe true love was worth his time or energy. I'd already been aware of the fact that he didn't date and that he was too grouchy to be a womanizer, but it wasn't as if

Mason lacked allure. He was sexy and incredibly good in bed. Plus, even if he couldn't see it himself, I could tell he had a good heart.

He was just afraid. He'd never admit it out loud, but he had said it in so many words just moments ago. His grandparents had lost their romance, leading him to lose his faith in love.

More than that, however, was the reality that Mason's parents were tragically killed before their time. They died together, and from what I had read and heard about them, were very much in love. I couldn't imagine what it felt like to have a beautiful guiding light like that ripped away from you. No wonder Mason didn't believe in love. Even though his parents had it with each other, it didn't last. It wasn't enough to keep his hope alive.

It wasn't my intention to psychoanalyze my boss in the middle of an elegant ballroom at a fancy gala. I definitely wasn't about to voice my opinions out loud. I kept them to myself, wishing there was a way I could prove Mason wrong.

Because the truth was, despite knowing better, I was falling for him. There was always a part of me that was drawn to him, that was loyal to him, that had faith in him … and maybe that was why I found it so easy for such fondness to grow into something stronger.

It's a waste of time …

I didn't agree. Love was worth all its risks. I'd been unlucky in love myself, but had never lost faith that I would one day find the right person for me. Was it pure optimism that kept me going?

Or, was it merely the fact that there were unchangeable qualities about Mason and me that would never be compatible?

I gently pulled my hand out of Mason's and took a small step away from him as the music shifted.

"I need to run to the ladies' room," I told him. "Go mingle. I'll come find you in a few minutes."

Mason looked as though he wanted to say something, but he didn't utter a word. Instead, he watched me go as I separated myself from him and hurried toward an archway that appeared to lead to a hallway beyond the main room.

I had no idea where the bathroom was, but I didn't actually need it. Rather, I was suddenly overcome with the need for a breath of fresh air. I needed to clear my head. The realization that I had genuine feelings for Mason was overwhelming to say the least, especially since nothing about this relationship was real.

As I meandered down a back hallway that was almost entirely empty, I stopped short at the sound of a woman crying nearby.

Peering nervously around the corner, I found myself at the entrance of an intimate reception room lavishly decorated with velvet drapes and antique furniture.

Marina was sitting on a silk ottoman, leaning forward with her elbows on her knees and her head in her hands. Her slender shoulders heaved with sobs as a tall, blond-haired man stood over her with his hands shoved uselessly in his pockets. I recognized the back of his head immediately.

Aiden. Of course. He was dating Marina. It made sense that he was accompanying her to her grandmother's memorial gala. I hadn't even considered it, especially since he hadn't showed his face earlier when Marina approached us at the entrance.

"Why don't you love me?" Marina cried.

"Marina—" sighed Aiden. He wasn't comforting her. He wasn't even sitting beside her or crouching in front of her, choosing instead to loom over her like an imposing judge.

"If you would just realize that we're perfect for each other, we could get married and claim the inheritance. I could throw together a wedding *so* much faster than—"

Aiden scoffed and spun around, stalking away from Marina while raking his fingers through his hair in frustration. I sank into the shadows, too afraid that running away would draw attention to me.

"That's a vile reason to get married," he growled.

Admittedly, those words cut deep. That was exactly what I was doing, faking a marriage so that Mason could gain the contents of Ruth Baldwin's estate. In Aiden's eyes, that was *vile*.

But, it was different for Mason and me. Even professionally speaking, we had a deeper and longer relationship than Aiden and Marina. Plus, Mason deserved that inheritance. It was supposed to be his. It was only because of his grandmother's ridiculous, last-minute stipulation that he hadn't received it right away.

"People have gotten married for worse reasons!" Marina protested, clearly not caring about keeping the volume of her voice low. She lifted her face, revealing streaks of mascara on her cheeks. "Is it really so awful, the thought of marrying me? You would benefit, too—"

"Enough!" snapped Aiden. "I've heard enough. I'm going home."

Aiden stalked toward the exit. I stumbled backward, but my heel caught on the long skirt of the gown I was wearing. Reaching out for the wall, I desperately tried to right myself in time to disappear from sight before Aiden emerged from his and Marina's private makeshift argument area.

Unfortunately, it was too late.

Aiden saw me right away, leaning against the opposite wall of the hallway just outside the private parlor. He froze, the anger in his expression morphing swiftly into surprise.

"Daisy?"

"I—" Whatever excuse I was about to offer immediately died on my lips. Apparently, Marina had decided she wasn't done begging her boyfriend of three months to marry her and chose to run after him.

The moment her gaze landed on me, her eyes narrowed menacingly.

"You!" she hissed. "This is your fault! I should've realized this before!"

"Me? What are you talking about?" I inquired, wishing that I'd simply stayed back in the ballroom with Mason.

"Him!" Marina snapped, pointing her finger at Aiden. He stood there dumbly between us, too baffled to say a word. "He's your ex-boyfriend! He's still in love with *you* and it's ruining *my* life!"

Chapter Fourteen: *Reed*

About one minute after Daisy excused herself from the dance floor, it occurred to me that letting her walk away was not the correct response to the situation. She seemed troubled by something. Plus, the ladies room was on the other side of the building. If she got lost, she was going to end up being cornered by one of my overeager relatives. From a contractual standpoint, it wasn't fair of me to leave her to fend for herself in that situation.

I headed off in the direction she'd disappeared, sidestepping an incoming distant relative as politely as I could manage. I'd been to this venue a handful of times before for various other galas and fundraisers over the years, so I knew it well.

She was harder to find than I thought. The back hallways were fairly empty—it was still too early in the evening for people to scatter outward from the main hub of the ballroom.

It wasn't until I heard the familiar sound of my cousin's voice that I had any indication of Daisy's location.

"—still in love with you and it's ruining my life!" Marina shouted.

I stopped short before turning the corner. It sounded as if she'd been crying. While she was family, I wasn't interested in offering her any kind of emotional support. She'd sooner see me suffer for her own sake, so I didn't feel guilty about such sentiments.

Stiletto heels clicked rapidly in the opposite direction of where I stood, signaling that Marina had run away immediately following her outburst. I had no idea who she was yelling at, but the next person to speak clued me in on exactly what was going on.

"Why aren't you going after her, Aiden?" Daisy asked.

Aiden Plourde. Her ex-boyfriend and fellow Yale alum. We'd met briefly at my grandmother's wake and he had made it very clear that he was an admirer of my financial success. It shocked me that someone who had once fallen in love with Daisy could also be interested in someone like Marina, but from what Daisy had said about their relationship, he wasn't a great guy to begin with.

"Why would I?" Aiden scoffed. "I'm assuming you heard her in there. She's a fraud. I don't think I can do this anymore."

Marina was a fraud at heart, but I suppose I couldn't judge too harshly given my current situation.

"Why would she say that to me? Why would she think that—that you—is this why you called me last week?"

I quirked an eyebrow, eavesdropping like a schoolboy as I dared to creep a few steps closer. At the mention of Daisy's ex-boyfriend calling her recently, I felt a sharp flare of annoyance. Not so much because she never mentioned it to me, but because the type of man who dated one girl while secretly contacting his ex was not someone I wanted near any woman I cared about.

"Daisy, if you'd just let me talk to you. I know you're engaged, but—"

I'd heard about enough at that point. I wasn't interested in listening to Aiden plead his case pathetically when the woman who was supposed to be his girlfriend had just run off crying.

I stepped around the corner of the hallway and cleared my throat, making my presence known. Immediately, both Daisy and Aiden whirled around to gape at me. Daisy looked more shocked than anything else, but I was pretty sure that one of the many emotions on Aiden's face upon seeing me was disappointment. Despite being a fan of mine, I was also his ex-girlfriend's current fiancé, so perhaps he had a difficult time figuring out what he truly thought about me.

"Mason," Daisy murmured. "What are you doing?"

"I realized you wandered off in the wrong direction of the bathrooms, so I thought I would come to your rescue," I explained. Then, with a cold glance in Aiden's direction, I asked, "Have we met before?"

"Yes," Aiden replied. "At the late Mrs. Baldwin's wake. I was accompanying Marina."

"So, you're my cousin's boyfriend?" I pressed, my voice loaded with accusation. I didn't try to hide the fact that I'd overheard the last part of their conversation.

Aiden looked as if the last thing he wanted to do was give an affirmative answer to my question, either because he didn't want to be Marina's boyfriend anymore or because he genuinely thought he had a chance to win Daisy back. In truth, I was offended by the implication that Aiden thought he had the right to speak to my fiancée. Regardless of the fact that Daisy and I weren't actually in love, and that our marriage wouldn't last very long, I had no respect for a man who couldn't keep his hands to himself. I wasn't normally possessive, but Daisy was certainly mine. He might have had her at one point, but not anymore. He was the idiot who'd messed it up and that wasn't my problem.

"We've been seeing each other casually," Aiden replied after a long pause.

I snorted quietly, then angled my body away from his, turning to give Daisy my full attention. It didn't take a genius to see that she was relieved by my arrival on the scene. It was safe to assume that she hadn't meant to get caught speaking alone with this idiot and was in the process of trying to get herself out of it when I stumbled upon them.

"Babe, have I told you how absolutely, breathtakingly stunning you look tonight?" I murmured. "I only wish my grandmother had the opportunity to meet you and see you wear this gorgeous dress named after her."

For a second, Daisy looked utterly baffled by the compliments pouring from my lips, then she caught on. As Aiden shuffled his feet awkwardly, she smiled softly and batted her eyelashes.

"You're always such a smooth talker," she whispered to me.

Aiden cleared his throat. "Daisy—"

He really didn't give up. It was pathetic. Even the most ambitious men had to know when it was their time to step out of the ring. Regardless of the inauthenticity of mine and Daisy's relationship, I was a far more deserving match for her than he was.

I decided to stop whatever words were about to spill out of his bumbling mouth with actions. Lifting my hand to cradle Daisy's face gently, I ducked my head and pulled her into a tender kiss. Daisy didn't hesitate to respond, melting into my touch. There was another awkward clearing of the throat behind us, but I ignored it and deepened the kiss.

Daisy was the first to pull away, glancing around my shoulder. The fool was still standing there as if waiting for his turn at the kissing booth.

"Would you mind excusing us, Aiden?" Daisy muttered sternly.

I kept my back to the younger man, making it clear that I had no intention of acknowledging his presence or showing respect for him in any regard.

"Right. I suppose I'll go find Marina," replied Aiden.

There was another moment of hesitation, then the sound of his footsteps disappearing down the otherwise empty hall confirmed his retreat.

Daisy took a slight step back from me, but kept her hands on my arms. She'd been gripping my suit jacket to keep herself steady during the kiss.

"What was that for?" she whispered.

I shrugged. "It kind of seemed like you needed some help making him scram. What was all that about anyway?"

Daisy sighed and leaned back against the wall. Just behind her, there was a private lounge. It was small but expensively decorated with soft furniture.

She nodded her head in the direction of the room. "I was looking for the bathroom when I overheard Marina and Aiden fighting. I'm a bit embarrassed to admit it, but I couldn't help myself and ended up listening in."

"What were they fighting about?" I asked.

Daisy bit her lip. "Your cousin was trying to convince Aiden to marry her before our wedding."

I chuckled humorlessly. I wasn't surprised at all. I had no ground to stand on when it came to judging people for arranging last-minute loveless marriages, but that inheritance was always supposed to be *mine*. Marina was merely leaping at the chance to claim something she didn't deserve.

"And, he wasn't buying it?" I inquired.

"No," she answered. "He called it 'vile' and stormed out of there, and saw me standing here. Marina came after him, but when she noticed me she claimed that the reason Aiden doesn't want to marry her is because he's still in love with me, which is absolutely ridiculous because I haven't seen Aiden in years. Prior to your grandmother's wake, at least."

"It certainly seems like that's the role he's eager to play, though," I commented, wandering into the intimate parlor.

Daisy followed after me. "What do you mean?"

"Well, clearly, Aiden wants you back. Not because he's had some kind of emotional awakening, I'm sure, but more so because he strikes me as the type of man who likes to win prizes. Not that you're a prize, Daisy. I don't mean to objectify you—"

"No, no. I know what you mean," she replied softly, dropping down onto a velvet upholstered loveseat with a rustle of satin. "You're right. I think Aiden wants to win me like a trophy. He cares a lot about status and image. I think, in his head, I am a more impressive win than Marina Baldwin because, as far as everyone else is concerned, Mason Reed is in love with me. Maybe he doesn't even realize he's thinking it."

"Now *that's* vile," I remarked.

I sat beside her on the sofa. She looked troubled, but I wasn't sure if I was her first choice for the person she wanted to open up to. We weren't friends. Daisy and I shared a lot of things, but a friendship wasn't one of them.

"Do you think we're bad people for doing this?" Daisy whispered, glancing beyond the entrance to check that no one was hovering outside now that we both knew how easy it was to eavesdrop in this part of the venue.

"Why do you ask?"

"I don't know. We're lying to a lot of people. I know that we have our reasons and I wholeheartedly agree with them—I'm not getting cold feet, so please don't take this wrong—but if anyone found out, I can't help imagining what they would think of me."

"Who cares what other people think of you?" I countered.

"I do," Daisy said. "I really do. Maybe it's childish, but I want people to like me. If I was an outside observer of this situation, my first thought wouldn't be that I was acting altruistically. Rather, I would assume I was in it for something. A promotion or cash or upward mobility."

"Is that not why you're doing this?" I asked, cocking my head to the side in confusion.

Daisy let out a bubble of laughter. "No, actually. It's not. I told you before that I want to earn my career success the old-fashioned way. I'm doing this because I'm loyal to you as your assistant and I care about you getting your rightful inheritance. Not only for the sake of the company, but also because you deserve it so much more than the alternative options."

"So, this is a moral situation for you?"

"I don't know. I guess so."

"It doesn't have anything to do with the fact that you think I'm hot?" I joked, eager to somehow diffuse the tension in her shoulders. Humor had worked before, so it was worth a shot.

Daisy swatted my leg. It was a gesture she never would have dared to do just a couple of weeks ago, but I found her new playfulness amusing.

"Excuse me?" she gasped.

"You said it yourself when we were at my place the other night," I said. "You always thought I was handsome."

"Are you suggesting that I agreed to this charade merely because of your looks? Do you really think I'm that shallow, Mr. Reed?"

There was a deliciously sexy smirk on her face that was driving me wild.

"Not at all, Miss Campbell."

We sat there in silence for a moment. Undoubtedly, people would wonder where we'd disappeared to if we stayed gone too long. Unlike Daisy, however, I didn't care what other people thought about me. They could go ahead and miss me, make their judgments, and draw their own conclusions. It was what they would do regardless if I tried to convince them otherwise. Daisy was too optimistic about life and people in general to realize that, though.

"That kiss—" she murmured. "It was unexpected."

"It felt necessary."

"I think it was. Aiden doesn't easily take no for an answer."

"I don't like him," I said.

Daisy laughed quietly. "I'm not surprised. I don't like him very much either. Not anymore."

Another beat of tense silence passed between us, our eyes locked together. Kissing her had felt amazing. Other than accidental brushes here and there, we hadn't touched since that unintentional sleepover at my place a week ago. I'd almost forgotten how much electric chemistry there was between Daisy and me.

"I'm sorry you had to deal with my cousin on your own," I told her. "I should've gone after you sooner."

She shook her head. "It's okay. I can take care of myself. Actually, I'm the one who is sorry. After all, you're the one who is related to her."

I huffed out a laugh. "True."

"Mason, I—"

Daisy trailed off, biting her lip as she glanced away. She looked so beautiful that I felt a flare of annoyance at not being able to see her lovely face anymore, so I reached out and coaxed her attention back toward me with a finger under her chin.

"What is it?" I asked.

Her answer did not come in the form of words. Instead, she leaned forward and kissed me hard. Whatever thoughts might have been in the process of forming inside my head at that moment disappeared into thin air. Her lips were so soft, so insistent, so tender … it consumed me.

Wrapping my arms around her waist, I shifted our bodies so that she was lying back against the cushions of the sofa and I was hovering over her. She sighed into the kiss, fighting against the long skirt of her gown to wrap her legs around my waist. Even though all I wanted to do was rip the dress off her and have my way with her right there on the floor, the measured voice of logic in my head reminded me that we couldn't go any further than this. I was hardly an exhibitionist and I definitely didn't want to embarrass Daisy by potentially exposing her in a compromising position.

"Mm, fancy galas aren't so bad," Daisy gasped as I trailed my lips down her feverish throat. I smiled and peppered kisses along her collarbone.

This was enough. Hearing her quiet moans and feeling the way she clutched at my body as if she'd never needed anything more in her life—there was no need to go all the way with her. The physical chemistry between us was deeply intimate no matter the level of intensity. I'd never met anyone who cleared my congested thoughts with just one kiss, who could stop my mind in its tracks when it was usually running a mile a minute.

So, for now, just being able to kiss her in this secret alcove was enough.

Chapter Fifteen: *Campbell*

"Sweetie, are you eating well? Getting in three square meals every day? You work so hard and it's wonderful, but I always worry if you're taking care of yourself."

"Yes, Mom. I'm eating just fine. Anyway, there's something I need to tell you—"

"Honey, did you get a haircut? You look so pretty! I can't believe we made a daughter as lovely as Daisy, Sharon. How did we do that?"

"Dad—"

"We must've worked some kind of magic, Jim."

"Ew, guys. Can you please—"

"Daisy, I heard there was some trouble in New York on the news. A robbery in Queens, I think. You're staying safe, right? You've got that mace I sent you?"

"Dad, of course I—"

"No, Jim, it was definitely the Bronx. Not Queens. Sweetie, you're not spending time in the Bronx, are you? I don't mean to judge places I've never seen, but—"

"Why would I go to the Bronx?" I sighed, fighting the urge to pinch the bridge of my nose or roll my eyes or otherwise indicate that having a conversation with my parents was utterly exhausting at times. I loved them dearly, but they really knew how to talk someone's ear off. "Mom. Dad. I really need to tell you something."

Both my parents paused on the screen of my phone, their pixelated faces pinching into subtle confusion at the evident anxiety in my tone.

"What is it, sweetie?"

"Did you get a promotion?"

"Is your boss being rude to you?"

"Do you need money? You know you can always ask for help if you need it."

"No, it's not that," I replied. "I don't need money. I'm very financially secure—"

"That's great, honey—"

"I need you both to stop peppering me with questions so I can just tell you this, okay? I love you guys, but I need you to put on your listening hats," I said, doing my best to keep my voice light and playful. Meanwhile, just below the screen where my parents couldn't see, I was wringing my hands nervously.

They smiled at my choice of words. When I was little, we used to play a game at the dinner table where we would tell a story about our day in the most theatrical way possible. However, because my parents were so bad at not interrupting, they had to devise the rules of *listening hats* and *talking hats*. Basically, the person with the talking hat was the only one allowed to speak, though the other participants could gasp and laugh to their hearts' content.

"Sorry, sweetie," said my mother. "Of course. You are officially wearing the talking hat."

"Thanks," I murmured. "Okay, so … I'm not really sure how to say this, but I've been seeing someone."

I paused when my father's mouth popped open, but he stopped himself before uttering a single noise. I'd crafted a decently convincing lie that ran somewhat parallel to the truth about Mason's and my situation. After all, I had been seeing Mason. At work, as his employee … but still seeing him.

"We've been involved for a while," I continued. "I didn't want to mention it until I was sure that it was serious because I didn't want to get your hopes up. I know how eager you both are for grandchildren and all that. Plus, you've been traveling so much that I didn't want to interrupt your adventures—"

"Oh, honey, a phone call from you is never an interruption!" crooned my mother.

Mischievously, my father placed a hand over her mouth. "You've got your listening hat on, Sharon!"

I snorted. My parents were goofballs. They always had been. Just as I'd told Mason, they were totally normal people from a totally normal suburb in Vermont, but they definitely had their quirks. Poppy reminded me a lot of them because they shared a tendency to prefer going with the flow rather than meticulously planning out the next decade of their life. They were easygoing, patient, open-minded, and unceasingly supportive. In spite of that, I was terrified to tell them the news that absolutely had to be delivered.

Both of my parents were retired now, so they spent most of their time traveling around the world with other older couples, going on yoga retreats, and enjoying the peace of a fairly stress-free existence. They'd just gotten back from a month-long stint in Bali a couple of days ago, so I had to take advantage of them being stateside before they whisked themselves away again.

"So, I know this is going to sound insane or like I'm playing a practical joke on you, but this man and I are now engaged to be married," I carried on. "And now, I'm officially handing you guys the talking hat."

"Engaged?" gasped my mother immediately. "As in, to be married?"

"How long have you been seeing this young man?" asked my father before she was barely done speaking.

"Yes, engaged to be married, Mom. In September. We've been seeing each other for a long time, Dad. Over a year." Technically, it wasn't a lie.

"What's his name?"

"Mason."

"How did you meet?"

"Work."

"He works at that fancy-shmancy investment company?"

"Well, it's actually a consulting company *for* fancy-shmancy private equity investment firms, but … yes."

"Honey, I think I speak for both your mom and me when I say we're absolutely floored right now. This isn't like you at all," said my father. "You usually do everything by the book, but we didn't even know you had a boyfriend!"

"I know, and I'm sorry—"

"That being said, I did notice even through this tiny screen that you're absolutely glowing, Daisy," he continued. "We know that you have a good head on your shoulders and we trust your judgment, so if you think accepting this man's proposal is the best way to follow your heart, we're with you all the way."

"Absolutely, sweetie," my mother agreed.

I was speechless. That wasn't the reaction I was expecting. I thought they would go red in the face or clutch their chests in horror and lecture me about the dangers of reckless decision making. Even though that wasn't like them at all, it wasn't as if I'd ever unloaded an announcement as big as this before. I was the perfect child. I'd attended an Ivy League school on scholarship, accepted a competitive internship, and eventually landed the kind of job that would hopefully unlock a very long and successful career. When the time was right, I planned on getting married and having kids just like everyone else. I never thought I would stumble into a fake engagement with my boss … but who could ever plan for something like that?

Still, I knew my parents were different than me. Somehow, two of the most relaxed and carefree people had produced one of the most neurotic young women in New England.

"Wait … what?"

They burst out laughing.

"Well, you were bound to do something unconventional eventually," giggled my mother. "I'm just glad it's an untraditional approach to courting rather than getting a neck tattoo! But, dear, you're not pregnant are you? That's not why this is so sudden?"

"Mom!"

"I have to ask!"

"No, I'm not pregnant," I gasped. "That definitely would've been the first thing I mentioned."

"Good to know," chuckled my mother. "How exciting! Let me see the ring!"

For the next few minutes, I sat torturously still on my sofa and twisted my left hand every which way so that my mother could admire Rose Reed's diamond. Even my father was impressed, adjusting his glasses and leaning close to the screen to get a better look as the massive gem caught the sunlight.

"That looks like it cost a pretty penny," remarked my father. "He must make good money if he's working at that big company. I'm a little confused, though."

"About what?"

"Well, it looks like you're still in that same studio apartment you moved into last year. Did he move in with you? Is there enough space for the two of you? Shouldn't you at least get a one-bedroom?"

I hadn't planned for that question, so I had no choice but to think on my feet.

"No, he—we—we haven't moved in together yet. He's ... traditional."

"Traditional, huh? If that was the case, wouldn't he have asked for my blessing before getting down on one knee?"

"Well—"

"I'm just kidding, honey. I'm sure moving in Manhattan is a nightmare. You've got to work around the market and your leases, all that stuff."

I breathed a sigh of relief.

"If the wedding is in September, surely we'll get a chance to meet him before then, right?" my mother added. "This is a pretty brief engagement."

I shrugged. "He's the one. I'm sure of it. Why waste time?"

It was the first direct lie I told. I might not have felt too guilty about saying something like that in front of one of Mason's family members, but convincing my parents I'd met my soulmate when I had every intention of signing divorce papers shortly after saying *I do* made me feel a bit sheepish. Hopefully, they wouldn't grow too fond of him. My parents had a lot of love to give, so it was unlikely they'd withhold from someone they believed to be the love of my life. It was still worth hoping for, I suppose.

Then again, it wasn't that far from the truth. Last night at the gala, when I realized that I genuinely did have feelings for Mason, it occurred to me that I was in much deeper than I thought. Only, he made it crystal clear that he didn't feel the same way, and that he would likely never feel the same way. From his perspective, love was a waste of time.

I was better off forgetting the soft, golden side of Mason that I caught glimpses of, similar to shafts of sunlight peeking through the clouds. That was better said than done, though. In truth, I wasn't the kind of person who could easily forget how they felt about another person. At least, not when it was real.

Forcing myself out of my reverie, I tried to remember what question my parents were still waiting for me to answer.

"Of course you can meet him," I told them. "I already told him that we'll have to come to Vermont before the summer ends."

"Oh, he doesn't want to come here!" my mother protested good-naturedly. "This place is just mosquito-infested woodlands and humidity in July. We'll come to New York, won't we, Jim? Actually, I was just thinking it's been too long since we took a trip to the city. We've got a bunch of hotel rewards points saved up, too."

The idea of my parents coming to New York to meet Mason for the first time instead of us going to see them in Vermont was less than ideal. There was more room for error in New York. I couldn't even imagine the horror of running into someone from Reed Capital and having them witness the CEO and his executive assistant hanging out with my parents in an obvious couple-y way. That would ruin everything.

Then again, I couldn't ever recall accidentally crossing paths with a coworker on the streets of New York once during the past two years. If we were careful, it shouldn't be a problem. My parents were going to have to come to New York for the actual wedding eventually, anyway.

"Sure," I replied. "That would be great. When do you—"

"How about next weekend?" my father cut in.

"Next weekend?"

"Yeah, no time like the present, right, Daisy? We might as well take a page out of your book and get this show on the road!"

"Great idea, Jim!" sang my mother. "Next weekend would be perfect. I'm too excited to meet this fella to wait any longer than that, so don't you even think about saying no, Daisy."

I suppose it was best for me to simply count my blessings. I had gone into this video call thinking my parents would be shocked into an early grave as soon as I told them I was getting married in less than two months. The fact that they wanted to meet Mason as soon as next weekend was not the worst possible outcome of this conversation.

"Sure, guys. Next weekend will be great. I'll let Mason know."

"Perfect!" chirped my mother. "This is going to be so fun! Will Poppy be around? I miss that girl. We can have a girls' outing while your father grills Mason."

I knew she was only joking, but the thought of leaving my father alone with Mason made me feel more anxious than anything else in the past couple of weeks. My father was hardly the type of person to grill someone, but Mason was so prone to impatience and grouchiness that I feared my father would get the wrong impression.

Not that it mattered if my parents truly liked Mason. In fact, when it came down to it, it was probably for the best if they weren't too fond of him. It would only make things easier when everything ended.

Still, I couldn't help wishing that my parents would like him as much as I did. Mason deserved to be seen as more than a surly businessman, because he *was* more than that.

"I'll ask Poppy what her plans are," I told my mother. "I should probably get going, though. I need to run some errands."

"Alright, sweetie. We'll see you next weekend! We love you!"

"I love you, too. See you next weekend."

When I disconnected the call, I sat there in silence for several long minutes. This was getting real. Almost too real. I was actually getting married. Never mind how genuine the relationship was … the marriage itself was going to be very real. I would really be walking down the aisle in a dress, really reciting vows to another person. My parents would be there. The Baldwin family attorney would be there.

God, what was I doing?

I couldn't think too hard about it. That was the key to making it through this. If I allowed myself to overthink, then I would panic.

Thus, I shook the anxious thoughts from my head and went about carrying on with the rest of my Sunday.

***

On Monday morning, I picked up Mason's coffee from Jennie at the front desk and made my way directly to his office. He glanced up from his computer, already slaving away at the helm of his empire, raising an eyebrow as I shut the door behind me.

"Hello," he said, a question in his tone.

I cut right to the chase. "My parents are coming to New York next weekend."

Mason sighed and slowly stood up, accepting his coffee from me by hand even though I usually set it down on a coaster for him.

"I see."

"They want to meet you."

"Naturally."

"You, as in—my fiancé."

"Right."

"You don't seem the least bit nervous," I remarked.

Mason smirked. "Why would I be? I meet with some of the wealthiest, most influential people in the world on a daily basis. Your parents will be like a breath of fresh air."

"Why? Because they're middle class and unimportant?"

His smirk grew more pronounced at my accusation. "No, Daisy, because they're *your* parents. I can't imagine anyone who created someone as unfailingly optimistic as you to be particularly intimidating. In fact, now that you mention it, I'm looking forward to it."

Why wasn't anyone reacting the way I expected them to? And, why did the fact that Mason truly wanted to meet my parents make me feel like the happiest woman in the world?

The marriage is real, but the romance isn't, I reminded myself. *Mason doesn't believe in love.*

"Okay then," I said, deflating slightly now that I wouldn't have to deliver any of the defenses or arguments I had mentally prepared on the subway ride to work that morning. "Great."

I turned to go, reaching for the knob.

"Wait."

Mason's voice stopped me in my tracks.

"Yes?"

"Come here."

I obeyed the gentle command without thinking, approaching his desk. He came around the front of it and perched casually on the edge. I expected him to ask me to reschedule one of his meetings or prepare a report—something related to my job, since we were in the workplace—but he surprised me.

"How are you feeling? After the fiasco at the gala and all that?"

I couldn't recall Mason ever asking me about my feelings. From what I'd observed over the past couple of years, emotions weren't something he took into consideration if he could help it.

"I'm fine," I answered. "It was really no big deal."

After Mason and I had finally stopped kissing in that little parlor where Marina and Aiden had been arguing, we returned to the main ballroom. Marina was nowhere to be seen after that, so we mingled with a few of Mason's family members, then he wrote a donation check to the charity being honored in his grandmother's name, and we left. He dropped me off at Poppy's place, where I spent the night and tried not to drown under my best friend's deluge of questions. It was simple and easy. The dress was already on its way to being held in the Baldwin Foundation art archives, too.

"I think it went fairly well despite that," Mason said.

I nodded. "I think so, too."

Was I losing my mind or had the tension suddenly shifted?

"My only regret is that we didn't finish what we started in that private room," he murmured.

I swallowed. He was coming onto me, flirting with me at seven-thirty on a Monday morning. We had agreed to keep our physical chemistry separate from our professional lives, but I couldn't deny I found it nearly impossible.

"Me, too," I admitted. I dared to take a step closer, biting my lip when he spread his knees and made room for me to stand between his thighs.

"Is there anyone else here yet?" he asked, eyes trailing down the length of my body as he spoke.

"Just Jennie and a few early birds on the lower floors."

"What time is my first obligation of the day scheduled?"

"Eight-thirty," I answered automatically, my voice becoming more breathless as I inched closer to him. "You have a call with—"

"With Kershaw, right?"

"Yes, Sir."

His hands rested on my hips, the warmth of them easily permeating through the thin fabric of my linen skirt.

"Sounds like we have plenty of time," Mason whispered, tilting his head to the side and ghosting his lips just below my jaw.

"Plenty of time?" I gasped, goosebumps erupting on my skin.

"To finish what we started, of course. Only if you'd like to, though."

"I would very much like to."

The moment I voiced my desire, Mason burst into action. He gripped me tighter, kissing me deeply without hesitation. Suddenly, I didn't care that we were on the top floor of Reed Capital headquarters. All I wanted was to feel him closer.

Clearly, he felt the same way. In a split second, he grabbed my thighs and flipped us around so that I was the one sitting on his desk and he was standing before me. His hand slipped below the hem of my skirt, wasting no time. He rubbed soft circles in my center through the fabric of my panties. I couldn't help myself. I threw my head back and let out a moan.

He chuckled low. "It's a good thing my office is soundproof."

Chapter Sixteen: *Reed*

"Oh! Mason! Yes! Right there!"

Suffice it to say, I'd never had sex in my office before. I'd definitely never had sex with an employee in my office before, and certainly not as business hours were dawning upon us and the building was slowly filling with Reed Capital staff on the floors below us.

I cursed under my breath. "You feel so good."

In response, Daisy moaned in my ear.

It was clumsy and uncomfortable, but the pleasure that coursed through my veins was too intense to even think about stopping. Daisy sat atop my desk, one hand braced behind her and her legs wrapped securely around my hips as I thrust into her hard and fast. The door to my office locked automatically when it was closed, so I wasn't worried about being interrupted, but I also didn't want to let this moment cut too deeply into the work day.

"Mason—" Daisy whimpered. "Harder."

I didn't care that she wasn't the boss of me. When I was inside her, I'd do anything she asked.

Unfortunately, the angle we were currently in wasn't very conducive to fucking her harder. Not unless I wanted to knock my computer down and possibly break the desk in the process—which I wasn't entirely opposed to in the heat of the moment—but that would be difficult to explain to the IT guy who would have to clean up the mess.

Instead of creating a disaster, I lifted Daisy up and carried her over to the chaise stationed against the far wall. No one ever sat there, but I was grateful Daisy had insisted on ordering it for me last year now more than ever. I laid her down on the soft leather cushions and positioned myself on top of her. It wasn't quite as pleasant as an actual mattress, but it was better than the hard surface of the desk.

I groaned low in my throat when I pushed into her once more, remembering her prior request and immediately increasing the strength of my thrusts. Before, when the moment first heated up, we didn't waste time undressing. All I did was push up the hem of Daisy's skirt and nudge her flimsy panties aside while she undid the zipper of my pants and yanked the waistband of my underwear down a few inches. I didn't mind; it felt so good to be inside her that I was grateful to be like this with her. Still, I wished I could do this properly. I wanted to take my time undressing her and enjoying every inch of her body. That singular night we'd spent at my place was always on my mind, even during the most somber of moments.

At the memory of Daisy naked and sighing in my bed sheets, I let out a low groan. I was reaching my climax fast, which normally would have been annoying, but it was probably best if we wrapped things up as soon as possible given our current location.

"I'm close," I growled into the warm skin of her throat.

In reply, she merely whimpered and clutched me tighter. I shifted onto one arm, deepening my movements and reaching my free hand between us to rub circles on Daisy's warm bud with my thumb. She trembled, eyes going wide. Unable to hold on to me any longer, she clutched the sides of the chaise for support.

"Mason," she moaned. "Mason, I'm going to—"

With a sharp gasp, Daisy's eyes rolled back. Her body curved off the cushion beneath her, bending closer to mine as she shoved her face into the fabric of my shirt and whined through her orgasm. As soon as I felt her clenching around me, my release soon followed.

I pumped into her twice more, clenching my jaw to stop myself from cursing out loud as I emptied myself into her. In a perfect world, we would have used a condom, but Daisy was on birth control and desperate times called for desperate measures.

For a moment, I lay there on top of her, hovering somewhat awkwardly with one shoe still braced on the floor. Once I caught my breath, I stood up and tucked myself back into my trousers, zipping myself up and buckling my belt once more. Daisy sat up slowly, squirming to pull her skirt back down. She ran her fingers through her hair, smoothing out the tangles that had formed during all that motion.

"Sorry," I said all of a sudden. It just hit me that we were literally in the office, the place where we worked—the building of the company *I* owned and operated. This was inappropriate. Even if Daisy really was my girlfriend—or rather, fiancée—having a quickie with her before business hours was tacky.

Or, was it? Honestly, I felt too invigorated to care much for morals and decorum.

Daisy burst out laughing. "Jesus Christ."

I raised my eyebrows at her. "What?"

"Please don't tell me you make a habit out of apologizing to women immediately after having sex with them."

I snorted. "That's not why—I'm not sorry for that. I guess I'm apologizing for being the one to initiate that after we agreed to keep our arrangement separate from our work lives."

"It's not even eight yet. I don't mind."

Checking my watch, I laughed again. "It's seven fifty-nine. Perfect timing, I guess."

Daisy giggled and stood, smoothing out the fabric of her clothing. There was a light blush in her cheeks and her blue eyes were even brighter than usual, but I didn't think anyone would suspect it was because she'd just broken at least three human resources violations with me. Everyone at Reed Capital knew that Daisy was a rule-abiding people pleaser.

"Why are you looking at me like that?" she asked softly, sauntering over to me. Without waiting for permission, she adjusted my tie and straightened my collar.

"Like what?"

She shrugged. "Like I said something that confused you."

"I suppose I'm merely coming to terms with the fact that you're full of surprises."

"Oh?"

Trying and failing to hide a smirk, I stepped away from her and settled into my desk chair. "For the past two years, I've been under the impression that you're an incurable goody-two-shoes. Apparently, I was wrong."

"I guess we all have our vices."

"So, I'm your vice?"

I hadn't meant to ask the question out loud. The fact that it spilled past my lips before I could stop it was alarming enough. I never spoke without thinking first. Every single word I said had a careful purpose. Lately, it had been harder to keep my composure, but the slip-ups only happened when Daisy was around. I didn't know what that meant, nor was I interested in psychoanalyzing myself any further than that.

Daisy chose not to answer, instead glancing at her own watch.

"It's 8:02," she announced. "Kershaw will want to start the meeting five minutes early, as usual, which means you only have twenty-three minutes to get sufficient caffeine into your system and review the metrics accounting sent to you last week."

"Yes, ma'am," I replied with a chuckle.

For some reason, Daisy furrowed her brow at that. "Are you okay?"

"I just had sex with a beautiful woman. Why wouldn't I be okay?"

"I've just never seen you in such an optimistic mood about an upcoming meeting with Kershaw. You normally dread them."

"There's a first time for everything."

"Right. Well, I suppose I'll go to my office now. Let me know if you need anything."

"Will do."

Daisy tossed me one last slightly baffled glance over her shoulder before she departed from the room, leaving the door open on her way out. Was she really that confused by my pleasant demeanor? How could I not be in a good mood when we had just started the day with mutual orgasms?

That was the upside of being attracted to my fake fiancée. When we were both stressed out, we could blow off some steam the old fashioned way. I was lucky that Daisy didn't press charges the very first day I pretended to be engaged to her at my grandmother's wake, and even luckier that she agreed to play along. The fact that she was also sexy seemed too convenient to be lucky. There had to be something fateful about the circumstances we had stumbled into.

Little did she know, I'd already reviewed the aforementioned metrics in preparation for my first meeting of the day, so I spent the next twenty minutes relaxing in solitude with my coffee, observing the hectic world outside the windows. It was a good thing they were designed to be transparent from the inside but impermeable from the outside, otherwise the residents of the neighboring skyscrapers might have caught a glimpse of Daisy and me acting less than professional.

Chuckling under my breath, I thought about how horrified my grandmother would be if she knew I'd discovered a loophole to her unexpected stipulation. It was hard to imagine she truly believed her little footnote in the will would be enough to finally convince me to settle down and live the life she wanted for me. She knew how devoted I was to Reed Capital and how uninterested I was in marriage. Yet, at the same time, Ruth Baldwin was also totally aware of how disappointing her other two grandchildren were. The fact that she was requiring me to be married in order to receive my inheritance wasn't because she didn't understand, but because she *did.* By adding the condition that either Marina or Bradley could claim the estate if they should wed before me was the true motivator.

That old crone knew I'd never be able to sleep at night if it was my fault one of those brats ran off with millions of dollars in both cash and equity. That was the real trick. It wasn't the money that would get me to bend to her will, but my pride that would spur me into action. It was clever. Stubbornly, I respected her for it.

Ruth Baldwin hadn't won, though. She had no idea I had a faithful assistant who was clearly willing to do anything to help me, a woman who was beautiful and charming and quick-witted. She didn't know I would dare to fake a romance with someone for that elusive inheritance. It wasn't as if Mr. Henderson was going to subject Daisy and me to an in-depth interview to determine the authenticity of our relationship. That wasn't one of the requirements noted in the will. He may have been a longtime ally of the Baldwin family, but he was an attorney at the end of the day. He wanted to cash his check, too.

Suddenly realizing how much of my brain was occupied with thoughts related to Daisy, I forced myself to snap out of it and went about the next hour of my morning as usual. I logged into my digital meeting with the pesky and demanding Kershaw, one of our wealthiest clients, and carried on as usual for the most part. By the time mid-morning came around, the routine schedule of the day was feeling so normal that I had almost forgotten what had happened mere hours ago right on the surface of my desk.

But then, my computer *pinged* with a notification from Daisy.

My parents are arriving Saturday at 10 a.m. I've already informed them we'll be picking them up from Penn Station, she'd written in the instant messaging system we used on the office computers.

Ten in the morning was a fairly early arrival from Vermont. That meant they were likely getting on the train before sunrise. I suppose they were eager to see their daughter and wanted as much time with her as possible. Or rather, with her and her new fiancé.

I felt a bubble of uncharacteristic nervousness form in the pit of my gut. Even though I played it off like it was no big deal to meet Mr. and Mrs. Campbell, it suddenly didn't feel like such a simple thing. I wish I knew why. I tussled with some of the most influential people on the planet on a weekly basis. A cheerful old couple from a small town in New England should have been the least intimidating prospect in my schedule.

Then again, it was undeniable that I didn't like disappointing people. At least, when it came to the wealthy and powerful, I knew exactly how to handle them. Unfortunately, because of my tendency to avoid romance and relationships in general, I didn't have as much experience engaging in discourse with parents.

On top of that, Daisy was their pride and joy. She didn't have to explicitly say that for me to know it was true. Daisy was an only child, so her mother and father had only ever had her to pour their attention and affection into. Plus, she was a Yale graduate, currently working for a billion-dollar company, and one of the kindest people you'd ever meet. I could only imagine how special she was to her parents and thus how much they wanted the best for her.

Not that it mattered if they thought I was good enough for her. Actually, it was probably better if they didn't like me all that much. In that case, it would be easier once Daisy and I eventually broke things off. Yet, the thought of simply letting her parents think the worst of me drove me crazy. At the very basis of our relationship, Daisy was extremely valuable to me as an employee. I didn't want her parents' disapproval to mar that.

Realizing that Daisy was waiting for a response from me, I quickly typed out a reply.

I'll let Maurice know, was all I answered. She didn't have anything else to say after that, allowing me to tumble right back into my minor mental crisis.

Feeling agitated all of a sudden, I started pacing back and forth across the room.

I was going to have to convince two complete strangers that I was in love with Daisy and would be a good husband to her. This was all so much easier when it was just a stupid game. When we were at my grandmother's house in Connecticut, smiling and nodding while assuming that announcing a nonexistent engagement would be enough for me to secure the inheritance, there was less pressure. That moment in time was short-lived, but I missed it, nonetheless.

Now, it was too real. I was going to have to dress up in a tuxedo and stand at the altar in front of everyone. I would have to say vows—promises that I never had any intention of fulfilling.

Then, when the marriage was annulled, my reputation would be tarnished. We might be able to avoid an official divorce if we moved quickly enough. Then again, an annulment might actually be worse, because that would imply our marriage was never legal in the first place, unraveling my access to the Baldwin estate.

So, divorce it was. I was going to be a divorcee. I'd no longer be New York's favorite billionaire bachelor, but New York's recklessly divorced bachelor. If I didn't handle my image properly, such a reputation could affect the company. Some of our clients were conservative and traditional. Others merely wanted to know that I was trustworthy; divorcing a woman I'd married after a two-month engagement hardly suggested that I was someone worth putting your faith in.

With a quiet groan, I sank onto the chaise. The cushions that had once cradled Daisy's supple body beneath mine now halfheartedly held my slumped form.

"What am I doing?" I muttered under my breath.

The fact of the matter was, once the news of my marriage and divorce made it onto page six, it would be almost impossible to keep Daisy's name out of the press. That meant people at Reed Capital would find out about us. Daisy would have to get a different job. I would lose the best assistant I'd ever had. Unless a real celebrity decided to have a mind-blowing scandal at the exact same time, the media would have a field day.

Was all of that really worth forty-two million dollars? Was it worth a few million-dollar properties, some stock holdings, and a significant stake in the Baldwin Foundation? It was a hefty sum and I wouldn't take it for granted, but I couldn't see any other way around the price of it all. If I were anyone else, this situation would be easier to keep quiet. However, I was Mason Reed. I was profiled in Forbes Magazine, quoted in various finance journals, and had a vast network of international colleagues. It wasn't easy for me to hide.

Part of me wondered if I should march down the hall to Daisy's office and call the whole thing off.

Except, the thought of meeting her parents reminded me of mine.

I was just a kid when they passed away, but that didn't mean they were easy to forget. I loved my mother and father more than anything. They were patient and affectionate. I never questioned how much they cared for me.

When they died in that plane crash, it felt as if someone had ripped my heart out of my chest and replaced it with a heavy brick of iron. My cousins were younger than me when it happened; Marina and Bradley barely five years old. They were lucky because they didn't have as many memories as me, but the truth was, their parents also weren't as loving as mine. My uncle, my mother's older brother and Ruth Baldwin's eldest son, was a drunkard. He never grew out of his party boy phase, which was probably why Bradley was the way that he was—it was genetic.

The thing was, Uncle Daniel was the one flying the plane. He'd earned his pilot's license in his twenties as a joke, though he wasn't known to be a particularly skilled aviator. While he and his wife Jane were on vacation with my parents in California, he convinced them to join him for a scenic ride over the valley. According to the staff they left behind at the vineyard before taking off, nobody knew how drunk Daniel Baldwin actually was, including my parents.

They were in the air for less than thirty minutes before going down in an open field just a few miles away.

How could I not hate my uncle for being so reckless? How could I not curse at my parents for not being more careful?

Marina and Bradley may have lost their parents that day, too, but it wasn't my father who was flying the plane. Furthermore, neither one of them tried to atone for their legacy. As they had grown older, they had become spiteful and selfish. They were spoiled brats. They didn't care about working hard and making meaningful progress in the world of business. The way I saw it, they were still the same children they had been the day the plane went down. They'd never grown up.

They didn't deserve our grandmother's inheritance. Daniel Baldwin muddied the family name, and as his children, neither of my cousins tried to be better people to account for his mistakes. I was a Reed, but I had Baldwin blood.

The estate belonged to me. I had earned it, fair and square.

So, I had to do this. No matter what the eventual consequences would be, I had to put on a brave face and keep moving forward. This wedding had to happen.

All in all, it wasn't as if it was torturous to pretend to love Daisy. In truth, she made it easy.

Chapter Seventeen: *Campbell*

"There's so many options! How do we even know where to begin?" crooned my mother, almost entirely engulfed by a rack of frilly white gowns.

The consultant who was assigned to us when Mason pulled several strings to get me this last-minute dress appointment smiled patiently at my mother. She'd introduced herself as Carla and had a pleasant aura, though I had suspicions that most of her kindness was due to the fact that she could tell the diamond on my finger was worth more than the shop's entire stock of wedding dresses.

"It's natural to feel overwhelmed when shopping for the perfect dress for your big day," Carla replied.

"I'll say!" chuckled my mother, running her fingers over the length of a long satin train spilling onto the carpet of our private lounge. "Daisy, when I was engaged to your father, we didn't have all these options! Even if we did, I never would've been able to afford it on my teacher's salary!"

"God, I've missed her," Poppy giggled beside me. While my mother was running around frantically, my best friend was perched next to me on the sofa. I was so relieved that she was able to make it today, not only because she was my not-so-fake maid of honor, but also because she was in on the secret and would be able to help me field questions as they came up.

"Daisy, let's first chat about what kinds of design features you're most drawn to," Carla continued, choosing to ignore my mother and sitting on a cushioned ottoman in front of me. "When you imagine yourself walking down the aisle, what silhouette do you see? What kind of fabric? What accessories do you envision?"

"Um—" was all I could utter in response. It wasn't as if I'd never fantasized about my wedding day, but being suddenly confronted with the reality of it had me feeling so overwhelmed, I was practically brain-dead.

As soon as Mason and I had picked up my parents from Penn Station that morning, we'd taken them to their hotel and had a quick brunch in a cafe across the street. Things went reasonably well, with both Mason and my parents being pleasant and polite. My father even managed to make Mason laugh, which was a feat in itself.

Earlier that week, Mason mentioned rather unexpectedly that it would be a good idea for me to find a dress while my mother was in town. After all, it was customary for the mother of the bride to attend an event like that. Therefore, that afternoon while Mason was charming my father's socks off on a golf course on Long Island, I was in one of the most exclusive dress shops in Manhattan with Poppy and my mother.

I felt dizzy.

When I didn't say anything for a full minute, Carla started to look concerned. Thankfully, Poppy came to my rescue.

"Daisy is very feminine," she explained to the consultant. "Not girly-girl, but definitely ladylike. I can picture her in something classic. She's also got a great figure, so I think something that shows that off without being too flaunty would be ideal."

God, I loved my best friend.

My mother flitted back over to us, nodding at Poppy's suggestions.

"You have such lovely collarbones, Daisy," she commented. "I'm not sure I would suggest something strapless, but definitely something with a wider neck."

Both of them offering their opinions with ease helped me kickstart my brain into functioning properly.

"I agree," I said to Carla. "I like traditional silhouettes, but I don't want it to be boring. I love embroidery, but no sparkles or rhinestones. Lace is okay, but not too much because I don't want to look like a doily."

Carla cracked a smile. "Understood. That's all really helpful information, ladies. How about I go pull a few gowns for you to start with? In the meantime, please help yourself to the complimentary champagne."

She stood and sashayed out of the room, ignoring the racks my mother had been combing through in favor of some selections toward the back of the store.

I sat back on the couch and closed my eyes. When my parents had made their last-minute plans to come to the city for the weekend, I didn't think I would be shopping for the dress I'd be wearing while walking down the aisle. Of course, I knew that I would have to find a dress eventually, but I figured I could just order something online like I did for the gala. It wasn't as if it were my real wedding.

"I can't believe this is happening," sang my mother giddily. "My little girl is getting married! I thought I'd still have to wait years before I got to experience this day!"

I forced a smile, but it wasn't hard to mirror my mother's cheerfulness. She was easily excitable and had an infectious laugh that, coupled with her brilliant smile, caused most people to fall for her charm within the first two minutes of meeting her. Before she retired, she won teacher of the year nearly every school year simply because the students loved her so much.

I liked to think I got my positive spirit from her, but I wasn't quite at her caliber. I was optimistic more often than not, but my mother could make you believe in unicorns and fairies and magic in the blink of an eye.

"It's definitely very surreal," I replied.

"What about you, Poppy?" my mother chirped. "When am I going to see a ring on your finger?"

Poppy laughed. "I'm still sampling as many fish in the sea as I can before reeling in the right one, Sharon."

"Good for you, sweetheart. Never settle for less than what you deserve! I imagine the dating pool in New York is full of many handsome, successful men. You've got your work cut out for you!"

"I certainly do," Poppy giggled. "You and Jim were high school sweethearts, weren't you?"

"Oh, yes," sighed my mother, settling onto the sofa on my other side with a wistful smile. "He was the first boy I ever kissed. I knew I was in love with him when I was only seventeen years old. Even back then, he was the one for me."

"Did you ever regret marrying so young?" Poppy asked. "Or, have you ever worried if you missed out on something?"

I could tell she was keeping the conversation going for my sake. While my mother was too consumed in her own delight to notice that I was falling apart on the inside, Poppy picked up on my cues easily. I couldn't stop fidgeting and whenever I smiled, it was hard not to feel as if I was doing so in a panic, as if there was a gun being held to my head.

"Never," my mother answered her. "Of course, Jim and I had our rough patches here and there, but that's normal for every couple. Still, I couldn't imagine being with anyone but Daisy's father. He's my soulmate."

"That's beautiful," Poppy sighed.

My mother squeezed my shoulder. "I haven't spent much time in Mason's presence, but I can tell he's got a good spirit. His soul is golden just like Daisy's. I understand now why they're so eager to tie the knot."

Saving me from having to formulate a reply to her tender statement, Carla came bustling back into the room. She was wheeling a rack full of garment bags in front of her. Pausing in front of the sofa, she gestured for me to stand up. I did so timidly, childishly thinking that something in one of those bags might bite me if I got too close.

"Let's try this one first, Daisy," Carla suggested, carrying one of the garment bags into a dressing room and holding open the curtain for me. "We'll be waiting out here for you, but let me know if you need me to help you get it on, okay?"

"Sure," I replied quietly, ducking alone into the small space. Carla shut the curtains abruptly, leaving me alone with the ominous, cream-colored bag. Beyond the privacy barrier, I overheard the consultant engaging in small talk with Poppy and my mother.

With shaking fingers, I lowered the zipper of the bag to reveal the first dress on the menu.

It's not real. None of this is real, I reminded myself. *There's no reason to freak out.*

All I had to do was make my mother smile a few times, then pick a dress that I liked well enough. I could worry about being picky when my actual wedding day was on the horizon.

The first dress Carla had chosen for me had a vintage flair to it. The material was pure ivory satin, shimmering in the fluorescent light as I slowly undressed and wrestled it off the hanger. It was heavier than I thought, but not particularly complicated to maneuver myself into. The sample was a little too big for me around the waist and I had some trouble getting the zipper up myself. Just as I was about to call for help, I heard Carla's rapid footsteps approaching on the other side of the curtain.

"How are you doing in there, Daisy?"

"I'm all right, but I need some help with the zipper," I replied.

Carla slipped past the curtain with a smile.

"This is beautiful," she whispered, immediately moving to finish up the zipper at my back. Then, armed with a handful of fabric clips, she pinned back the excess satin around the bodice to show how the dress would fit once it was tailored to my size. "Let's go show them, okay?"

I nodded wordlessly. Following her out of the alcove woodenly like a well-dressed robot, I barely registered my mother's or Poppy's reactions as I stepped up onto a circular platform in front of a large trifold of mirrors.

The other two women rushed to me to get a closer look. Poppy cursed under her breath and my mother started talking a mile a minute, but as I caught a glimpse of my reflection, the world seemed to go silent.

I'd worn white plenty of times in my life. It suited my skin tone, and I also liked the way white clothes paired with my golden-blonde hair, making me look exactly like a daisy. Still, for all the days of my life that I'd donned a white dress, I wasn't prepared for the image in front of me.

I looked beautiful. The dress had a smooth, fitted bodice that accentuated my small waist before blossoming into a full, flawlessly pleated skirt. It looked like a waterfall of pure, fresh cream. The short-sleeves were capped, feminine without being girlish, and the sweetheart neckline allowed my bare collarbones and slender neck to be stars of the show.

"You look like a goddess," breathed Poppy, shyly reaching out to touch the fabric with her fingertips.

"It's perfect," gasped my mother. "Literally perfect. Carla, how did you do that?"

Carla chuckled. "I'm the fairy godmother of wedding dresses."

"You certainly are. You ticked every single box we mentioned!"

I remained still and silent as Carla approached with a gossamer veil. She fixed it into my hair, which I'd tied back in a loose bun before getting undressed, and fluffed out the pleats until the hem rested flawlessly around the platform. I looked like a doll inside a music box.

While my mother continued to gush, all I could do was stare.

I should have been happy. The dress was gorgeous. I could call it a day after trying on the first one with a single swipe of Mason's credit card. Then, I could rest easy knowing that I'd ticked off another item on the long list of things to do before the so-called big day.

Yet, instead of feeling joy, I felt pain.

I wished it was real.

I hated that such a thought crept through my careful boundaries, but it was impossible to deny. I wanted the wedding to be real. I wanted this moment, with my mother tearing up and my best friend grinning ear-to-ear, to be genuine. I wanted to know for certain that the man I was walking down the aisle to meet at the altar would see me as the absolute love of his life. I wanted to meet my soulmate.

My mother had said that Mason's soul was golden like mine. She saw him the way that I did. Rather than being distracted by his gruffness, she discovered what was beneath the surface of his moody persona. Did that mean she thought Mason was my soulmate? How crushed would she be if she knew such a thing could never be true?

Marrying Mason—or rather, staying married to him—wouldn't be so bad. In fact, I'd be bold enough to consider it a wonderful fate. Mason was hardworking, passionate, and moral. He cared about fairness and doing things the right way. He didn't treat people poorly just because he could, and he took care of the people who worked for him. Sure, he was a little rough around the edges, but I couldn't help thinking that he would be a really amazing father one day. Children would bring out the softness that Mason tried to hide from everyone around him.

I could picture it, and the image was torture.

He didn't want that. He didn't want smiling kids or a happily ever after. He made that clear.

Catching Poppy's eye in the mirror, I noticed her smile falter ever so slightly. Somehow, she knew exactly what I was thinking. I started tearing up, my heart breaking while I was still encased in swaths of pure white satin.

"Daisy, dear," Poppy murmured, taking my hand and squeezing it tightly.

"She's crying!" gasped my mother. "That must mean it's the one!"

Carla chuckled, similarly mistaking my tears for ones of happiness rather than despair. "That is often the case."

"How often does this happen? Surely not every bride finds the perfect dress the first time around?"

"It's more common than you think, actually."

While the older women chatted, Poppy helped me down from the platform. I sniffled, accepting a tissue from her as I subtly turned away from my mother.

"I'm fine," I whispered to Poppy.

"It's okay if you're not," she replied softly.

That only made me want to cry more. I wanted to be fine. I wanted to be more than fine. I wished more than anything in the world that I was the happiest woman in New York City.

Only, that wasn't the truth. None of this was the truth. When Mason and I said our vows, they wouldn't have any honesty behind them. At least, his wouldn't.

Was I about to ruin my life? I was falling harder for Mason every single day. Seeing the way my parents smiled at him only made things more difficult because it let me imagine for a moment that Mason might actually fall for me also.

But, he wouldn't. I was going to be walking down the aisle toward a man who didn't see the value in love. It was a waste of time, he claimed.

My mother wrapped me in a tight hug. "I'm so happy for you, Daisy. You're going to be such a beautiful bride. I love you so much."

"Thank you, Mom," I replied automatically. "I love you, too."

Numbly, I followed Carla back to the dressing room. As I changed into a simple slip so that the tailor could take my measurements, I tumbled deeply into my agonizing thought spiral.

I wondered, if Benjamin and Rose Reed were still alive, would Mason be as jaded about love? If he never lost his parents, would he still believe in the value of romance and promises and soulmates? Or, was this who Mason was deep down at the very core of his being?

Desperately, I hoped it was the former. The thought that Mason's refusal to fall in love came from a place of trauma was easier to swallow than the idea that it was ingrained in his genetic code. Then again, if his parents were still alive, we wouldn't be in this situation. Ruth Baldwin's estate would have likely been split between her two children, Daniel Baldwin and Rose Reed, with only smaller inheritances trickling their way down to Mason and his cousins. He wouldn't have to force his heart into an unwilling marriage. He wouldn't have to pretend to love me.

In that impossible scenario, I would be nothing more than his dutiful executive assistant. Things would be easier that way. Things *were* easier that way. It was mere weeks ago when, despite acknowledging how handsome my boss was, I never dared to imagine he would have passionate, urgent sex with me on top of his desk.

I should have wanted to go back to that. It was the logical desire. It was best for my career and my mental stability.

Except, I no longer wanted to be Mason's employee and nothing else. Now that I'd gotten a taste of what it was like to be *more* in his eyes, I was ravenous. It felt good to be adored by him, even if it was a lie.

I suppose it was true that love makes fools out of all of us.

Chapter Eighteen: *Reed*

"—but Mason is an impressive golfer. I have a feeling that he let me win!" chortled Mr. Campbell. He was recounting the events of our afternoon on the golf course where I usually took my clients over the dinner table to the girls.

"Not at all, sir," I countered good-naturedly. "You won fair and square."

"We'll have a rematch sometime soon just to be sure," Daisy's father replied with a friendly smile. "We have all the time in the world for it."

It took me a second to realize what he meant. Then I remember that he was under the impression that Daisy was truly going to become my wife and therefore be part of my life forever, which meant, in his eyes, we could schedule our golf rematch for next week, next year, or ten years from now.

"Absolutely, sir."

"I appreciate the politeness, Mason, but please call me Jim."

"No problem ... Jim."

Satisfied, Mr. Campbell took a sip of wine and grinned at his wife and daughter. "I trust you girls had a productive day as well?"

Mrs. Campbell's face lit up. "We did! It was so nice to see Poppy again. Plus, we found the perfect dress. I'm shocked at how quick the whole process was. It was almost too easy! I think the universe is on Daisy and Mason's side—"

While Mrs. Campbell continued chatting about their time at the wedding dress shop, I glanced at Daisy beside me. We were at The Smith, a stylish yet relaxed American-style restaurant in East Village. Reed Capital represented many of the establishment's investors, so I was always guaranteed the best table in the house whenever I called for a reservation.

Ever since Mr. Campbell and I reunited with the girls, I noticed that Daisy was more solemn and subdued than usual. To anyone who didn't know her well, she would appear perfectly normal, but I was familiar enough with her quirks to recognize that she wasn't smiling or laughing nearly as much as usual. Her parents didn't seem to pick up on it, but they were probably so overwhelmed with the hustle and bustle of New York City, not to mention the thrill of meeting someone they believed to be their future son-in-law, that they weren't paying as close attention to Daisy as they normally would.

I could only guess what was bothering Daisy, but I figured it was safe to assume that she was uncomfortable about having to lie to her parents. I felt bad for forcing her to do so, even if she insisted time and time again that I wasn't forcing her to do anything.

Meeting Daisy's parents was going surprisingly well so far. I thought I'd done a fairly good job of charming them, especially while being left to fend for myself with Daisy's father on the golf course. They were easy to get along with, not because they were fools, but because they were truly nice people.

I genuinely liked them. Mr. and Mrs. Campbell were funny and easygoing. Earlier that morning at brunch, they'd told me the story of how they were high school sweethearts and had been together ever since. They had an obvious bond, the kind of thing that couldn't be forced. In that respect, they reminded me a lot of my parents. I didn't want to think too much about that, though.

Once the food arrived, conversation died down as everyone dug into their meals. At least, mostly everyone. I noticed that Daisy was merely picking at her food. Usually, she wasn't a fussy eater. Nudging her knee with mine under the table, I offered her a subtle smile when she glanced my way. She mirrored the expression, but it didn't reach her eyes.

She took a sip of water, her ring catching the light as she lifted the glass to her lips.

"Mason!" gasped Mrs. Campbell. "Before I forget—since we've been traveling all over the place and haven't had the chance to meet you until now, I prepared ahead of time—"

"Prepared what?" I inquired.

Daisy's mother fumbled around in her purse, finally withdrawing her phone with a victorious grin. "I couldn't bring the family photo albums with me, so I took some snaps with my phone. Wait until you see how cute Daisy was as a baby!"

"Mom!" Daisy protested as Mrs. Campbell scooted her chair closer to mine. Her father chuckled, cutting into his steak as his wife began the traditional task of embarrassing their kid in front of their significant other.

I chuckled when Mrs. Campbell showed me the screen of her phone, revealing a picture of a little girl with curly blonde pigtails and a missing front tooth. Little Daisy was grinning brightly at the camera, dressed in a frilly pink tutu and posing like a tiny ballerina.

"This is Daisy when she was about three or four at her ballet recital," explained Mrs. Campbell, ignoring when Daisy groaned quietly and pinched the bridge of her nose. "Isn't she just adorable?"

Smirking, I felt like Daisy and I were sharing an inside joke at that moment, but I was enjoying it much more than she was. It wasn't often that a boss got to see his employees' baby pictures.

"She is very cute," I replied.

"This one is from Daisy's fifth birthday party," her mother continued, flipping to the next picture. "Funny enough, despite her sweet nature, Daisy isn't a big fan of cake or frosting. If you'd believe it, she requested nachos instead of a birthday cake that year."

It was impossible not to laugh. I had no idea Daisy didn't like sweets.

"What are you doing about that, by the way?" her father piped up. "Will you still have a cake at the reception?"

The question was directed at Daisy, but I was prepared to come up with a quick response if she wasn't in the mood to lie. Much to my surprise, she beat me to it.

"Of course we'll have cake," she told her father. "I think I can handle eating one bite of it for the sake of a picture. Then, everyone else can enjoy it without me."

"Good compromise," replied Mr. Campbell. "That's what marriage is all about."

"Mason, look at this picture," Mrs. Campbell continued, beckoning my attention back to her. "This is Daisy at one of her piano recitals. She must've been in eighth grade because that was the year she insisted on getting bangs."

"Oh, my God," grumbled Daisy, setting down her fork and pouting at her mother.

The photo was endearing. Preteen Daisy was scrawny and her hair was styled in a way that I remember being popular at the time but would raise eyebrows nowadays, but even at that age she was a beautiful girl.

"The two of you are going to make such adorable kids," sighed Mrs. Campbell, pausing the trip down memory lane in favor of continuing her meal. "They'll definitely have blue eyes, and no matter who they take after, they'll have fantastic bone structure!"

"Mom, seriously?" whined Daisy. "Kids? How do you even know we're planning on having kids?"

"Well, I hope you are! You can't deny me and your father the joy of being grandparents!"

"It's my womb. I'll be the one making the decisions," she snapped back a little too harshly.

Her mother frowned. "Honey, I thought you always wanted to be a mom—"

Daisy clenched her jaw and glared down at her plate. Knowing that I needed to come to the rescue to diffuse the tension, I placed my hand over Daisy's on top of the tablecloth and smiled at her parents as calmly as possible.

"We'd both like to be parents one day, but we're taking things one step at a time," I responded diplomatically.

"Of course," her mother replied.

I'd had a feeling that potential grandchildren would come up in the conversation at some point, but I hadn't expected it to be so awkward. Usually, Daisy was so good at laughing things off and pretending to be unbothered, her dark mood was turning her into a completely different person.

It was my fault. Here she was, a woman who—according to her mother—wanted to have a family of her own one day, having to act as if it might actually happen with the man beside her … who happened to be her employer, not her fiancé. It was uncomfortable on so many levels, and also somewhat sad. It didn't take a genius to see that Daisy would make an incredible mother one day. In truth, I felt sorry that I was wasting her time while she could be out there meeting a man who could give her the blue-eyed children she deserved.

After a couple more minutes of quiet eating, Mr. Campbell cleared his throat.

"Mason, I wasn't sure when the best time to say this was, but seeing as how Sharon and I won't be seeing you again until the wedding, I figured it was important to tell you sooner rather than later," he began. Daisy furrowed her brow at him in confusion, clearly having no idea what he was about to say.

"I'm all ears, sir—I mean, Jim."

He placed his cutlery down and folded his fingers together in his lap. The tone suddenly felt somber. Even Mrs. Campbell had dampened her own smile in preparation for whatever speech her husband was about to give.

"Daisy told us that your parents passed away when you were a boy," he murmured. "Sharon and I are deeply sorry for your loss. It is truly unfair that the people who brought you into this world don't have the privilege of witnessing the warm, intelligent, and successful man that you are today. I know it takes a lot of hard work to get a position at that company where you and Daisy work, so I am certain they would be incredibly proud of you."

I was stunned. I hadn't expected that at all. Suffice it to say, no one had ever said anything like that to me before in my life. Plenty of people had paid me compliments or admitted they were impressed by my accomplishments, but I couldn't name a single person who would assert that my parents would be proud of me if they were still alive.

"Thank you," I said. "That's very kind of you."

Apparently, he wasn't done.

"I know that in-laws can't replace what you have lost, but we hope, in time, as we get to know each other better, you can learn to depend on us as a mother and father. Although it's not been twenty-four hours since we first shook hands, I can confidently say that officially welcoming you into this family is something I truly look forward to."

Embarrassingly, my throat was too tight for me to speak. Mr. Campbell was speaking from his heart without an ounce of hesitation. From the expression on Mrs. Campbell's face, I could see that she was in full agreement with his words.

It was difficult for me to make sense of their sentiments. After my parents died, my paternal grandparents had adopted me and raised me as their son. I loved and respected them, but they weren't anything like Daisy's parents. The dissolution of their marriage and ensuing divorce took up quite a large portion of my teenage years. Just when I was getting past the worst of the grief from losing my parents, my new guardians rocked the boat all over again.

It was no wonder why Daisy was so bright and happy. The people who raised her radiated sunshine and stability. The foundation upon which she had grown up had never once been shaken. She was lucky. I didn't resent her for it, either. I wouldn't wish what I had been through on anyone.

Now, Mr. and Mrs. Campbell were offering that same support to me. They handed it to me so effortlessly and without question that I almost thought they might be lying. They barely knew me. How could they be sure that treating me like a son would be worth it to them in the end?

The answer was obvious. Daisy's parents didn't see the world through a transactional lens. Their acts of kindness didn't have to be mutually beneficial in order for them to be meaningful. They simply handed it out left and right to anyone in need because they had a bottomless supply of it. I'd never met anyone like them, so it shouldn't have caught me off guard that I wasn't sure how to respond.

However, staying silent wasn't an option. That kind of declaration deserved a heartfelt response.

"Thank you, Jim and Sharon," I said, squeezing Daisy's hand even though she continued to offer me limpness in return. "I wish I could more eloquently explain how much that means to me, but please know that I don't take your words lightly. It is my greatest happiness that you have accepted me so warmly into your lives."

"Well, if our Daisy loves you, then we know you're a good man," said Mrs. Campbell.

I tried not to flinch. Daisy definitely didn't love me, so the compliment fell short, but her mother didn't need to know that.

Daisy shifted in her chair and voluntarily spoke for the first time since arriving at the restaurant. "Mom, Dad, how about you tell us about your trip to Bali?"

The deflection was perfect. Instantly, the older couple launched into a detailed description of their recent vacation. I listened avidly not only to be polite, but also because they were entertaining. They were constantly finishing each other's sentences and slipping jokes into the narrative. Even the waiters appeared amused by their chatter.

Still, it was hard not to reply to Mr. Campbell's words over and over again in the back of my mind. They left me feeling shattered and vulnerable, but not because they were hurtful. It was the sheer generosity of the words that broke through my impenetrable barriers.

They were under the impression that their daughter wanted to spend the rest of her life with me. Because they loved her, they trusted her heart, and therefore trusted me. They barely knew me—they didn't even know I was the CEO of Reed Capital, not just an upper-level employee—but they'd laid out all their affection and support for me to help myself to. Given time, which was an assumed factor in a marriage, they wanted me to consider them as surrogate parents. In turn, they were eager and willing to treat me as their son.

I'd spent so many years ignoring the grief of losing my parents and the pain of my guardians' divorce that I'd forgotten what it was like to yearn for things I was convinced I would never have. It was Daisy who had brought me to this point. Simultaneously, I wanted to thank her, and run away from her.

Instead, I did my duty as her fiancé and stayed at the table. Each time Daisy let slip a bubble of laughter at her parents' antics, I felt a glimmer of hope that her stormy mood was a figment of my imagination.

When the meal was finished, I playfully argued with Mr. Campbell over who would pay for it before humbly admitting that the owner was a friend of mine and the bill was already taken care of. After that, I put Daisy in a cab with her parents back to their hotel, kissing her chastely on the cheek. I stayed on the curb until the taxi disappeared into the smog further up the avenue.

Rather than calling Maurice to pick me up, I walked home. It wasn't far and I needed to clear my head.

I felt sad. It was a foreign emotion to me, so unfamiliar that it took me several blocks' worth of thinking to recognize what it was. Even when Ruth died a few weeks ago, I wasn't sure I felt sad. My emotions regarding the death of my grandmother were closer to disappointment and melancholy acceptance.

There were a hundred things making me feel sad as I walked home. I was sad that Daisy's determination to help me earn my grandmother's inheritance resulted in her having to lie to almost every single person in her life. I was sad that Jim and Sharon Campbell weren't going to be my parents-in-law for longer than a month or so, and that they would shortly perceive me as their daughter's disgraced ex-husband. I wanted them to keep smiling at me. I was a grown man, but I craved their warmth like a baby.

On top of that, I was sad that I didn't have anyone special to introduce Daisy to. My grandparents were still St. Lucia with their respective partners, engaging in their weird new version of friendship. I hadn't told them about the wedding yet. The family members of mine that Daisy had met were either abundantly rude, shamefully nosy, or childishly spiteful. Nobody from my family tree was offering Daisy the kind of love that her parents doled out to me with ease.

She deserved better than me and what I could offer. Hopefully, one day, she would find that with someone. When this was all over, Daisy had a bright future ahead of her. She'd fall in love with a good man, get married after a traditional engagement, and have cute blonde children with him.

Maybe it was the wine I'd had with dinner, but there was a tiny voice in the back of my head that insisted I was also sad because I couldn't be that man for Daisy. My house wasn't the one she would come home to at the end of the day.

What did that mean? I didn't have feelings for Daisy. She was gorgeous and funny and smart—the ideal woman, actually—but those were facts, not softhearted admirations. Daisy possessed good qualities. She was a good person. We had physical and intellectual chemistry, and I enjoyed having sex with her. I liked her parents. I had fun looking at her baby pictures. I was looking forward to seeing which wedding dress she had picked out today.

But, that didn't mean I was falling for her. Just because I enjoyed her company in a variety of contexts didn't imply I thought of her as anything other than a friendly colleague.

Right?

"Pathetic loser," I muttered under my breath as I wrestled with my keys. It took me several tries to get the front door of my townhouse open. I wasn't drunk; just distracted.

I climbed the stairs and got ready for bed. Normally, I would check in and do a bit of work before crawling under the duvet, but my thoughts were too jumbled to do Reed Capital any favors that evening.

I wish she were here, I thought to myself when I laid my head down on the pillows. It was lame, but it was true. I wished Daisy was in my bed with me. Not to fuck, but just to be there.

As stupid and naive as it was, I simply wanted to be close to her.

Chapter Nineteen: *Campbell*

"I didn't know you wanted kids."

The words spilled out of me before I could stop them. It was something I hadn't stopped thinking about since the dinner with my parents at The Smith.

We'd both like to be parents one day, but we're taking things one step at a time ...

I should have anticipated that my mother would be bold enough to bring up the topic of grandchildren. My emotions were such a mess after visiting the dress shop that I wasn't able to fend off the attack without Mason's help. His answer had been vague, but I'd been fixating on it for days.

"Sorry?" Mason replied, raising an eyebrow at me.

I bit my lip. "Last weekend you mentioned that we'd *both* like to be parents one day."

"I see—"

"Unless that was just a fib to fend off my mother's prying."

Mason paused, staring down at the table between us. It was late on a Wednesday night and we were back at his townhouse, tucked away on the second floor in an informal sitting room with a load of wedding-related paraphernalia between us. The discreet wedding planner, who had dutifully signed a nondisclosure agreement, had sent us dozens of things to approve. She had instructions to make our fake wedding as classic and simple as possible, but we still had to offer our input on smaller details.

So far, we had agreed on accents of mauve and sage green for the reception decor, as well as dahlia and purple acacia as compliments to the floral arrangements. The cake would be vanilla with traditional buttercream frosting. The place settings would be clean and minimalistic.

It should have been easy to make decisions about a wedding that was all for show. It wasn't my real wedding, after all. However, as it had been with the dress, I found myself caring a little too much about how perfect I wanted it to be. I blamed it on the fact that I was a perfectionist, but I wasn't foolish enough to think that it wasn't also because I wanted the day to be special. If divorce was inevitable, the wedding might as well be as pleasant a memory as possible.

"It wasn't a fib."

Mason's voice startled me out of my reverie. I'd almost forgotten what I had asked him.

"It wasn't?"

He shook his head, tapping his fingers on a bundle of fabric swatches for the tablecloths. "The idea of being a father isn't totally abhorrent."

I snorted. "That's convincing."

"I mean it. I don't really have the time to become a parent at this point in my career, but if the timing was right further down the road, it sounds nice."

"I thought you said love was a waste of time," I remarked, once again blurting out my thoughts before I could stop myself.

Mason frowned. "When did I say that?"

"At the gala."

"Did I?"

"Yes."

"Well, I guess what I meant to say is that romance requires a lot of time and energy, neither of which I have much to spare. I have other priorities."

There was no use toeing the lines of professionalism at that point. I was barefoot in his house, steps away from the bedroom where I had spent the night before.

"Why don't you see love as a priority in your life?" I asked him.

Mason furrowed his brow at me. "Why would I?"

I stood my ground. "Why wouldn't you?"

"What has love brought me?" he countered. "I have a successful career because of hard work and perseverance, not love."

"But, your career isn't your entire life. Or rather, it shouldn't be."

"That's rich coming from you."

"I'm not talking about me."

"Fine. Outside of my personal experience, what has love brought the people around me?" Mason argued. "Loss. Frustration. Disappointment. Betrayal. The list goes on, Daisy."

"So you've never been in love?" I dared to ask.

"No."

"Then, how do you know you'll meet the same fate? Other people's bad experiences are universal, Mason."

"I suppose I don't have the time to take my chances."

"What if time was infinite?" I don't know why I was pressing the issue so hard. It felt as if I was digging for something that might not be there.

"Excuse me?"

"What if the days were twice as long and humans didn't have to sleep for eight hours of them? Would you still consider love a waste of time?"

Mason cocked his head to the side. "If the days were twice as long, I'd devote the extra time to the company."

"Of course you would," I sighed.

In a transparent attempt to change the topic, Mason held up two different name tags for the table settings. "Which font do you prefer?"

"I hate them both."

"Me, too."

Against my will, I smiled. Even when it came to the most inconsequential things, we were on the same wavelength.

Feeling antsy, I stood up from the table and wandered over to the window that overlooked Mason's compact backyard. Beyond the tall garden walls, Manhattan was pulsing with vibrancy. The city breathed deeply around us, holding us tight in its embrace. I always loved the way it felt to simply *be* in New York City. It was a place that could be mercilessly ugly, cold, and dark, but it was also unfailingly alive. Those who dared to call it home were rewarded with a spark of energy that couldn't be found anywhere else in the world.

I liked sharing the city with Mason. I liked being here with him. I liked that I could hear the gentle cadence of his breathing in harmony with the distant rush of traffic out on the hectic avenues. I liked that, when we were apart, the lights from the windows of his townhouse and my apartment belonged together in the mosaic of brilliance that created New York's iconic skyline.

More than any of that, I liked him.

Things were going extremely well. My parents approved of him and the people who mattered believed that our relationship was real. Mason was on track to securing the inheritance from his wicked cousins. He'd have the money to grow his firm far beyond what the current budget allowed, and then, he'd help me transition out of my current role into a flourishing career of my own. Soon, this would all be in the past.

Unfortunately, I wasn't sure I could walk away so easily.

When I'd tried to explain my feelings to Poppy during another margarita meetup the night before, she urged me once again to *go with the flow.*

"Do what feels right," she had said to me, eyes wide with earnestness.

What felt right in the present moment was telling Mason the truth. I was glad I had the guts to interrogate him about his previous statement regarding the wastefulness of pursuing love. He wasn't as fatigued by the thought of romance as I'd previously assumed. There was still hope for him. Mason just needed someone to prove to him that true love could be worth it. Love wasn't destined to end in disaster. My parents were living proof of that, but perhaps he needed more evidence.

My heart told me that the right thing to do was to tell Mason that I had feelings for him, that I could see myself inching closer to being in love with him every day. The optimist in me had faith that, if Mason knew I felt that way, he might start to see value in love and romance. He had inarguable proof that I was loyal to him. I was on his side. I had no intention of leaving him or betraying him.

He needed to know that.

Yet, I was frozen to the spot with my back to him. Several minutes of silence passed until Mason stood and made his way toward me with measured steps. If I wanted to, I could watch his approach through the reflection in the window before me, but I kept my eyes focused on the dark garden below.

Mason stopped just a few inches away to lean against the wall.

"Penny for your thoughts?" His tone was low and deep. I felt goosebumps rise on my arms at the sound of it.

"Are you sure you want to know?"

"I'm sure."

"I'm thinking about love."

He huffed. "You're stubborn."

"Not as stubborn as you."

With a smirk, Mason brushed a strand of my hair off my bare shoulder.

"You've been in love before." It wasn't a question. We both knew he was referring to my near-engagement to Aiden years ago. In most cases, you don't get engaged to someone unless you love them. *Most* cases.

"Yes, I have."

"And, it turned out to be a waste of time, didn't it?"

I pouted at him. "No, it didn't. I still have some great memories from that relationship that I cherish. Plus, with the way things happened, I was able to learn more about myself and what I wanted."

"So, you have no regrets?"

"Not really," I replied with a shrug. "The feelings I used to have for Aiden died out a long time ago, but that doesn't mean the period of time we spent in love wasn't worth it."

Mason pursed his lips and crossed his arms against his chest. I'd never felt more casual with him before. Our suit jackets were lying abandoned downstairs, our shoes were off, and our hair was equally messy from hours of running our fingers through it while dealing with the monotonous wedding responsibilities. He'd taken off his tie a while ago, leaving the top few buttons of his shirt undone, and rolled up his sleeves. Like a fool, I had a fleeting thought that this was the version of Mason I would see after a long day if I really did become his wife in the long-term. I'd get to see all the hidden sides of him.

"Were you on the debate team in high school?" he asked suddenly.

"Why do you ask?" I laughed.

"It seems like you have a lot of experience winning arguments."

"Have you considered that I'm simply always right?"

He offered me a crooked smile. "I have, actually. It seems like a reasonable conclusion."

Tell him, I commanded myself. *Tell him how you feel.*

"You know—" I trailed off. I wanted to kick myself. I rarely struggled to find the words to explain myself. Surviving through four years at an Ivy League university and gaining a position at an exclusive, competitive company required boldness. I was no stranger to speaking my mind.

"What is it?"

"You know, you're really not so bad to have as a fake fiancé."

What the hell? I internally cursed at myself. That was beyond lame. I'd been trying to find the words to tell him that I was falling for him, that marrying him felt like more than simply following through on a promise I'd made to my employer. Instead, I cracked a joke. What was wrong with me?

Mason looked amused. "You're not so bad yourself."

Staring into his eyes was making me feel lightheaded, so I looked down at my feet. "Thanks."

"No, seriously," he continued, tilting my face toward his. "I hope you know how lucky I consider myself that you've agreed to all of this insanity. If I was looking to get married for real, I'd feel fortunate if it was with a woman like you."

I didn't know what to make of that. It seemed as if even he wasn't fully aware of what he was implying. From the way it sounded, it was almost as if he was saying that I was his ideal woman. His dream girl. That, if he was the kind of person who saw value in romance, he would want to marry me for real.

I felt the same way about him. If I had to marry someone, I would be grateful that it was him.

Didn't that mean we were perfect for each other?

"A woman like me?" I asked him.

"Yes. A woman who is witty, but doesn't tell jokes at others' expense," he hummed, ducking his head to press a kiss to my jaw. "A woman who is beautiful and knows it, but doesn't boast about it."

I shivered as he turned his face and kissed the other side of my neck. "Go on."

"A woman who is loyal and supportive, but isn't afraid to speak her mind," he continued, trailing his lips up to my cheekbone. "A woman who—"

"Okay, okay," I giggled. "I get it. I'm perfect."

Mason chuckled. "And humble."

Before I could rebut, his lips were on mine. I had a feeling the evening would lead to this. The physical chemistry between us was heating up to higher temperatures every time we were alone together. I melted into his touch, forgetting the blooming city around us as the warmth of his lips and pressure of his tongue nudging against mine overwhelmed me.

There was no going back from something like this. Neither one of us had said it aloud, but he couldn't actually think that, once the inheritance was deposited into his account and we were safe to file for a discreet divorce, we would be able to go back to normal. Although it had been the norm for two years, I couldn't imagine returning to the role of Mr. Reed's executive assistant—plain and simple. How could I stand in his office and go over his schedule for the day knowing that we'd once had sex on multiple surfaces there? How could I sit in the back of his town car with him on the way to another meeting or event knowing that our first kiss had taken place there?

How could I ever forget the clean cotton scent of his bedsheets, the dimples at the base of his spine, or the particular way his wavy hair curled around my fingers when I gripped it in my hands? This wasn't the kind of magic that could disappear easily.

But now wasn't the best time for a panicked thought spiral, not while his hands were roaming down the curve of my waist to my hips and around to the rise of my butt through my dress.

"Bedroom," he muttered against my lips.

I moaned an affirmative, taking a step backward toward the arched doorway with my arms wrapped around his shoulders. Mason followed after me, firmly holding on to my waist. We almost made it out of the room, but I stumbled on the edge of the carpet. He caught me at the last minute, pressing me up against the doorframe gracefully.

Smiling into the kiss, I wriggled as he pulled up the hem of my dress, shimmying out of it as he yanked it over my head. He tossed it somewhere in the hallway, then flipped us around so that he was the one leading the way to his room. Using his shoulders to shove open his bedroom door, I left feverish kisses along his neck and made quick work of the buttons on his shirt.

By the time we collapsed in a tangled heap on the bed, he was shirtless and I was needier than ever. Mason moved fast, tossing me onto my back as if I were a doll and sliding off my panties in one quick motion. I wasn't wearing a bra that day, since the dress I was wearing provided enough support on its own.

"Why am I always the first one to be naked?" I pouted jokingly.

Mason smirked, whipping off his belt and standing up briefly to take off his trousers and underwear. He paused before getting back on the bed, holding up his hands in surrender while fully nude.

"Happy now?" he asked.

I giggled. "I'm sufficiently satisfied, yes."

He rolled his eyes and climbed onto the mattress. However, instead of getting on top of me as I expected, he lay down on his back beside me and reached greedily for my hips, tugging upward.

"Come on. All aboard," he murmured playfully.

"What are you doing?" I laughed, straddling his lap as he continued pulling my hips toward his chest insistently.

"Let me taste you," he whispered. "Come sit up here."

A pleasant chill ran through me when I realized what he wanted. Biting my lip to hide a nervous smile, I readjusted my body so that I was straddling his shoulders and his face was between my legs.

Without hesitation, he wrapped his arms around my thighs and pressed my center flush against his mouth. My muscles tensed as if electrified, but only because the sudden rush of pleasure was almost too much to bear. Tossing my head back, I held on to the headboard for support and tried not to scream as his tongue worked magic on my most sensitive spot.

My thighs were shaking and I worried that I was crushing him, but each time I tried to lessen my weight, Mason grunted and gripped me tighter. When I reached my climax, I had to clap my hand over my mouth to muffle the whimper of ecstasy that escaped against my will. It wasn't as if we were in danger of anyone overhearing us, but what I really wanted to do was shout out a string of expletives, and I wasn't sure if that would kill the mood or not.

When I recovered, I tried to wiggle off of him, but he laughed, his breath fanning out across my thighs, and pulled away just long enough to say one word.

"No."

"Mason, I just came. You made me—I—"

"Again."

"Wha—"

The rest of my protest was cut off as he lapped his tongue against me once more. I mewled at the overstimulation, shivering when he didn't stop. It felt too good, too deliciously overwhelming, to fight.

When I unraveled into my second orgasm barely a minute later, Mason grinned crookedly and set me free. I dropped onto the sheets beside him, trying to catch my breath.

"I like watching you squirm," he muttered in my ear.

His eyes were dark and hungry like a predator, twinkling with wicked mischief. My stomach flipped, my breath stuttering into a gasp on the next inhale. Not once in all our ill-advised trysts had I seen him like this. It was as if something new had awakened in him. Something that craved me in ways neither of us thought possible.

"You're unbelievably sexy," I breathed.

"You're one to talk. I could go down on you for hours just to listen to the sounds you make—"

"You're sadistic."

"Maybe so, but I think you like it."

"Maybe I do."

He laughed once more before taking hold of my waist and flipping me onto my stomach as if I was utterly weightless. Mason smiled so much these days that I barely recognized him, but I was grateful for whatever had triggered the change in him.

I let him be in control, mostly because I had a feeling there was no way to gain dominance over the situation when he was in his current state. I spread my knees apart and lifted my lower half off the mattress, arching my spine because I thought that was the position Mason wanted, but he pressed me down flat.

"Stay," he whispered.

I smiled, one side of my face pressed into a pillow. "Yes, sir."

He rested his weight on top of me, settling between my thighs and pressing into me with both of our bodies lying flat on the sheets. At first, the angle felt strange and surely had to be uncomfortable for him, but then he started thrusting and I immediately understood the appeal.

Shoving my entire face into the pillow to stifle a loud groan, I gripped the sheets in both of my fists as Mason's hands locked over mine and he increased the pace. There was so much beautiful friction everywhere—him inside me, on top of me, and all around me. Not to mention the way my center rubbed against the fabric beneath my hips. I felt trapped in the most exquisite way, so overwhelmed with rapture coming from every direction that I thought I might cry.

Mason was fierce, but not rough. Firm, but not forceful. His quiet groans echoed in my ear, coupled with kisses to my neck, my shoulders, and my spine.

Eventually, he turned us over so that we were face-to-face again, but I had no idea how much time had passed until that moment. I was too enraptured in the moment, too lost in him.

It felt different this time, the way he touched me. Before, each time we allowed ourselves to indulge in one another, it was chaotic and desperate and needy. We were giving in to the undeniable physical chemistry between us, falling victim to the forces of nature that refused to keep us apart. This time, however, it was more like we were in control of the magnetism.

Perhaps I was a fool for thinking it, but it was more like we were making love.

Chapter Twenty: *Reed*

I was in a good mood.

It wasn't that feeling good was a rare occurrence for me. Most days, I was decently content when I wasn't busy being frustrated by somebody else's incompetence. Usually, it was more like I didn't waste my time looking too deeply into my own psyche to determine which emotions were swimming closest to the surface.

Lately, however, despite the stress of the lies I was balancing left and right, it was impossible to ignore how good I felt. I chalked it up to two things: my inheritance was definitely within my reach, and I was regularly having sex with the hottest woman in New York City. Before I stumbled into the affair with Daisy, I didn't place much importance on sex. It was nice every once in a while, but I had more crucial things to focus on. If I gave in to my physical desires as often as most men did, I'd never be able to nurture Reed Capital into the company it was born to become.

Thus, it was a blessing that the person I was being intimate with was my assistant. It was an incredibly convenient arrangement, one I wasn't sure I was willing to let go of. Daisy was the total package in a variety of ways. Once this was all over and she went back to being nothing more than my employee, I'd be disappointed … to say the least.

Until then, I preferred to enjoy the perks of this convoluted situation while I still could.

While my chauffeur maneuvered the car through the congested streets of lower Manhattan, I opened an email from the wedding planner I'd booked for the big day. She confirmed that she had received Daisy's and my input the other night and thanked us for guiding her in the right direction.

The wedding was in one month. Thirty days. A little over four weeks. The guest list was extremely short, but thanks to my status, we were able to easily pass it off as my wanting to keep a low profile in the press. Hopefully, the divorce could be kept just as secret. If everything went smoothly, the media wouldn't even catch wind of it. I'd been worrying so much about Daisy's and my reputations being tarnished, but there was no reason to think anyone would give a damn, let alone find out in the first place. The Baldwin family in general preferred to stay off the front page, especially after the plane crash, and it wasn't as if Daisy's loved ones were going to make a call to the tabloids once they found out our marriage fell apart. All signs pointed to the entire thing being over in the blink of an eye.

The best part was that Mr. Henderson had already confirmed his attendance at the wedding, though he regretfully informed us he wouldn't be able to stay for the reception. It was ideal. Daisy and I would put on a show for him at the altar, sign our names at the bottom of a contract, and Mr. Henderson would run off to signal the green light on the transfer of Ruth Baldwin's estate.

Of course I was in a good mood. How could I not be optimistic when my partner in crime was as magnificent, efficient, and dependable as Daisy Campbell?

Maurice parked outside my townhouse.

"One minute," I said to him, my attention still focused on my email inbox.

"No problem, sir."

It was a shame that Daisy wasn't able to come over to my place that night, but she did have an entire separate life to attend to that had nothing to do with me. It wasn't as if she were actually my significant other. When there were no work or wedding obligations, she had no reason to be in my company. Yet, it was strange how empty my home felt when she wasn't in it.

I was sure I'd learn to get used to it again, though.

"Sir—" Maurice piped up again.

"Hmm?"

"There's someone waiting for you on your front stoop."

It was hard to resist the instant hope that sprang to life within me that it was Daisy, perhaps surprising me with an unannounced visit even though she had literally no reason to.

Unfortunately, when I finally looked out the window, the woman waiting for me was not a welcome revelation.

I sighed. "Thank you, Maurice. That'll be all. See you in the morning."

I climbed out of the car, briefcase in hand, and glared at my guest from the sidewalk.

Marina Baldwin was sitting on the top step of the stoop, her ankles crossed neatly and her elbows resting on her knees. She was dressed entirely in black, clearly trying to appear more chic than funereal and only somewhat succeeding at it.

"What do you want?" I asked her.

She pursed her lips and unfolded her long limbs slowly to stand in front of the entrance to my house. She'd never been here before, but I wasn't entirely concerned about how she managed to get my address. Even for someone less nosy and conniving than her, it wouldn't be that difficult to figure out where one of the youngest billionaires in the city owned property.

"Seriously? I don't even get a 'hello'?" she snapped, placing her hands on her hips.

My good mood dissipated. "Why would you? I didn't invite you here."

Marina flung her dark hair over her shoulder. "Why do you hate me so much?"

Still standing on the pavement, I rolled my eyes and exhaled quietly. I did not have the patience to deal with whatever insecurity-based temper tantrum Marina was on the verge of. It was exactly why I preferred to avoid both of my cousins at all costs. They caused more frustration and annoyance than what the so-called bonds of family were worth.

"I don't hate you," I told her truthfully. "Hate is not an emotion I would expend my energy on in your regard."

She narrowed her eyes. "You're heartless. Can't a relative simply drop by when they're in the neighborhood?"

"Not in this day and age, and not when we've quite literally never been the type of relatives to spend time together unless we can help it."

I climbed the steps, pulling the electric key fob out of my pocket that opened the highly secure door.

"So, you're really not going to invite me inside?" she scoffed.

"You're incredibly entitled if you believe that waiting for me at my front door after I've had a very long and tiring day at work will instantly earn you a warm embrace and a cup of tea."

Marina fell quiet for a minute, but I knew it wasn't because she was acknowledging the truth in my statement. I angled my body to block her line of sight as I typed in the code to unlock the deadbolt. With a dull *clunk*, the knob gave way under my hand and the door swung open.

In spite of my irritation, I'd never been the type of man who could slam the door in someone's face. Thus, I simply let the door hang open on its hinges as I stepped into the foyer and kicked off my shoes. Just as I suspected, Marina let herself in. She kept her stiletto heels on, stomping after me as I wandered into the kitchen.

"Where's Daisy?" she asked, her tone dripping with sarcastic spite.

"At her apartment."

"You two don't live together yet?"

"We value tradition, and I wish you valued minding your business."

Reaching into the fridge, I grabbed one of the pre-bottled green juices my chef prepared for me on a weekly basis. Out of the corner of my eye, I watched Marina help herself to a stool at the granite island in the center of the room.

"You're not going to offer me a drink?" she inquired, ignoring my dig. "You're not a very good host."

"You're not a very polite guest," I quipped, setting the juice on the counter across from her a little too harshly. "Seriously, Marina, what the hell do you want?"

She furrowed her brow and glanced away. For a second, I thought she was about to cry, but then, she took a deep breath and crossed her arms against her chest.

"Aiden broke up with me," she announced.

I quirked an eyebrow at her. "Okay? Why would I care?"

"You're such an asshole."

"You go through boyfriends faster than anyone can keep track. Furthermore, when have I ever been considered a shoulder for you to cry on? Frankly, Marina, I don't care. That man is garbage anyway."

"How would *you* know? Just because he's your fiancée's ex-boyfriend doesn't mean you're an expert on him. I really thought this relationship would last."

To her credit, it was clear that she was telling the truth. That was the problem. Marina always believed her temporary flings were the foundation for a genuine, mature relationship. She didn't understand that coupling up with foreign millionaires in exclusive clubs and on party yachts wasn't the right way to go about finding a dependable partner. Somehow, she also didn't realize that most of the men who dated her read her last name and saw her as nothing but a walking dollar sign. From what Daisy had told me about Aiden, I figured that was how he ended up with my cousin in the first place.

"I don't know what you expect me to say," I sighed. "You're twenty-seven years old. Maybe it's time you spent your days doing something useful instead of crying over boys who never wanted you in the first place."

Marina slapped her hands on the granite countertop and narrowed her eyes at me.

"Do you want to know why he broke up with me?" she hissed.

"Not particularly," I muttered.

She ignored the comment, as I figured she would. "He gave me a bullshit speech about how he doesn't think it's fair to me to stay in a relationship while he's still hung up on somebody else."

I was bored and I wanted her to leave. There was no part of me that was interested in stupid, girlish woes. However, I also knew that, unless I literally dragged her out by her hair, Marina wasn't leaving until she'd gotten what she came for. I had no idea what that was, but the sooner she finished her whining, the sooner she'd tire herself out and leave on her own accord.

"So, you'd rather your boyfriend stay with you even though he's in love with someone else?" I replied. Obviously, the vague reference being made here was to Daisy, but I wasn't bothered or threatened in the slightest by him. The way she'd moaned my name last night told me everything I needed to know about her feelings on the topic.

"No! It's just that he apparently didn't realize he was still obsessed with that bitch until she waltzed back into his life out of the blue!"

"Do not talk about Daisy like that," I growled.

Marina sneered at me. "Have I touched a nerve?"

"You're a jealous child. Grow up, Marina."

"Why is everyone so obsessed with her?" she shouted, throwing her hands up. She stood abruptly and whirled away, angrily pacing across the tile floor. "Daisy, Daisy, Daisy! That's all anybody ever seems to want to talk about! If it's not Aiden, it's Auntie Kat or someone else! Even Bradley barely shuts up about her allegedly *killer body*. Like, oh, please. She's an eight out of ten, at best."

It didn't surprise me that Bradley made disgusting comments about how hot Daisy was, but that did nothing to quell my fury.

"Well, I'm marrying her, so if you're expecting me to react any other way right now, you're more delusional than I thought," I told her.

I was doing my best to keep my tone measured and patient. Marina was a year younger than Daisy, an entire seven years younger than me, and her personality made her come across as a child more often than not. I couldn't lose my temper at a petulant kid. I was better than that.

"That's what doesn't make sense!" Marina continued ranting, jabbing her index finger in my direction. "I've seen you turn down models and heiresses and literal royalty! Why her? Am I really supposed to believe that you've suddenly changed your ways because you love *that woman* so much? When there's forty-two million dollars at stake? Yeah, right!"

"Marina, you need to go," I responded. "You're not welcome in my home. I won't tolerate you storming in here and insulting my fiancée like this."

I moved toward her in an attempt to usher her to the door, but she shoved me away. Her sharp nails scratched at my arms as she stomped out of my reach into the front parlor. She glared at her surroundings as if trying to decide what she wanted to destroy first. I really didn't want to call the police on my hysterical cousin, but I wasn't about to let her rip apart my house for no reason except that she was heartbroken by a man whom she never should have been stupid enough to give her heart to in the first place.

"I mean, what's so special about her?" Marina exclaimed shrilly. "Pretty girls with Ivy League educations are a dime a dozen in New York! It's not like she has any real value. She has no pedigree. She's just an ordinary, middle-class social climber!"

"Shut your mouth, Marina. Or else."

Suddenly, she burst into tears. The sharp, angry sobs and redness in her cheeks told me they were born from fury rather than sadness. She was crying because she was frustrated, because she couldn't handle her own emotions. It was pathetic to witness and I desperately wanted it to end.

Marina stalked toward me menacingly, tears streaming down her face with reckless abandon. "You know, my parents died in that plane crash, too!"

"What are you talking about?" I scoffed. I softly pushed her away, but she pushed me back twice as hard.

"You always acted like you were the only one who lost something that day," she cried. "I may have been young, but I remember the way you basically cut Bradley and me off. *You* were the eldest. You should've been there for us."

"I was twelve!" I replied with an incredulous laugh. "I wasn't equipped to support the emotions of two orphans! Just because your new guardians were less attentive than mine, doesn't mean it was my fault you—"

"Screw you!" she shrieked. "Screw you, Mason! You got the best of everything! The best adoptive parents, the best schooling, the best opportunities. You were clearly our grandmother's favorite—you're *everyone's* favorite. Everyone always treated you like you were special because your parents died and meanwhile me and my brother were handed the leftover scraps! It's like people don't even remember our mom and dad died, too."

There was a tiny pang in my chest at what Marina was saying. In truth, it was all valid. I really did get lucky in the aftermath of the tragedy, but my life wasn't perfect. It wasn't my fault that I was easier to like than Marina and Bradley, while it was definitely their fault that they were insufferable brats.

Marina looked like a madwoman. Her hair was tangled from the way she gripped it in frustration. Her eyes were wild and unable to focus on anything for longer than a few seconds. I had half a mind to assume she'd taken some kind of drug, but I also knew Marina was always on the verge of becoming completely unhinged. The thing was, she'd simply become very good at hiding it from everyone else. Those of us who had grown up with Marina knew that she was emotionally volatile on a good day, but she was absolutely batshit this evening.

"Your dad was driving the plane," I reminded her cruelly. "It was his fault."

Her eyes flashed with rage. She balled her hands into fists as if she planned to hit me, but I could also tell from the subtle deflation in her shoulders that she knew I was right. The reason that the Baldwin family didn't mourn her parents as deeply as they mourned mine was because, at the end of the day, Uncle Daniel was the reason they were all dead. The plane didn't experience a random engine failure or machine malfunction. The weather wasn't blustery or stormy. There was nothing else in the sky that might have caused the pilot to lose control. The fact of the matter was that Daniel Baldwin had pretended to be in a state of sobriety, settled into the pilot's seat of a tiny aircraft, and paid out the consequences with his life and that of three others.

Sure, it wasn't fair that Marina and Bradley might have been treated with less tenderness in the beginning because they were Daniel's children, but that wasn't the reason why Marina was miserable in her current situation.

Instead of going completely postal, Marina became eerily calm.

"You'll pay for that comment," she whispered.

Without another word, she spun on her heel and marched toward the exit.

"What the hell is that supposed to mean?" I called after her retreating form.

Marina was an idiot child, but she always made good on her threats. I didn't like the sound of the one she just delivered. There was too much at stake.

She didn't answer. In fact, she didn't even offer a backward glance as she threw open the door and walked out into the humid August evening. It slammed shut loudly behind her.

In the utter silence that followed, a flare of frustration struck me with such force, it was all I could do not to punch my fist through the plaster wall or chuck the nearest table lamp across the room.

Be a man, I thought to myself, pressing my fingertips to my temples. *Men don't throw temper tantrums.*

I took a deep breath and lowered onto the sofa. I should have held my tongue. Marina knew it was her father's fault that both our parents were dead. She'd known that for the past twenty-two years of her life. I didn't need to point it out, but I knew doing so would push her to her breaking point. That's what I wanted. I wanted her visit to be over.

Now that it was, I was riddled with regret. I couldn't stand my cousin, but maybe I should have been more patient with her. Maybe I should have swallowed my pride, offered her some hollow yet comforting words about Aiden, and sent her on her way in a taxi on my dime.

But then, I remembered the way Marina had gotten in Daisy's face at the gala just because a nobody like Aiden Plourde preferred Daisy over her. Marina's insecurity was what marred her natural beauty. She saw everyone around her as competition because she never received enough attention as a child. Therefore, as a mature adult, she was still spitting out insults at people who didn't deserve them. Daisy wasn't a bitch, nor was she ordinary, nor a social climber. Marina didn't know her at all, but she had drawn these conclusions because it was easier than accepting the truth that Daisy was extraordinarily kind, humble, and patient.

I only hoped that whatever Marina meant by making me pay for my harsh reminder didn't involve using Daisy as a target. Not only for Daisy's sake, but for Marina's, too.

Because, if anyone hurt Daisy, I would personally and single-handedly ruin them.

Chapter Twenty-One: *Campbell*

"That's seriously the sexiest thing I've ever heard. Like, he lay right on top of you? It didn't hurt?"

"No, not the way he did it."

"That's basically bondage. He was holding you down, forcing you to handle the overwhelming pleasure of his—"

"Jesus, Poppy," I snorted, covering my face with my hands. "Don't make me regret telling you about it."

Poppy giggled and playfully pinched my arm. We were curled up on my tiny sofa, a bottle of wine sitting mostly untouched on the coffee table as I recounted everything that had happened with Mason since that emotional afternoon in the wedding dress shop.

"I really think you need to tell him how you feel," Poppy said earnestly. "Just hearing you talk about it, I can tell that you're head over heels. Even if he doesn't feel the same way—which I highly doubt, for the record—you'll feel better knowing that you actually said something."

I flinched. "I think it'll freak him out. Mason really isn't the romance kind of guy. I've told you before."

"People can change, Daisy. Maybe he's in the process of seeing the light. Even Belle wore the beast down over time."

"What?"

"*Beauty and the Beast.* Duh."

"Right."

"It's not like he's going to be disgusted by the thought of a young, gorgeous woman with a big, sexy brain telling him that she's into him," she continued. "I mean, is it really a bad thing that you're falling for him when you're about to get married anyway? Who knows? Maybe this is fate."

"You're out of your mind."

"Just tell him. What's the worst that can happen?"

I chewed on the inside of my lip. "He fires me?"

"He's not going to fire you because you admitted to falling for him. You're the best executive assistant in Manhattan."

"I guess so."

"And, he wouldn't call off the wedding, either," she argued. "It's gone too far at this point and it needs to happen in order for him to get that money. He doesn't strike me as the kind of guy who gives up just because he feels a tiny bit emotionally uncomfortable."

"True—"

"So, tell me, Daisy—realistically speaking, what is the worst thing that could happen if you tell Mason how you feel about him?"

I shrugged. The planet wouldn't implode. The building wouldn't collapse. I wouldn't spontaneously combust. I'd still have my job and still be able to follow through on my promise to be his fake fiancée.

"I guess the worst that could happen is that he doesn't feel the same way," I admitted.

"Exactly! And, if he's not totally crazy about you, then he's utterly demented and should probably be institutionalized."

"Is that your professional opinion? Your official legal advice?"

"It sure is."

Poppy was grinning. She'd made a great point, just as she always did, and she knew it.

"Fine," I told her. "You win. Case closed. I'll tell Mason that I have feelings for him."

"Thank God. You know, I think I might have a future as a marriage counselor."

"Or, a divorce attorney."

"Hey!"

***

The next morning, fueled by Poppy's pep talk, I tapped my foot impatiently in the elevator on my way to the top floor of Reed Capital. It was a quarter to eight in the morning. I was early compared to the rest of the staff, but late according to my usual seven-thirty arrival time. Not because the subway system failed me again, but because I'd spent too long nervously pacing back and forth in my apartment before finally forcing myself to leave.

But, I couldn't back down. I had to tell Mason the truth. Even if he didn't feel as strongly as I did, he had to feel *something,* right? You didn't sleep with someone as much as he had with me and not develop a single ounce of fondness as a result. His cold, allegedly anti-romance heart couldn't resist the most basic human instincts, could it?

I suppose I was about to find out.

The elevator doors slid open. I straightened my spine and marched out.

"Morning, Daisy!" sang Jennie, who looked as if she'd only just gotten to her desk minutes prior.

"Morning, Jennie!"

"You look absolutely radiant today!"

"So do you—oh! Hi, Mr. Holt. How are you today?"

I stopped short, hesitating by the front desk where Jennie was shuffling around various stacks of files. Although his office was also on the top floor, I rarely saw Mr. Holt. He was the CHO, head of Human Resources, and his own executive assistant Michael never had any reason to cross paths with me. We ran in different circles in the C-suite, which I was grateful for because Mr. Holt was downright rude and Michael was an insufferable snob.

As far as I knew, Mr. Holt was rarely in the office before nine. That was practically noon by my standards, but I suppose he got away with a lot because he'd been in the role when the company was still operated by Abe Reed, Mason's grandfather.

"Miss Campbell," he grumbled sternly in greeting before turning to Jennie, who was doing her best not to flinch under the weight of his imposing gaze. "Miss James, have you had the chance to check your email yet this morning?"

"No, sir," she replied immediately. "I've just booted my computer up, but I can check on my phone. Is there something you'd like me to do for y—"

"No. Please do not open your email until eight o'clock. This is a serious matter."

"Yes, sir."

This was why I didn't understand why people found Mason so grouchy and intimidating. His personality was rainbows and sunshine compared to Mr. Holt. It was an odd request that Jennie not check her email for the next fifteen minutes, but she was right not to question it. Hopefully, Mason would make good on his promise to give Jennie a promotion soon and she would be able to stay far away from the CHO and his cryptic demands.

"Miss Campbell, please come with me."

"Sir, I should go let Mr. Reed know that I—"

"It was not a request, Miss Campbell. Come with me."

The air was thick with tension. Without another word, Mr. Holt turned and strode away. I glanced at Jennie, who offered me a wide-eyed shrug. It made no sense for Mr. Holt to be giving me commands, let alone speaking to me at all. If he was upset about something, it certainly wasn't my fault. Perhaps he was trying to poach me from Mason, fed up with the string of inadequate assistants he hired and fired like clockwork.

I knew better than to disobey, but I was also curious, so I set a quick pace and hurried after Mr. Holt. It had certainly thrown a wrench in my plans for the morning, but I could always talk to Mason later.

Except, when I stepped through the door of Mr. Holt's cluttered office, I saw that Mason was already there. He was sitting in a chair across from Mr. Holt's desk, leaning over with his hands on his knees. Beside him sat Mrs. Porter, a Human Resources representative from one of the lower floors. She was normally friendly and warm, but today she had a pinched expression on her face.

Mason glanced up only once Mr. Holt had sat down at his desk and pointed to the third available chair.

"Take a seat, Miss Campbell, and please close the door behind you."

My stomach dropped. Something was wrong. I'd never gotten in trouble in my life, but I knew the signs. I was outnumbered by executives, everyone was frowning, and I'd just been asked to make the meeting a private one.

I sat down, holding Mason's gaze. He looked angry, embarrassed, and horrified all at once. Also, the seats had been arranged to place Mrs. Porter between the two of us, which had to be intentional because my position was always supposed to be right at Mason's side.

When I was settled, I expected Mason to say something, but it was Mr. Holt who spoke.

"Miss Campbell, I'm going to ask you the same question I asked Miss James a moment ago. Have you checked your email yet this morning?"

"No, sir," I replied. It wasn't normal behavior for me. Usually, I checked my inbox before I even left my apartment for work, but I'd been so preoccupied by thoughts of what I was going to say to Mason that I didn't get a chance.

"I assumed as much. Mrs. Porter, would you like to summarize the situation for Miss Campbell?"

Mrs. Porter frowned at me. She seemed conflicted, like a mother who had no choice but to chastise her child for something that wasn't their fault.

"Miss Campbell, I'm afraid there's been a rather serious breach of HR protocol," she began. Her tone was gentler than Mr. Holt's, but I still got the sense that she was disappointed in me.

"I see," I replied.

"At approximately seven-fifteen this morning, a mass email was circulated to every single Reed Capital employee's account. This email contained a series of photographs of you and Mr. Reed at a formal event engaging in … an intimate embrace."

My blood ran cold. When I looked at Mason, I realized his gaze had returned to the floor. He couldn't even look me in the eye.

"What you do in your private life is none of our business, of course, but given the nature of your position in this company, such a relationship brings up an issue with our official code of conduct," Mr. Holt added. "We have been unable to confirm who initiated the mass email, as the address seems to have been deactivated within minutes after the person hit send."

Mrs. Porter nodded. "As far as we know, it was Mr. Hamwell—Mr. Holt's assistant—who first noticed the unexpected content in his inbox. Luckily, he called the head of the IT department immediately, then contacted Mr. Holt. Right now, IT is in the process of deleting the emails from the employee database, which should be completed by the time business hours officially start at eight. All personnel involved with the cleanup have already agreed to sign nondisclosure agreements. However, we obviously cannot make any guarantees that no other employee at Reed Capital might notice the email before its deletion."

I didn't know what to say. This was a nightmare. It was my worst fears come to life. I felt as if the floor beneath me was caving in, dragging me down into the boiling center of the earth. My heart hammered in my chest so loudly that I had to strain to hear what Mr. Holt and Mrs. Porter were saying.

"The Reed Capital code of conduct clearly states that all personal relationships between employees of differing status must be registered with Human Resources in order to ensure the safety and wellbeing of all individuals involved," Mr. Holt recited. "Despite the uniqueness of the situation, a violation has been made. The main issue, however, is the semi-public dissemination of the photographs. It is apparent that they were taken without your consent, but the damage is undeniable. Reed Capital has always prided itself on being a moral, clean-cut company. It is unfortunate that its reputation is under threat of being tarnished."

Violation. Damage. Tarnished. I'd never been associated with words like that before. It made me feel dirty and out of control.

This isn't me, I wanted to scream. *Daisy Campbell doesn't cause trouble. You know that. Everyone knows that!*

But I couldn't even open my mouth. I was still as stone.

Finally, Mason spoke.

"I take full responsibility for everything," he said, his voice low and measured. "I am Miss Campbell's superior, and therefore I should be the sole recipient of whatever negative consequences arise from this."

He was looking directly at Mr. Holt when he spoke, ignoring me entirely. Maybe he was doing it for my own good, knowing that showing me anything close to affection in this context would only make things worse, but it definitely didn't help me to feel any better about myself.

"That's very noble of you, Mr. Reed, but the fact of the matter is that the photographs unquestionably reveal Daisy's identity," replied Mr. Holt. He might not have been CEO, but he was two decades older than Mason and held a chief position in the company, so they were as close to equals as anyone could get. "Of course, we cannot tell the Chief Executive Officer what to do nor can I reasonably question your choice of partner."

Mrs. Porter cleared her throat. "That being said, we have some recommendations on how to handle the situation. Firstly, we believe that terminating Miss Campbell's employment will benefit everyone involved. I also recommend that we hire a public relations consultant just in case this scandal hits the public."

Scandal. That's what this was. I'd done something scandalous. I'd caused a disgraceful outcome.

I didn't dare ask to see the pictures that had been released to the entire company. I could already guess that they were from the memorial gala for Ruth Baldwin. From the way Mrs. Porter described them, they must have been taken when Mason and I were making out in the private lounge before returning to the party.

There was only one person who would do something like that. Well, two people, technically, but only one of them knew that Mason and I would have been in that back hallway. It was Marina. She must have looped back around after she ran away crying. Snapping photos of a couple having a private intimate moment was grimy behavior, but I assumed Marina thought that it might be useful to her plight even if it was proof that Mason and I were attracted to each other. Her evil nature wouldn't allow her to mind her own business.

I hated that her creepy spying had paid off for her in the end.

How had she found out what my real job was? As soon as Mason and I made the arrangement official, I made my LinkedIn profile, which named me as his executive assistant, private. It wasn't as if it were listed on the company website, either. The only thing I could think of was that Bradley mentioned how awkward it was the day he delivered the gala invitation. Maybe he walked past my office, which had my name written on a plague next to the door.

Or, perhaps Marina was just very good at digging up dirt on people. It didn't really matter how she knew. There was no going back now. Time machines had yet to be invented. What was done had been done.

"You can't be serious," Mason replied to Mrs. Porter. "Firing Daisy would only make things worse."

My head spun. This couldn't be happening. They wanted to fire me. Gravity was pressing in harder, crushing me alive. My life was ruined. I'd never recover from this. If I had an involuntary termination on my employment record, I would never be able to make a name for myself in another reputable company. I'd be a disgrace, the slutty assistant who couldn't keep her hands off her boss. It didn't matter that the relationship we were hiding was fake. Even if Michael had the good sense to keep his mouth shut, Reed Capital had hundreds of employees. Someone else was bound to have seen the pictures, too, but they weren't bold enough to admit it.

Once the news broke about me being fired, I would be implicated as an immoral, sleazy woman. It was inevitable. I didn't have the money or influence to fight off wrongful rumors like Mason did. The man always fared better in situations like this. No matter what, from now on, everyone would always gossip about how I was the girl who seduced her way into Mr. Reed's favor.

I never should have taken the risk.

Nausea struck me. Gripping the arms of the chair, I tried to slow my rapid heartbeat to no avail. Three pairs of eyes turned on me, adding to the weight of the world that was breaking me down into dust before them.

I couldn't take it anymore. I had to get out of there. Standing so abruptly that I nearly knocked the chair over backward, I whirled toward the door. I ignored the chorus of protests as I flung myself out into the hallway.

And then, I ran.

Chapter Twenty-Two: *Reed*

"No!" I barked when Mr. Holt stood up to follow after Daisy. My tone was louder and more menacing than I intended, but it suited the situation. The CHO halted immediately, raising his eyebrows at me.

"Mr. Reed—"

"No," I repeated. "I'll go find her."

"Someone should speak to her—" Mrs. Porter began.

"As her direct supervisor, that should be me," I interrupted.

"As her romantic partner, you might not be the best—"

"Enough," I growled, glaring at both of them. "Neither one of you has the right to speak to me like I am a child. Now, it is seven-fifty-eight. Make yourselves useful and confirm what progress IT has been able to make."

I left them like that, gaping at each other like idiots, and went after Daisy.

I never pegged Daisy as the type of person who ran from things. She functioned extremely well under pressure in the workplace. I figured her silence had more to do with the fact that she was trying to formulate a logical solution to the problems being presented to her. Daisy was unfailingly quick-witted, after all.

Apparently, people were full of surprises.

Jogging past Daisy's office, I checked that it was empty and kept going. It was safe to assume that, if she was choosing flight over fight, she would want to get out of the C-suite altogether.

"Did she leave?" I demanded of the front desk secretary.

"Yes, sir," replied the young brunette woman. "Is everything all right?"

I ignored her questions, running to the elevator bank and impatiently punching the down button. Unfortunately, this was the time of morning when everyone was arriving for the day, so all of the elevators were busy traveling upward. I tapped my foot impatiently, briefly considering taking the stairs down several dozen floors, until one of the elevators finally burst open for me.

A small crowd of non-executive staff who nonetheless worked on the executive floor piled out, stumbling with surprise when I pushed past them roughly and slammed my fist into the button for the first floor.

Tapping my foot impatiently, I hoped Daisy's descent was just as painstakingly slow as mine and that I actually might be able to catch up with her. While I waited, I took out my phone and confirmed that the IT department had been successful in wiping the damning email from my inbox. Yet, just as Mrs. Porter said, there was no way of knowing if someone other than Mr. Holt's assistant had seen the photos and was already spreading them across the lower levels of the company.

I should have known better than to push Marina to her breaking point. She had a quick temper and no morals. Plus, socializing and gossiping were her favorite pastimes. How could I forget to ensure Marina wouldn't befriend the right person and find out that Daisy's and my relationship was professional rather than romantic?

At last, the elevator arrived on the ground floor. I lunged out into the lobby, startling several staff members and security personnel, but I paid them no mind. Whipping my head around wildly, I caught the shimmer of long, golden hair twirling around one of the revolving doors.

"Daisy!" I called out, breaking into a run. The crowd parted for me. They recognized their CEO even though they'd never seen me act like this, and they knew better than to get in my way.

She didn't stop, but I had longer legs than her. Once I made it to the street, I caught up to her on the busy sidewalk and reached out to grab her wrist.

"Daisy, stop!" I exclaimed. "Where are you going?"

"Why do you care?" she snapped. She spun around and harshly yanked her arm out of my grasp. "You're the reason I just got fired, and yet all you did was sit there quietly and let them act like I just ruined the company!"

"First of all, you're not fired. That decision rests with me and me alone," I told her.

Around us, pedestrians gave us a small berth. We earned a few curious glances, but people minded their business for the most part. This was New York. No one wanted to get themselves involved in whatever drama might be going down in the streets if they could help it.

"Well, I definitely can't be your executive assistant anymore! Do you really think people are going to let this drop? This is irresistible gossip, Mason."

"What's the big deal?" I sighed.

"Are you serious right now?" she exclaimed.

I shrugged. "Yeah, I guess so."

I'd already dealt with one young woman's dramatics in the past twenty-four hours. I really didn't have the energy to do it all over again, especially since Daisy had never been the melodramatic type.

"I don't understand why you're acting like this *isn't* a big deal. Do you really not care that I've just lost my job? Or, is the fact that your reputation will obviously survive this enough to make you completely unbothered? Is that it?"

Pinching the bridge of my nose, I leaned against the side of the building.

"There's no reason to overreact like this," I argued. "It's not like Marina sent out a press release to the major media outlets. Now we don't have to keep the engagement a secret at work anymore. I'll get you a high position at one of Reed Capital's subsidiaries and we can carry on as we were. It'll be easier this way! I know it's a little embarrassing that a few people have seen some intimate photos of us, but it's not like we were indecent—"

Daisy stared at me with a furious expression, her lips parted in shock. I was at a loss. I didn't think I'd said anything wrong, but she was acting as if I'd just cursed her entire bloodline.

"You're so clueless," she muttered, throwing her hands up in exasperation. "I am not overreacting. What if my parents find out that you're not just my coworker, but the CEO of the company where I work? And, I don't want you to hand me a new position on a silver platter, Mason. You should know by now that I like to *earn* my successes. Not all of us come from rich, privileged families, so I know that might seem like a foreign concept to you."

"Now, hold on—"

"And anyway, that doesn't even matter anymore because as soon as word spreads that I fucked my boss, I'll only be hired by the trashiest, creepiest firms in the city."

"Daisy—"

"What was I thinking?" she muttered, taking a step away from me. "I mean, obviously, I wasn't thinking at all. That's my problem. I'm such an insufferable people pleaser that I can't say no even when it's the more reasonable decision. No wonder you want to keep me around so badly, huh? No wonder you're barely upset right now! The only way I'm going to be taken seriously now is if you force people to! You have complete control over me! God, I'm so stupid—"

For the first time in my life, I was speechless. I had never heard Daisy speak in such a manner. She was always gentle and careful with her words, always gracious and complimentary even when she was clearly frustrated or stressed out. Daisy was a ray of sunshine; no cloud was dense enough to dull her shine. At least, that's what I had always thought.

Apparently, I was the dark cloud in Daisy's life that had the power to twist her into something mean and spiteful. Unfortunately, for all her rude accusations, I knew she had a point. I was privileged. I often forgot that the chances I'd had in life were much easier for me to grab than if I'd been born into a different family.

Perhaps, there was also a part of me that wanted to stay in control of Daisy. I didn't want her to leave me. It wasn't just because she was a good assistant, either. I liked having her around. She was one of the few people who didn't annoy me on a daily basis.

"I think you're letting all the stress get to your head," I suggested. "Maybe you should take the day off. Go home and try to relax. Everything will be taken care of here. You don't have to worry. The power of NDAs and PR teams is strong. I'll speak with Mr. Holt and inform him you'll be staying in your current role, and when we are married in September, I'll arrange for you to move to a more separate position in the company."

"No."

Daisy's answer was so forceful and immediate that it almost felt like a slap in the face.

"No?"

"No," she repeated. "I'm done. I'm going home and I'm not coming back. You can find a different executive assistant and a different fiancée. I should've known better from the very beginning. This whole thing is over, Mason."

She turned to go and almost slipped away from me thanks to a sudden gaggle of tourists who wormed their way between us when I tried to reach out and stop her again. By the time I managed to wriggle past them, she was already halfway across the street. I rushed after her, dodging a bicyclist who wasn't minding the red light.

"Daisy!"

"Leave me alone!" she called over her shoulder.

"Daisy, don't be so hasty," I begged, grabbing her arm and tugging her toward me. Once again, she slapped me away, but she stopped walking.

"Touch me again, I dare you. Just because I'm a nice person doesn't mean I'm not capable of biting back."

"Why are you being like this? If you'd just stop freaking out and listen to me when I say everything's going to be fine–"

I trailed off when I noticed that she was blinking back tears. Daisy had shown me a lot of different emotions since the professional barriers were broken down between us, but I hadn't yet seen her cry. I never knew what to do when people cried. It made me feel helpless.

"Do you even care about me at all?" she asked, her voice frail and stuttering.

"What?"

"Do you? Do you care about me?"

"I—"

"Are you even capable of caring about anyone but yourself? That's why you care so much about your company, after all. It's a reflection of you."

"What are you talking about?"

"Answer the question! It's an easy one!" she snapped, her lower lip trembling. She looked nothing like the frantic, wild-eyed version of Marina who had confronted me last night, but I still couldn't believe I was dealing with something like this from two different people, one after the other.

"I don't understand why you're asking me that," I admitted.

Daisy rolled her eyes, nodding to herself as if that alone was enough of an answer for her. "Of course you don't. You know what? I'm not even mad at you right now. I'm mad at myself.

I'm the one who was stupid enough to think that someone who has made it his life mission not to waste his time on love would care about me as anything other than a means to an end."

"Stop using my words against me. I already explained what I meant by that."

"Well, that's why you don't really care that at least half the company is going to know you're fucking your assistant, isn't it? Because it makes your life easier! You won't have to keep your fake fiancée a secret anymore! The only reason you came running after me is because you only care about me when I serve a purpose for you. I see that now."

Utterly stunned, I stared at her for several long seconds. The street was less congested where we stood, but there was a group of construction workers nearby who were eyeing us and muttering amongst themselves. I turned my back to them and did my best to shield Daisy from view as a single tear dripped down her face.

"Daisy, that's not how I think of you," I sighed. "Yes, you're very helpful to me, but that's not your sole value. I don't just care about you because you manage my schedule and lie for me. I enjoy your company and I appreciate all that you've risked on my behalf. Can we continue this conversation somewhere more private?"

Daisy snorted. "Listen to you. You're talking to me like I'm your business partner. I'm so embarrassed right now. Maybe I'd be okay if I knew that my reputation was sullied for the sake of a meaningful, genuine relationship. This is really just a game to you, isn't it?"

All of a sudden, it dawned on me why Daisy was so upset. She was ashamed that a handful of her colleagues and superiors had seen those pictures and she was embarrassed to have been caught breaking a rule for once in her life, but that wasn't the grand issue.

She liked me. She had feelings for me. She'd gotten caught up in the fake romance and the sex and the wedding plans, allowing it to drag her under. That was why she'd argued with me the other night about the importance of love and all that nonsense. She'd been attempting to gauge if there was a chance I could feel the same way.

I'd be lying to myself if I said the answer to that was an absolute *no*. There were numerous times when I'd thought, if I was the kind of man who settled down, doing so with a woman like Daisy wouldn't be so bad. There were times when I watched her from across the room doing something utterly mundane—taking notes or frowning at her iPad screen—and thought she was the most beautiful person I'd ever seen. There were times when I looked at my mother's engagement ring on her finger and couldn't stop myself from thinking that my parents would love Daisy if they were still alive to meet her.

We worked well together, and not just in the workplace. We had incredible physical chemistry. Our intellect was fairly matched. We often understood each other without having to verbally announce our needs or desires. Although we disagreed about some things, it was the type of disagreement that created a necessary balance between us. If things were different, if life had happened another way for both of us, maybe we would have met and fallen madly in love years ago.

But Daisy deserved better than me. If she was the sun, I was the earth. We worked in tandem, but she didn't need me the way I needed her. She was too bright for me and I wasn't strong enough to handle it. I was moments away from bursting into flames and it wasn't her fault in the slightest.

This is really just a game to you, isn't it?

It wasn't a game to me. Not anymore. At one point, it was a risky tournament that overwhelmed me with anxiety. I spent every minute cursing my grandmother for putting me in a position like this. However, over time, my perspective changed in infinitesimal ways. Every time she tucked her hand into the crook of my elbow and smiled at someone unimportant. Every time she pressed her body to mine and sighed with pleasure. Every time she smirked and talked back to me playfully, giggling even when I gave her nothing but grouchy retorts. Daisy filled me with life … with *hope*. She made me want to believe that love was worth the trouble. That was no small feat.

The problem was that I offered Daisy nothing in return. I was a troublesome burden, a heavy and dying planet that orbited her incessantly. I soaked in all the benefits of her energy and never repaid the favor.

I had to let her go. When I suggested that this inconvenient trick orchestrated by Marina was a blessing in disguise, I was right, but for the wrong reasons. It was a blessing because it gave Daisy the opportunity to walk away from me with no regrets. Without me, she'd be able to shine brightly somewhere else. She could create a whole new solar system if I allowed her to shake me off.

That was why I couldn't tell her I stopped playing the game ages ago. If I hinted that I might care for her the same way that she cared for me, she'd keep getting weighed down by me. She'd turn into a falling star, collapsing into a blinding explosion and then going dark forever.

It didn't matter if my feelings were real. They obviously were, considering I'd never thought so poetically about another person in my entire life, but I had to ignore them for her sake.

I took a deep breath and fixed her with a firm stare.

"Of course it's just a game," I told her, forcing the emotion out of my voice as I gazed down at her. "What else would it be? It's all for show, Daisy. It's for the money. This was never real. I thought you understood that."

Daisy appeared speechless. All around, the city shrieked and groaned the way it always did, though I didn't hear any of it. For all I knew, we were standing on a desolate asteroid, utterly alone, floating through empty space.

"This was never real," she whispered, repeating my words back to me. "You're right. I am the fool. I shouldn't be upset with you. It's clear that I am not the appropriate candidate for the role of your fake fiancée. I'm not heartless enough. I apologize for causing you trouble today with all of these dramatics. I'll ask Jennie to pack up my office for me and—"

"Wait, you don't have to quit," I protested. "You can still stay at Reed Capital. That doesn't have to change."

"Yes, it does. Everything has to change and you know it."

In spite of the fact that I had just decided to let her go, it felt as if I'd been hit by a ton of bricks as she moved away from me and waved her arm to call a cab on the avenue.

Let her walk away, I urged myself. *It's best for both of you. You're a burden and she's a distraction.*

"Daisy, at least let me call Maurice for you," I sighed, taking a step toward her.

She shot me a glare so piercing that I instinctively halted.

"No," she replied. "Don't do me any more favors, Mr. Reed."

That was the final blow. It really was over—over before it had truly begun. I was no longer Mason in her eyes, but Mr. Reed once again.

A yellow cab pulled up to the curb and Daisy yanked open the door, practically falling into the backseat in her rush to get away from me as quickly as possible. All I could do was stand there like a useless fool as the driver slammed on the gas and peeled away as if he were filming a getaway scene in an action movie.

Thus, I was alone again.

Chapter Twenty-Three: *Campbell*

"Where to?" asked the taxi driver.

I didn't want to go home. The thought of being alone in my quiet little apartment made me feel suffocated and pathetic. Thinking fast, I remembered Poppy mentioning she was going to be at one of her firm's satellite offices in Brooklyn that morning. Even if it meant interrupting her workday, I wanted nothing more than to collapse into my best friend's arms.

"Dumbo," I answered.

"You want me to go to Brooklyn? At this hour? Gonna be tons of traffic, babes."

"I don't care, but if you'd like to let me out here, I'm more than happy to pay the fare to a different cab driver."

"Hey, it's all good! No worries. Brooklyn, it is."

"Thanks."

I settled in the seat, begging myself not to look back as we started inching down Seventh Avenue. Except, the more I tried not to think about what I was leaving behind, the more vivid my memory became. Mason looked shell-shocked when I'd left him standing alone on the street corner.

Suddenly, I no longer had the strength to hold back my tears. I started sobbing, dropping my face into my palms as if that would hide my emotional breakdown from the driver. My heart was shattered. How could so many bad things happen at once without warning? Everything was going so well. When I'd woken up that morning, I truly thought that I would walk into Mason's office, tell him how I felt, and we would get our happily ever after.

Apparently, even those of us who were educated at Yale were capable of being utter morons.

"Bit early in the morning to be crying, don't you think, babes?"

Despite his unapologetic nosiness, the driver's tone was oddly gentle. Sniffling loudly, I glanced up to find him peering at me with concern through the rearview mirror as he maneuvered through the dense traffic. Most of the time, cab drivers minded their business when they picked you up. You could be dressed in a feathered costume or speaking in tongues and they'd keep their mouth shut. But for some reason, I was grateful for ending up with one of the few drivers who paid a little too much attention to his temporary passengers.

"When is the best time to cry, in your opinion?" I asked him, my voice thick with tears.

He chuckled. "In my experience, at sunset. It's more romantic that way."

"At least I'm not the only one who thinks romance is a good thing."

"Did that dude in the suit back there break your heart or something?"

I sniffed again. "Something like that."

"Well, we've got a long ride ahead of us, babes. You want to talk about it?"

"I wouldn't want to burden you," I murmured with a shrug.

"Nah, it's no problem. Least you can do for dragging my ass to Dumbo on a Friday morning is offer me some gossip."

Despite my tears, I cracked a smile. This guy was rough around the edges, but he was a genuine New Yorker through and through. He talked tough, but he had a big heart. Maybe the best thing for my bruised ego was ranting to a stranger.

"Okay, but it's kind of a long story—"

"What's your name, babes?"

"Daisy."

"Like the flower?"

"Yeah."

"I'm Pauly. Nice to meet ya."

"Nice to meet you, Pauly."

"I'm all ears."

I swallowed hard and wiped my cheeks. My makeup was ruined even though I'd only applied it about an hour ago.

"So, that guy on the sidewalk—he's my boss—*was* my boss. His name is Mason. I've been working for him for almost two years."

"That young guy is your boss?"

"Yes. I'm his assistant. He's from a really wealthy family and his grandmother recently died. He was supposed to inherit all of her money and property and whatnot, but there was a stipulation in the will stating he had to be married first. I guess she always wanted him to get married and settle down instead of becoming a workaholic."

"Sounds like she had the right idea," Pauly remarked.

"I guess so. Anyway, Mason really isn't the marriage type. He's not even the relationship type. I mean, in all the time I've worked for him, he's never been on a single date. Just recently, he told me he thinks love is a waste of time."

"What?!"

"I know, right?" I cried, tearing up again. "Anyway, when he found out he had to be married to get the inheritance, I wanted to help him, so we lied to his family and said I was his fiancée. I thought it would be as simple as that, you know? Like, I could tell one little lie and the attorney would send the money to him and it would be over."

"Turned out more complicated than you thought, huh?"

"Yeah … I've always thought Mason was handsome, but we never even touched except by accident. Never. For some reason, the day I went to his grandmother's wake, we ended up, um, doing stuff in the backseat of his town car."

"Babes!"

"I know, I know. It was so trashy and we both kind of agreed to just forget about it. We would go about our lives as normal and keep it a secret from the rest of the company that we had to get married. Except, then we slept together. And then, we did it again. And again. I don't even know how it happened. I swear I'm telling you the truth when I say we never had sexual tension at all before this."

"Maybe you did, but you just ignored it."

"Maybe."

"So, what's with the tears? Sounds like you got a pretty sweet deal, cupcake."

"I thought so, too," I sighed. "I kind of started to fall for him, though. I knew he would never allow himself to feel the same way, but it happened anyway. I couldn't help it. He's just so … it's hard to explain. He's so deserving of love, but it's like he doesn't agree with that, so he pushes it away."

"He pushed you away? A sweet, pretty thing like you?" Pauly gasped, whipping the taxi into the next lane.

"Sort of. It's really complicated. Basically, he has an evil cousin who told the entire company that we were in a secret relationship, even though it was technically fake. I got all freaked about my reputation and my future career, so I ran out of the building. He came after me and told me I was overreacting, that he'd get me a new job somewhere else, and there was no reason why we couldn't still go through with the stupid, fake wedding."

"Damn … this is a lot."

"I know."

"Can I be honest?"

"Sure, Pauly."

"He sounds like a dick, Miss Daisy. Sociopathic, too. What kind of person doesn't believe in love? More than that, what kind of man lets a woman like you cry like this? You deserve better."

I burst into tears again. Pauly watched me nervously while he navigated the traffic. We'd barely made it twenty blocks at that point, and I was beginning to think that going all the way to Poppy was not the most productive decision.

Once I collected myself enough to talk, I automatically sought to defend Mason.

"It's deeper than that," I told Pauly. "He lost his parents when he was really young. They died in a plane crash. Then, his paternal grandparents adopted him, only to get divorced a few years later. It's no wonder he doesn't believe in love. He's never seen it last."

"I get it," Pauly mused. "It makes sense now. It's not that the kid doesn't believe in love. He's afraid of it."

"Afraid?"

"Think about it, babes. His parents were in love and they died. His grandparents were in love, but they divorced. In his eyes, love doesn't have a happy ending. You know, I studied psychology at the community college up in the Bronx. In my opinion, it also sounds like he's afraid that everyone he loves will leave him."

I gaped at the driver through the plexiglass divider. I hadn't expected him to say something so insightful.

"That's a good point," I admitted. "If he avoids love, then it can't hurt him. And, once he realized I might have feelings for him, he pushed me away before I could do the same to him."

"But, you weren't planning on pushing him away, were you?"

"No, not at all. It was the last thing I wanted."

"I think it's a two-way street, babes. He didn't just push you away because he thought you might love him. The guy had to have feelings for you in return. That's what I think."

"He has a funny way of showing it," I muttered.

Resting my head against the window, I exhaled in relief when we finally made it to the West Side Highway. Our progress to Brooklyn would move a little more quickly now that we had escaped Manhattan's congested grid. I was already on my way to Poppy, so it was best to follow through with the original plan. She'd be able to tell me what to do once I explained what happened. I wouldn't have to fill her in on all the details as I had to do with Pauly.

I thought the conversation had naturally drifted off when the quiet stretched on. My sobs had calmed into quiet hiccups and my eyes were drying. When we were closer to Dumbo, I'd fetch my mirror out of my bag and officially assess the damage to my makeup.

"I've got a question for you, Daisy," Pauly spoke after a short while.

"Hmm?"

"I'm just thinking—if your guy believes that everyone he loves will leave him, why did you prove him right?"

"What?"

"You hailed this cab and ran away, babes."

"Yeah, but he basically told me that he didn't want me around."

"Did he? Or, is that how you perceived it?"

I frowned, replaying the scene in my head. Mason was cruel when he told me that he saw our secret affair as nothing more than a game that would earn him a lot of money in the end, but there was a part of me that wasn't sure I believed the words coming out of his mouth. He was irritable and surly, but he wasn't mean. He didn't say things to purposefully hurt people, which meant that he had been lying.

Not only that, but the more I thought about it, the clearer it became that Mason wasn't driving me away. He was being stubborn and difficult, but he wasn't telling me to leave him alone or to quit my job. If that was what he wanted, he wouldn't have run after me. If Mason truly didn't care about me, he would have stayed up there on the executive floor and let me walk away.

In fact, when I hailed the cab, he tried to stop me. In the heat of the moment, I assumed that he offered his chauffeur so that he could maintain his control over me, but as the adrenaline faded from my system, I understood that he was only trying to hold on to me in the smallest possible ways. He didn't want me to go.

I cleared my throat. "I think you're right."

"Damn, really?"

"I shouldn't have left him. I've always been loyal to him, no matter what. He trusted me to stay by his side, but I threw that back in his face. I said a lot of really unfair things, though. He probably doesn't want to talk to me again."

"I doubt that. He's a grown man. Whatever you said, I'm sure he can find a way to get over it if you show him that you're still loyal."

I closed my eyes and pictured Mason's face in my mind. His dark, wavy-ish hair. His blue eyes, a few shades darker than mine. We were like the ocean and the sky in that regard. I liked the way his smile always shivered for a moment on the corners of his lips before he curved his mouth into a grin, that handsome hesitation that never failed to fill me with exquisite anticipation. I liked the way he laughed—unexpectedly, and with his whole body.

I thought about the way Mason held me, how he was simultaneously gentle and rough at the same time. He didn't treat me like a fragile little thing; rather, his sweetness felt like an intentional, wordless gift. He always kissed me as if he meant it. His touches were never halfhearted or obligatory. Mason made love to me with ambition—as with everything in his life, he was never satisfied with merely *good enough.*

He made me happy. Before, when I was just his assistant, I truly liked doting on him. Mason fascinated me. Even on his moodiest days, I was never discouraged because I was convinced there was something brighter behind those clouds. He wasn't miserable through and through.

Mason wanted to believe in love. He wanted to be happy. Despite being uncertain that he deserved such things, there was a part of him that hoped someone would prove him wrong.

God, I really shouldn't have walked away. I should have kept fighting with him. I should have been stubborn and relentless just like him, refusing to back down until he admitted that he cared about me. I shouldn't have let him lie to me or push me away.

"You're right, Pauly," I whispered. "Mason and I have something real. He's just too afraid to admit it and I was too proud to force him to. Underneath this big, stupid scheme we concocted together, there's a genuine bond between us. I've known it since the very first day I started working for him. We belong together."

"That's what I like to hear!"

"Screw the inheritance!" I continued, sitting upright. "Screw the wedding! Screw all of these lies! All I want is to be with him, honestly and publicly without any games. I don't care if I have to get a new job and I don't care what people whisper about me behind my back!"

"Hell yeah, cupcake!"

"I have to show him that I won't leave him!"

"Absolutely!"

"Pauly—"

"Yes, Miss Daisy?"

"Would you hate me if I asked you to turn this car around and head back to midtown?"

Pauly chuckled. "I'd hate you if you didn't, babes."

I grinned through the tears, suddenly renewed with hope. This random cab driver was right, oddly enough, and I was pretty sure that if I had actually made it all the way to Poppy, she would have told me the exact same things. Mason didn't need another person in his life who left him behind, whether by accident or not. Nobody could go back and save his parents from the plane crash, nor could anyone erase the demise of his grandparents' marriage. I couldn't bring Ruth Baldwin back from the dead, either. Nor could I magically turn Marina and Bradley into compassionate, altruistic cousins.

All I could do was be there for him. As infuriating as his stubbornness was, I knew I had to be the one who didn't let him down.

"Let's go, Pauly," I told him.

"Right away!"

Pauly changed lanes, switching from the faster paths of traffic racing toward Brooklyn to get closer to the next exit. I gripped the edges of the seat with anticipation as he sailed smoothly off the southbound highway and wound around the complex twists and turns to bring us back in a northbound direction. My heart was hammering fast, pounding in my chest and throbbing all the way up to my temples.

I needed a plan. I couldn't just waltz back into Reed Capital. Or, couldn't I? Whether or not I was still an employee there remained ambiguous, but it wasn't as if the security guards would toss me out. Yet, if I dared to march up to the top floor and barge into Mason's office armed with bold declarations, I had to think about what I was going to say.

He was a surprisingly good listener, but that didn't mean he'd take whatever I said to heart. In fact, from what I'd learned, Mason responded better to actions rather than words.

"What do I say Pauly?" I asked, leaning forward closer to the barrier as the northbound traffic closed around us like a swarm of impatient bees. "Do I just walk in there, declare that I'm in love with him, and kiss him right on the mouth?"

"I'd say that's as good a plan as any."

"Or, should I maybe be more careful about it? Maybe I should call first. Only, he might not pick up. Actually, it's nearly nine-thirty—he's supposed to be in a meeting right now. Oh, God. What am I doing? Pauly, maybe I should just have you bring me back home. Can we stop off in the East Village?"

"Absolutely not! I'm invested in this now, babes. We're going back to that big, fancy building and you're going to walk your pretty little butt back up to—oh, shit!"

What happened next played out in a matter of seconds, but my mind translated it into slow motion. The cars on the highway were practically bumper to bumper across the lanes, but that hardly slowed anyone down. New Yorkers were used to flirting with fate. Every once in the while, one of them flew too close to the sun. There was a large van to the right of us attempting to move into our lane. Without checking their blind spot, they shoved in front of us, but Pauly couldn't slam on his brakes without forcing the car behind us to rear-end the cab.

The van careened carelessly into the front end of the taxi with enough force to shove us into the lane to our left. I braced myself for impact seconds before we collided with a sedan. Pauly honked the horn loudly, the racket echoing as the traffic began knocking into each other and screeching out of control. I let out a panicked shout as two other cars slammed into each other before sliding into the cab's right side. It was a disaster in the making, a snowball event that nobody could stop.

Suddenly, a loud *bang* shattered the general cacophony. Something struck the van crunched against us, sending both them and us careening off the side of the highway and into the barrier wall.

No! I screamed internally as the concrete drew closer and closer, unbuckling my seatbelt and scrambling away from the side of the cab that would get the worst of the impact. I clung onto the right-hand side door handle as Pauly let out a string of curses, desperately trying to steer us out of the pileup.

When my head smacked against the window, I knew it was over for me.

"Mason—" I whimpered, my limbs growing weak as my vision became fuzzy around the edges.

A horrifying *crunch* reverberated dully as if coming from a faraway distance. It was the last thing I heard before the world turned dark and I drifted away into nothingness.

Chapter Twenty-Four: *Reed*

I kicked the side of my desk, regretting it instantly as pain shot up my calf. I settled for anxious pacing.

I'd just sat through a nine-thirty meeting without Daisy for the first time in over a year. I was distracted the entire time, barely registering what anyone was saying. All I could do was keep replaying the disastrous events of the morning.

She was gone.

I paced furiously, fighting the urge to kick every piece of furniture that stood in my way. The IT department was successful in erasing the email by eight o'clock, but that didn't mean Marina's scheme was unsuccessful. In fact, she'd gotten exactly what she wanted. She'd exposed me for the lying fool that I was, sullied Daisy's reputation, and ruined our relationship in the process.

I didn't know what to do. I shouldn't have let Daisy walk away from me. I should have forced my way into that taxi alongside her or stopped her from getting inside in the first place.

Then again, that was her choice. She chose to walk away from me. Everyone leaves eventually. That was a fact. Daisy proved it.

It's not a one-way street, you idiot, I cursed at myself, slamming my fists into the wall on the far side of my office. *You could've stopped her. You could've prevented her from running out of the building..*

I hated that the voice in the back of my head was right. I wasn't an unwitting victim. Maybe I couldn't bring my parents back to life or fix my grandparents' broken marriage, but there were other choices I could make to mend my heart from the losses I'd endured.

Call her, the hopeful side of my brain begged me. *Call her right now.*

Obediently, I grabbed my phone and tapped Daisy's contact information. She was the first option, the last person I'd texted. The last person I'd called. The only person I texted or called on a daily basis, for that matter. She was the closest thing I had to a friend, even when she was nothing more than my assistant.

I'd been so stupid.

The call didn't ring. It went straight to voicemail.

"Hi! This is Daisy Campbell! Sorry I missed you, but if you leave your name and—"

I hung up. I wasn't interested in leaving a message that she would likely delete before listening to. If her phone was going directly to voicemail—when she usually answered my calls before the first ring had finished—that meant she had turned off her phone. She didn't want to see if she was getting any missed calls or voicemails or text notifications.

Don't give up, pleaded the hopeful voice.

I shoved my phone into my pocket and rushed to my desk to retrieve my keys. If she wasn't answering calls, I'd go to her apartment. I'd never been there, but Maurice had dropped her off a few times before, so he knew the way. If she wasn't home, then I would wait on the stoop all night if I had to.

The fact of the matter was, I couldn't go on living my life like this—without her. I needed her for a multitude of reasons, but more than anything else, I cared about her. Deciding to push her away and let her go was cowardly. I regretted it the second the cab pulled away from the street corner.

I had to tell her the truth. She had to know that this wasn't a game to me anymore. Even if I'd only just figured it out myself a mere hour ago, I needed to tell Daisy that the thought of waiting for her at the altar next month made me feel like the luckiest man in the world. I didn't want to take that for granted anymore. I didn't want it to be a silly charade, a meaningless trick. I wanted it to be real.

It was real.

Just as I turned toward the door, I noticed someone was standing there. She jolted when I made eye contact with her, eyes going wide as if I'd spooked her. It was Daisy's friend, the petite brunette girl from the front desk.

"Sorry, sir," she murmured.

"Miss James," I greeted her. It took an immense amount of effort not to push past her and carry on my way, but that kind of behavior wouldn't serve anyone.

"I … I'm sorry for bothering you. It's just—well, I—I don't know how to—"

"Miss James, you don't have to be afraid of speaking candidly with me."

The young woman bit her lip and inched further into my office, clasping her hands nervously in front of her.

"I saw the photos," she admitted, staring down at the floor. She was much more timid than Daisy, but I was used to the lower ranking staff speaking to me as if I were the most intimidating person they'd ever met. "It wasn't my intention to disobey Mr. Holt's orders not to check my email yet, but curiosity got the better of me. They disappeared from my inbox a minute later, though. I only wanted to tell you because it didn't feel right to keep it a secret, and—"

"Yes, Miss James?"

"And, I figured that's why Daisy ran out of here earlier. She's been acting different lately," she muttered, sneaking glances at me nervously though she seemed to grow a little more confident with each word she uttered. "Not in a bad way. She seemed even happier, which I didn't think was possible. I really respect and admire Daisy, sir."

"That's kind, Miss James. I know she feels the same way about you."

"Oh?" She raised her eyebrows in innocent surprise at the realization that she might have come up in conversation between Daisy and me.

"Yes. Is there something I can help you with? I was just on my way out."

Patience. Kindness. Daisy taught you a few things. Don't forget them.

"Well, I—I was wondering, sir … did Daisy get fired?"

"She—"

"And, if she did, then I'd like to formally submit my intent to resign, as well."

I balked. That was the last thing I expected.

"I'm sorry?" I replied.

Miss James shrugged. "As I said, I have a lot of respect for Daisy. I'm not much younger than she is, but I consider her one of my role models. Please forgive my candor, but I don't want to work at a company that Daisy is not a part of."

The loyalty that the secretary showed to her colleague was remarkable, especially given that this industry was mercilessly competitive. The kind of faith that the two women had in each other was hard to come by in the professional world.

I cleared my throat. I wondered if Miss James had come to speak to me as Daisy's employer or as Daisy's alleged boyfriend, or if she now saw me as a combination of both. It was strange to think that I wasn't clear on the status of either of those things, but I was on my way to find out.

"Miss Campbell's employment at Reed Capital has not been officially terminated," I informed her. "However, should she choose to voluntarily end her contract, she is at will to do so and I wholeheartedly admire and support your decision to follow her wherever she may go."

"What? Really?"

"The loyalty you show your friend should not be discouraged. In fact, I think many of your seniors could learn from it," I explained. "I really do have to ask you to excuse me now, though, Miss James."

"Are you going to see her? I tried to text her, but she hasn't replied."

Before I could effectively put an end to the discussion, my phone started ringing. I had it pressed to my ear in a heartbeat, not even bothering to check who was calling first. If it was Daisy, I wanted her to know that I wasn't going to ignore her.

"Hello?"

Miss James hovered awkwardly at the threshold, stepping aside to make room as I moved toward her.

"Mason Reed? Is this Mason?" asked an unfamiliar feminine voice.

It wasn't Daisy.

"Who's asking?" I barked.

"It's Poppy. Poppy Maxwell. I'm Daisy's best friend. I got your number from her phone."

"Is something wrong?" The way Poppy spoke made me nervous. It sounded as if she'd had to hunt down a way to contact me, rather than getting it from Daisy herself.

"It's Daisy. There was an accident on FDR Drive. I don't know if you saw. She was in a taxi that was involved in a pile-up. She's at Mount Sinai. I was about to call her parents, but I thought you should know. I have to go, but she's in room 613. Text me if you get a chance to come by."

Poppy disconnected. I remembered Daisy mentioning that her friend was an attorney. It was obvious from one conversation with her. She relayed only the information I absolutely needed to know with limited emotion, and cut the discussion short.

I was left standing there, staring numbly at the C-suite secretary with my phone gripped tightly in my hand.

"Sir?" Miss James asked. "Is everything okay?"

No. She can't be ... not her, too ... I won't allow it.

"I have to go."

***

The second Maurice was told that the reason we needed to break at least a dozen traffic laws to get to the hospital on the Upper East Side, he obliged. I got the feeling that he'd grown more loyal to Daisy than me in the past weeks, but I couldn't fault him for that. I certainly liked her a lot more than I liked myself.

The town car had barely screeched to a halt in front of the hospital entrance before I stumbled out and darted into the lobby.

"Sir? Sir! Sir, you have to check in first!" shouted a nurse the moment she saw me rushing to the elevators.

"Mason Reed! I'm Daisy Campbell's fiancé! Patient in room 613!" I shouted over my shoulder, ignoring the confused security guards who looked as if they weren't sure if they should tackle me or let me go. I didn't wait around to find out.

I ran down the linoleum hallways, ignoring startled medical staff and civilians alike, taking back stairwells and reading the directional signs as quickly as I could. Poppy hadn't told me if she was okay, but at least I knew she was alive. As I dashed toward the last living person on earth keeping me in one piece, I tried not to fall victim to the worst of my imagination. The cruel half of my brain pictured her in a coma, her bones shattered, her body frail and tattered. I couldn't stand it.

By the time I made it to her room, I was panting for breath. The door was open, so I hurried inside without knocking.

"Mason?" gasped the most beautiful voice in the world.

I halted. She was awake. Daisy was sitting up on a hospital cot, a shallow cut on her forehead and a few bruises along her left cheekbone, but she otherwise looked as if she was in one piece. There was no one else in the room, but I knew it wouldn't be long until someone caught up to the madman running through the hospital as if his life depended on it. They could arrest me if they wanted to. It was worth it just to see Daisy's aquamarine gaze locking onto mine again.

"You're okay," I breathed.

"Did Poppy call you?" she asked. "I told her not to bother you."

"You're okay, right?" I repeated, paying no attention to her words as I rushed to her side and checked for any casts or large bandages. "Are you hurt? She said there was an accident. I saw … someone passed away … I thought—"

"I'm fine," Daisy replied, furrowing her brow at me. "Mason, I'm fine. I mean, they said I have a concussion, but I got lucky."

After that, I couldn't keep it together anymore. The relief that poured into me was so strong and absolute that it sent me falling to my knees. The range of emotions I'd endured since waking up was more immense than anyone could be expected to handle.

For the first time in over twenty years, I started crying.

"Daisy—" I sobbed. It was as if a levy had broken. I could barely get out the words as I clung to the bedsheets. Daisy stared down at me, utterly stunned. "Daisy, I'm so sorry."

"Mason, it's okay. Everything's okay."

"No, it's not," I argued, forcing my voice to work properly as tears streamed down my face. "It's not okay because I lied to you. This isn't a game to me, Daisy. It hasn't been for a while. I'm in love with you. I can't imagine my life without you. I was stupid for thinking I could let you walk away from me. I need you. I can't—I won't accept living in a world where you don't know that. It's okay if you don't want me anymore, though. I'll understand. But, it's true, Daisy … I love you."

Daisy teared up and glanced away, giving me a full view of the injury on the side of her face. Yet, even bruised and beaten, she was radiant.

"I wish you had told me that earlier," she murmured.

"I know. I know I should've told you. I'm an idiot. I'm an utter fool, Daisy, and I know I don't deserve you, but is there any chance you still love me, too?"

She turned back to me with a gasp. "Of course I love you. That didn't change in the few hours since our fight, Mason. Love doesn't come and go that easily. If it does, then it's not real. But, still—"

Daisy trailed off. I could hear the hesitation in her tone, could sense it in the tense set of her shoulders. Out in the hallway, the sound of several pairs of approaching footsteps echoed through the open door. I didn't have much longer to be alone with her.

I shifted where I had collapsed onto the floor, settling onto one knee before her for the second time.

"Marry me, Daisy."

"Stop it—"

"I mean it. Marry me. For real. Become my wife. It doesn't have to be next month or even next year. I don't give a damn about that stupid inheritance anymore. If my cousins want it, they can have it. I don't want anything else in this world but you."

"For God's sake, Mason, stand up," she laughed.

"Say yes," I begged her. "Please say yes."

"You've lost your mind," she whispered as I crawled back to my feet and leaned over her. She reached up and cradled my face with her palm, eyes wide with pure forgiveness. "We haven't even gone on a real date yet. You can't propose to me."

"Of course I can. I just did."

"My head hurts," she breathed, eyelashes fluttering. "Don't make me answer any big questions right now."

"Are you okay? Do you need me to get someone?"

"No, no … just kiss it better."

I chuckled. It wasn't quite the response I was hoping for, but she had admitted to being in love with me. There were a lot of unresolved issues floating around, but she was right—it was best if we didn't try to fix everything all at once. For now, acknowledging the beauty of the moment was all that mattered. I thought I had lost her, but she was still here.

"I'm not going anywhere, Daisy," I whispered to her. Gently, I pressed my lips to her forehead right above the jagged cut. She closed her eyes and sighed, relaxing back into the pillow.

"Neither am I, Mason. I promise."

"—he's in here!" barked a voice behind us. "Sir, you can't just run into a hospital like that. Who the hell do you think you are?"

Daisy blinked open her eyes and frowned at the security guard standing in the doorway, flanked by two nurses with panicked expressions.

"It's okay," she told them. "He's with me."

Epilogue: *Campbell*

One Year Later

"Imagine telling this story to your grandkids one day," Poppy giggled as she fussed over the pleats of the long, satin gown. "They'll be like, 'Grandma! Grandpa! Can you tell us the story of how you fell in love?' Then, you'll have to sit there on your quaint porch swing and explain to your innocent little grandchildren that their grandpa used to be your boss, but then you oh-so-romantically agreed to be his fake fiancée so he could inherit forty-million dollars. Except, then you became friends with benefits because neither of you could ignore how mind-blowingly attracted you were to each other. But we all know that's a slippery slope, so you ended up falling in love … and the rest is history!"

I snorted. "Forty-two."

"What?"

"It's forty-two million dollars."

"That's definitely not the point," Poppy laughed. "Anyway, with the way inflation is headed, by the time we have grandchildren, forty-two million dollars will be the equivalent of forty-two dollars."

"We're going to talk economics right now? Seriously?"

My best friend grinned and straightened up, admiring her handiwork. "You look so beautiful, Daisy. I'm so happy for you."

"Thanks, Poppy," I sighed, hugging her tightly.

There was a light knock on the door. Pat Maybell, the wedding planner who had been hired over a year ago and since then been asked to readjust the nuptial plans more than once, poked her head through the crack with a bright smile.

"Ready, ladies? It's time. I need the maid of honor."

"I'll be right there," Poppy promised.

Pat nodded and disappeared once more.

I smiled at Poppy. She wore a long gown the color of peonies, layers of taffeta spilling down to the floor like water. Her hair was pulled back with flower-shaped pins that matched the ones in my own hair. We'd decided to keep the wedding party small and simple, so Poppy was the only one dressed in the same shade of pink that matched the flowers in my bouquet. Jackson Gallagher, a longtime colleague and friend of Mason's, was the best man and would be accompanying Poppy down the aisle. They'd been hitting it off the last few times they crossed paths, hinting at the possibility for a budding romance.

But, I suppose we'd have to wait and see.

"Go on," I told her softly. "You know how much I dislike tardiness."

Poppy hugged me one last time and slipped out the door. I was left alone in the dressing room, dolled up in the same white dress I'd bought thirteen months ago on an unexpectedly melancholy day. It really was the perfect dress. Nothing else would do.

I took a deep breath, waiting for Pat to come collect me. Soon enough, I would walk down the aisle at last, but this time it would be real. There were no divorce papers prepared and ready to be signed, no more lies to maintain.

This was happening.

Not much had changed from the original plans. The wedding remained intimate and secure. The guest list was small and tidy, the pews rearranged to account for the lack of a crowd.

Mason and I preferred it that way. We didn't need the entire city gazing upon us to know that our love was genuine.

The truth was out, but we didn't bother unleashing it upon everyone involved. When I told my parents that we intended to push the wedding out a year, I explained that it was because we wanted more time to plan the event to our tastes. They didn't need to know that the original wedding was a farce or that the reason it was rescheduled was because Mason and I were actually in love this time around.

There were some things that we knew should be kept to ourselves. But, who knew? Maybe Poppy's prediction would come true, and one day, we would tell our grandchildren about the wild series of events that had brought us together. Perhaps they wouldn't believe us if we did.

Even I could hardly believe the destiny I'd been handed.

When I agreed to go on a proper first date with Mason and see how the relationship fared over time, I thought we would cancel the wedding altogether. After all, it wasn't customary to already have a marriage set in stone when you hadn't even declared yourself boyfriend and girlfriend yet.

But, I knew he was the one. I knew that, no matter what, I wanted to spend the rest of my life with him. A wedding was inevitably on the horizon, so we kept it in the books. The inheritance could wait. The threats that potentially stood in the way of Mason claiming it were gone now. Once it was proved that Marina Baldwin hacked the Reed Capital employee database and disseminated photographs against our consent, Mason sued her for defamation. Bradley Baldwin went down with her, too stupid to keep his mouth shut about his involvement in his younger sister's schemes.

Mr. Henderson, the Baldwin family attorney, took that as his cue to override Ruth Baldwin's declaration that another of her grandchildren could lay claim to the inheritance if they were married before Mason. Apparently, given that Marina and Bradley clearly tried to trick their way into receiving the inheritance before Mason, they could be legally disqualified.

Thus, Mason had no competition. He had all the time in the world. Sort of. He had to claim the estate eventually. Mr. Henderson couldn't be expected to handle it indefinitely. Thankfully, the time had come for the faithful attorney to pass the reins to Mason. He was waiting in the audience, delighted to finally be witnessing the wedding he'd always been led to believe was based on something real.

It was a relief that we weren't lying to him now. We weren't lying to anyone.

"Daisy?" Pat murmured. I jumped, so lost in thought that I hadn't registered her knocking. "It's time."

I nodded. "Okay."

She bustled into the room and gathered up the train of my dress as I wandered out into the grand, high-ceilinged hall that opened up to the sanctuary just around the corner. We were at a charming chapel in the suburbs, far away from the hustle and bustle of Manhattan.

Pat quickly arranged my dress once more, recreating Poppy's careful work from earlier as the organ played a cheerful tune. I imagined Poppy and Jackson walking down the aisle together, a bit sad that I couldn't witness it for myself. I hoped the photographer captured it perfectly so I could see later.

"There she is," chuckled my father quietly as Pat gave me a final thumbs-up and scurried away.

"Hi, Dad. Don't you look dapper?"

"Aw, shucks, sweetheart," he joked, pretending to wave off my compliment. "You look gorgeous, Daisy."

"Thanks, Dad."

"Ready to get hitched? Any last-minute doubts you need me to clear up? I'm on your side, honey, so if you want to make a run for it—"

I giggled and shook my head. He was joking, but there was truth to his words. If, for some reason, I chose to suddenly walk away from this wedding, I knew both he and my mother would stand proudly by my side as I did so. They always supported me and I was grateful for that. More than anything, though, I was overjoyed that they supported Mason now, too. They had taken him under their wings and showered him with the parental affection that was stolen from Mason when he was a teenager. Although, we knew it wouldn't replace that which he missed out on, it helped him glow a little bit brighter.

"Don't worry, Dad. I don't have any doubts. I love Mason."

He jokingly exhaled in relief. "That's good to hear. I like the guy a lot, so I'd be bummed if I had to start hating him on your behalf."

I nudged his arm with my elbow, smirking at his playfulness. He always was an emotional guy, but he tended to cover it up with humor.

"I love you, Dad."

"I love you, too, sweetheart."

The music in the sanctuary changed tempo. The recognizable melody of the classic wedding march filled the space. I held on to my father's arm and followed him to the massive archway.

In hindsight, I absorbed every lovely thing in the room. The petal-strewn aisle, the gleaming pews, the blooming wisteria dripping from the ceiling … I was aware of my mother standing at her place in the front row, crying and smiling at the same time as she caught sight of my father and me at the head of the aisle. I saw Poppy positioned in the maid of honor's place, as well as Jackson waiting patiently opposite her. And then, there was Mason's Auntie Kat, as well as a few other members of the Baldwin clan who weren't rotten like Marina and Bradley.

Jennie was there, too, grinning teary-eyed at me from the end of her row. She was a junior analyst in the finance department now, with her own private office located just one floor below the C-suite. Her date was the infamous Michael Hamwell, who was her boyfriend now.

Michael no longer worked for Mr. Holt—by choice, miraculously enough—and had moved on to work for one of the investment firms on Reed Capital's client list. He'd wormed his way into my good graces over the past few months. I didn't blame him for the way he reacted to the discovery of that fateful email. It was the appropriate thing to do. If I were in his shoes, I likely would have done the same thing.

All of these things I registered vaguely as I clung to my father and waited to take my first step.

However, at the moment, I only saw one person.

Mason.

He looked perfect, tall and glowing like a god. His tuxedo fit him flawlessly, hugging the body that I had gotten to know so much better in the time that we negotiated for our love to grow. Mason had gotten a haircut for the wedding, his glossy waves tamed slightly. I liked it better when they were a mess, but I could tousle them back to normal later.

He smiled at me with such brilliant happiness, it felt as if I were basking in pure sunlight. I'd never seen him look so exalted, so hopeful. All I wanted to do was forget the rhythm of the march and break into a run. I wanted to gallop down the aisle and throw myself into his arms, speak my vows as fast as I could, and kiss him until I couldn't breathe.

But, I was supposed to be the patient one in the relationship, so I stayed next to my father and continued walking toward the altar at a reasonable pace. It was agonizing. I swore that time was purposefully running slower just to test me. Each second that passed where the only thing that connected us were our gazes felt like an eternity.

Until, finally, my father delivered me to the altar and handed me off to Mason. I melted the moment Mason's hands folded over mine and had to fight the urge to burst into tears from joy.

"Hi," he whispered.

"Hi," I replied back as the organ player finished his dramatic crescendo.

"You're so beautiful."

"I love you."

"I love you, too."

When the song ended, the priest took his place between us.

"Ladies and gentlemen, we are gathered here today—" he began.

After that, everything was a blur. It was all I could do not to stutter my way through my vows or tremble with uncontainable glee as Mason slipped the wedding band onto my finger.

The entire future unraveled before us. There were still many uncertainties ahead of us, but I was confident that we would figure them out together.

Firstly, I was no longer Mr. Reed's executive assistant. Leaving the role felt like the best thing to do. Not because I was ashamed of Mason's and my affair, but because I was always meant to move on eventually and it seemed as if the universe was telling me that the time had come.

Naturally, I turned down every single offer Mason made to get me a spot in one of the most competitive companies in Manhattan. Instead, I took some time off and did some soul searching. What did I really want to do with the rest of my life? I'd always wanted to be successful. I'd always wanted to lead. Strangely, I'd never given much thought to the specifics of how those two things would happen, other than that it would involve the financial sector.

In the end, I didn't apply for any other companies. I started my own. When I sat down and asked myself what my greatest passion in life was, it wasn't anything like *earning money* or *gaining influence*. My passion was other people—caring for them, guiding them, and supporting them however they needed. I knew there were a lot of others out there like me, and that quite a few of them ended up as executive assistants.

So, that's what Campbell Consulting did. We recruited, trained, and advocated for personal assistants of executives and celebrities alike. So far, the staff was small and our clientele was limited, but I wasn't afraid of failing. I had Mason to guide me, Poppy to help me with the legal stuff, and my own talents to push me in the right direction.

Everything was going to work out in the end. I'd always believed that. Optimism wasn't just something I was born having faith in. It was something I worked toward every single day. No matter what, there was always a bright side.

And this was it. I'd found my silver lining.

I smiled up at Mason, thinking back to the very first day I had seen him. I was so much younger then. I was naive and awkward, but determined to make something of myself.

He and I were living proof that life rarely worked out the way you expected, but that was the beauty of it. Sometimes, life led you down a path that was even more wonderful than you could have imagined. If you trusted the process, you'd find your happy ending.

"I do," I said at last when the priest posed the final question. "I really, really do."

The audience laughed at my ad lib.

"In that case, with the power vested in me, I now pronounce you man and wife. You may kiss the bride."

Music and applause erupted to life when Mason and I kissed on the altar. I felt him smiling against my lips and couldn't stop myself from grinning in return. Kissing him now was just as magical as the first time, but better nonetheless because there were no question marks hovering in the air between us.

"I love you, Mrs. Campbell-Reed," he whispered to me.

"And I love you, Mr. Campbell-Reed."

He took my hand, holding tightly as we turned to face the smiling crowd of all the people we loved. Once upon a time, Mason thought he didn't believe in love. He thought there was no point to it. Now, he told me he loved me as many times a day as he could. It was as if he was making up for lost time.

Together, we walked down the aisle as a married couple, grinning and waving until we reached the exit. Everyone would follow after us eventually to the reception, but for now we were traveling on our own.

Outside, a familiar black town car with tinted windows waited for us. It idled in the gravel driveway. Mason helped gather my skirts as I ducked into the back, then slipped in beside me.

"Congratulations, kids," said the man in the driver's seat.

"Thanks, Pauly," I chuckled.

Right … one last thing. I was relieved to find out that Pauly survived the accident. Just like me, he managed to make it out of the rubble with nothing more than a few bruises and scratches. It was a true miracle, since the taxi was the first to strike the concrete barrier at the edge of the highway, and in the ensuing pileup, served as a buffer against all the other vehicles that tumbled into the action. According to the police, the way Pauly maneuvered the car at the last second—and the fact that I was smart enough to scramble to the other side of the backseat—saved our lives.

Maurice was getting old and was on the verge of retirement. When he informed Mason of his intentions to move on from being his personal chauffeur, I suggested Pauly as his replacement. It took a bit of convincing, seeing as how Pauly was much chattier than Maurice had ever been, but Mason eventually gave in. Marriage is all about compromise, right?

Mason held me close to him in the backseat as Pauly put the car into drive and pulled away from the chapel as the wedding guests started to trickle out little by little.

"Where to?" Pauly asked. It was a joke, one of the old phrases leftover from his cab driver days. He knew that he was tasked with delivering us to the reception venue, after which he would pick us up and bring us to the airport where we would jet off for our honeymoon. I was as surprised as anyone else that I actually convinced Mason to take time off from work. He truly was a changed man.

Mason chuckled at Pauly's joke. The past version of him would have rolled his eyes and barked out a grouchy response, but the man beside me was much more easygoing and good natured these days.

"Where to?" I repeated with a playful smirk. "Well, definitely not Brooklyn."

BOOK 2: *There's a bitter reason I don't wear jewelry...* join Nina & Dr. Ian Clark as they chase love and an international jewel thief with the FBI! Click to buy ***Dr. Clark*** on Amazon: geni.us/dr-clark

FREE NOVELLA: When my brother's cocky billionaire friend asked me to be his wife for the weekend, I never thought it'd be so hard to resist... Click to get exclusive content from me & ***The Billionaire's Secret Wife*** for FREE at maryjenningsauthor.com/secrets

About the Author

I am a contemporary romance author and guilty of being addicted to books, caffeine, wine, bad reality tv and even worse puns.

I'm also a cat mom and usually spend my days biking around my small town or staying in and writing a bit of romance for you to enjoy!

My favorite tropes that I can't seem to put down are second chance romances and enemies to lovers, but I'm always getting caught up in enjoying other tropes (and publish them too!)

I've always got something new planned and going on so please subscribe to my author newsletter for a FREE novella, exclusive content, and behind-the-scenes emails of what I'm doing □ □ maryjenningsauthor.com/secrets/